A rich and immersive sensory experience of Indian life, culture and history; a story of beauty and poetry of the 8th century interwoven with a contemporary search for self-enlightenment. The retelling of two women's lives and their unrequited love for god or man. Meticulously researched. Evocative description and sense of place.

— CASS MORIARTY

Saisha, an Australian traveling in India with her partner, Marcus, makes a chance purchase of a book of Tamil poetry from a Delhi market. The yearning verses precipitate her quest to discover more about their author Andal, the revered young tale-teller of a thousand years ago, a girl with goddess eyes in thrall to the sapphire-skinned Lord Vishnu. Saisha, questioning the faltering bonds of her own relationship, returns alone to southern India to trace this intriguing story. Helen Burns carries readers safely aloft amid scents of sacred basil and rose and the push and shove of temple towns as Saisha is wooed by the mystique of the revered poetess and succumbs to the irresistible pull of Mother India, that most divine of temptresses.

— SUSAN KUROSAWA

I have no doubt that Helen Burns writes under the immense and long-reaching aegis of Andal herself. Saisha's longings resonate with echoes from a distant time, in which a young poet learns to transcend the world through verses that reveal the secrets of the aching heart and the eager body. Gently philosophical and elegantly erotic, *Andal's Garland* has a narrative charge that spans centuries and continents with ease. What a lovely book this is. I could say it over and over, like Andal's own parrot might.

— SHARANYA MANIVANNAN, AUTHOR OF
THE QUEEN OF JASMINE COUNTRY

This is a book for pilgrims. Every so often in a life there's an urgent and mysterious summons, and – it can happen very abruptly – you find yourself on a pilgrimage. I read *Andal's Garland* at such a time in my own life. It's a wise, thoughtful, passionate and necessary companion.

— PETER BISHOP, CREATIVE DIRECTOR OF
VARUNA – THE WRITERS' HOUSE

ANDAL'S GARLAND

the fragrance of a young girl's love endures a thousand years

HELEN BURNS

ODYSSEY
BOOKS

Author's Note

Andal's Garland is a work of fiction, an intertwining of venerated themes, historical and mythic, with the experiences of a contemporary woman. Due to the intricate nature of culture and religion, I do not claim any ultimate authority and humbly apologise for any inadvertent error or misrepresentation. I remain ever thankful to the gracious people of South India.

Tirumal, in fire you are the heat
in flowers you are the scent
among stones you are the diamond

Kirantaiyar 500 BC

Oh heart! Meditate on Andal
born in Villiputtur where swans wander.
She took the flowers adorning her body
and garlanded the Lord of Arangam.
She sang to Him her Tiruppavai,
precious garland of songs.

Uyyakkondar 10th Century

South Indian Place Names

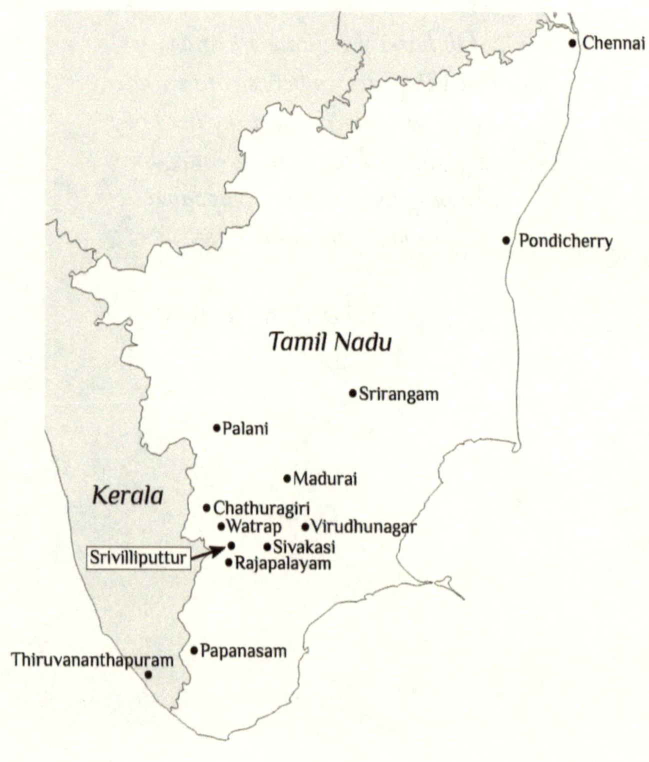

Prologue

On the first day in the month of early dew, Andal woke long before the sun. It was the hour of Brahma, when the gods were nearest, so close his breath might brush her cheek. Birds were still asleep in their nests, heads tucked into wings, eggs cosseted. Moon-flecked shadows of tree branches and tall houses laced the earthen streets outside her window. Andal lay for a moment in this quietest hour of all, sensing the imminence of something or someone quilting the air of her room, breathing into her, pounding her temples, beating at her ribs.

Stars still crowded the dark square of sky above the courtyard as she drew a pail from the well. The water was cold. She braced herself before splashing her face. She combed coconut oil through her raven curls and twirled them on top of her head, then tied a length of homespun cloth round her waist, pleating the end and tucking it in at the back. She laced her bodice and wrapped a shawl round her shoulders. She was twelve years old now, of a marriageable age, so she veiled her head before unlatching the gate of her father's house.

The oil lamps had burned dry, leaving the streets in delicious darkness. Andal felt reprieved, for a little longer, before the buds of the moon lilies closed in her father's garden, before the pleas of her mother, the neighbours' gossip and, from the only one who mattered, his stubborn silence. Except for the occasional bell of a foraging water buffalo and the skip of her feet through the night jasmine air, nothing else was perceptible. In the company of so many stars Andal felt an uncomplicated joy, free from the familiar despair that pooled in her throat like a pinch of salt dropped into a tumbler of water. Like the circle of ripples only ever rumouring his reflection at the bottom of her well.

Skipping faster to leave the thought behind, she followed Villiputtur's wide main street, past the entrances of its two-storey houses flanked by carvings of dragons rearing twice her height. Those giant elephant trunks hanging from their sculpted mouths —how she had shrieked with fear and delight hearing her father describe these guardians with their crocodile head and lion legs, their monkey eyes and peacock's tail. She passed the scents of sacred basil and roses, pungent and sweet, infusing the air of her *Appa's* temple garden and, on the other side of the wall, the gateway of a thousand gods leading to Lord Tirumal's temple. Then, through a labyrinth of alleyways and thatched dwellings, she skipped to the edge of town.

Andal balanced across the bunds of two paddy fields. Here, she could see for miles in ten directions. She looked to the eastern horizon beyond which, people said, were the waves of a great sea. Hints of lilac turning to crimson washed the sky, dismantling all of its stars. But there was one bright light rising as if it, and not the sun, claimed that particular morning, Venus. Andal turned around to face the dark red-rimmed peaks of the Western Ghats. Hovering in the crevice of two mountains was another bright star, Jupiter. After watching its descent, Andal turned again to Venus but she too had disappeared.

Women were already gathered at the low stone temple on the banks of a sacred river. Its source was a spring bubbling up through the floor of a cave deep within the ylang ylang forests of the mountains. From Villiputtur it snaked a slow path across the plains to the sea. For the next thirty dawns in this early dew month of Margazhi, they would bathe in its chilly waters offering rituals to Katyayani, the goddess their ancestors had invoked since the beginning of time. But now their drumbeats and incantations summoned the presence of a god as well—a blue-skinned god who flew between worlds on the back of an eagle and made his bed on the coils of a snake.

It was he who swung the pendulum of stars that morning with four arms raised holding a discus, a lotus, his conch and mace. He watched Andal unable to contain her excitement, standing midpoint in this rare conjunction of Venus and Jupiter.

Chapter One

Where Coromandel flowers entwine celestial worlds
there the primeval one holds a fiery discus.
Bring me close to its glow—but do not scorch me

Nacciyar Tirumoli 10:3

For the Love of God. I counted fifteen rupees into the book-*wallah's* hand. A playful title, was my first thought. Of all the paperbacks I had picked up and put down on that marathon Sunday morning this was the one I chose. Marcus and I had walked from Jamma Masjid to Chandi Chowk. It was the last day of June, pre-monsoon and dripping hot. Any moment my legs would crumble and I'd expire into a puddle right there on the pavement. But I didn't fall, because that was the moment I saw her. The book's cover was creased and faded, its thin spine torn, and there she was dancing on the front. A copper engraving of a girl, hands raised above her head, feet poised.

I skimmed the back cover. The title had nothing at all to do with the cry of a woman at wit's end, it was a book of Tamil poetry. Flipping through its yellowed pages, I stopped at the verses of a girl called Andal. She was the only female in the company of twelve poet saints, the *Azhwars*, who lived more than a thousand years ago.

Clouds, dark as clay moulds, I am the wax inside you. Rain down on Venkata where Tirumal lives, caress my body and soul, melt my heart, pour him into me.

I had no idea where Venkata was or who Tirumal might be and had never heard the name Andal, but there was a charge to the words, as if the entirety of love had been condensed into four lines. For the rest of the day, as we traipsed the streets of Old Delhi, all I felt was impatience to return to the quiet of our tiny hotel room. *I am the wax inside you.* I had dabbled with the I Ching and alignments of stars, but arriving at these words felt like an altogether different kind of divination.

I had lost count of the times we had come to India, Marcus and I. What mattered more were the twenty-five years stretching between us since meeting there. India was a land that bound us. Two days after our first encounter we were sharing a bed. The romance of those early years, roaming about in our cheese-cloth clothes and faded jeans, had all but disappeared and it seemed those wild-eyed days, when my young self recklessly poured into the body and mind of another, had never happened. And yet I continued to believe Marcus and I had staying power; we defied the odds and rode the changes. What was it keeping us together? For me it was more than an attachment to comforts and habits or the fear of living alone. More than companionship or convenience. The reason of us ran deeper. But love? I found myself asking more and more: was it love?

Thinking back to that night in the refuge of our hotel room, windows closed to Delhi's Armageddon air and the air-conditioner turned high, I took a long breath and picked up my new book. It fell open at the same page—*Caress my body and soul.* I closed my eyes and tried to imagine.

Marcus slept as I read by torchlight. Verse after verse, late into the night, I devoured the words of a girl. Then I read the legend of her life in a small annotation at the end. It was like a fairy tale, her birth from the red soil of a temple garden, and how she vanished at the age of sixteen. My mind swung between the reality of the lines I had bookmarked and the girl who composed them. How much of the myth was true? And what to make of her poems?

Love tortures me, I burn in its flames. All night I lie awake, a target for the southern breeze.

Love tortures—the words careered inside me.

I didn't know what dream it was to later jolt me awake, and what the lines I had scrawled in the dark meant: my heart an ocean of unuttered love, even in a sandstorm I sweep the threshold of my house.

I didn't know then that this girl, this revered Indian goddess, was the guest I had been waiting for.

For the Love of God became as constant a companion as Marcus until one perfect summer morning at home I felt the familiar pull to return, and he did not.

'We were only there four months ago. Look at the sky, Saisha, the sea,' he said, with his surfboard under his arm. 'No way am I leaving this for lungfuls of leaded air. I can't afford to get sick again. It took weeks to recover from whatever strain of Asian flu I caught last time.'

I sat there, staring at the ray of sunlight hovering near my feet, uncommonly sullen. I felt *her*—Andal—the sweep of her goddess eyes vibrating the air between us.

'*Come*,' she called from her temple garden thousands of miles away.

Marcus didn't hear the sound of her voice, but it was clear as a bellbird's for me.

'What about a summer in France? Ockitania. You've always said you wanted to return. Let's plan for next year.' He stood there, like a foreigner, and she called again.

'It's *Occ*itania!' I said, my gaze bypassing those penetrating eyes of his. The sea was not the only reason we had chosen this house, there was also Wollumbin, the view of its crooked peak through our kitchen window. On that day, like so many others, its tip was veiled in cloud and I remembered its second-hand name, Mt Warning.

'Your grandmother,' he said. I looked at him blankly, and at those clouds swirling behind him.

'She's given you the keys. Let's go before the roof falls in.' The roof was fine. But he was right, grand-mère had insisted her house wasn't to leave the family. My mother had no intention of returning, so I was it.

'The house is built of stone, Marcus. It's not going anywhere and now isn't the right time.'

Marcus surfed and Marcus returned, so sure of himself, sure that I would come to my senses. He stood there, wetsuit draped over his chest, diamonds of saltwater clinging to his skin. A long time ago I would have crossed the room for a taste of that ocean.

'It's Margazhi, the Tamil month of ancient bathing rituals. Just imagine,' I pleaded, 'golden chariot processions and all of Srivilliputtur's women chanting Andal's songs. Marcus! I really, really want to go.'

Life happened *to* me for the most part and I dealt with the consequences. Occasionally though, a set of circumstances might unfold answering a desire I harboured but lacked the courage to acknowledge, let alone speak. Close to midnight I pressed *pay* for my ticket. A thrill ran through my body, then a flood of relief.

❧

Mid-December to mid-January is a winter month. Tamilians call it the month of early dew. I stepped from an air-conditioned terminal into an onslaught of touts, taxi drivers and money changers, each with probing dark eyes, and smiles gleaming beneath manicured moustaches. Winter? Sweat had already beaded my forehead. Smoke-hazed, crow-call filled air assaulted my ears and nose.

It was impossible to prepare for the days, sometimes weeks, it took to navigate the portal into India, an unpredictable over-whelm of wonder, confusion, irritation, light-headedness, before emerging through to the other side charmed and surrendered. Perhaps this was the reason I kept returning since my first visit all those years ago. I knew by now, no matter how many times I dreamed my arrivals from the comfort of an Australian veranda, there was no safe passage, no alternative to the unravelling of a time and logic I took for granted in the West. Simple or compli-cated, most questions in India are met with the universal swim of a head. Did it signify yes or no? I was never sure. Three requests for a street direction and I'd be given three different answers. Sometimes none of them true.

Ensconced in the brown velvet seat of an Ambassador taxi, happy with the negotiation of a fare to Srirangam and the good-luck twinkle in Ganesha's gemstone eyes as he bobbed up and down on the dashboard, I let go into the life outside my window: wastelands of dust and auto shops, fruit stands and a shining new supermarket, an errant cow and a woman dressed in pink brocade gliding her hand over its back as their paths crossed. The driver sped us toward the Kavery River and the other side of town, a domain of tradition, of temple towers and Brahmin streets, pilgrims, and bicycle rickshaws.

Nearing the bridge, we slowed into the chaos of two lanes being widened into four. The driver made a comment in a tumbling of Tamil then pressed his horn as we crawled ahead, eventually coming to a scattering of onlookers lining the remains of a verge. A bulldozer was crushing the plastered walls and bamboo struts of an entire row of houses. The taxi driver released his hand. I watched the listless shape of an old woman on a bench marooned in a rubble of rocks, the palm fronds of a roof at her feet broken as a shipwrecked sail; one half of a house behind her. Unapologetically sliced in two. I shifted uncomfortably in my seat. Its three inside walls were painted blue, everything in order—a small kitchen, a chair, shelves neatly stacked with cooking utensils, and a calendar. I felt a prickling of goosebumps down my arms as if the tip of a knife was lifting my skin, testing its limits—one life severing into two.

Neat and ordered was how I had left our house. Everything in place, everything spotless—an attempt at wholeness, a way to make the leaving easier, to soften the unforgiving gaze of Marcus, as if a lint-free carpet meant anything to him. 'Why can't you be happy with what you've got? You think leaving is going to change things?' Over and over like a broken record. All it did was make me more determined.

It was enough, at first, our renovated house and trellises of vegetables, Marcus's carpentry and my part-time hours as a nurse's aide in a retirement home—each room a capsule of memories real and imagined, beside every bed a tableau of wedding photos, sons and daughters, grandchildren and great grandchildren. It was as much my job to listen, as it was to take a pulse, to bathe and feed the residents in my care; each story recounted, a way of circumventing their years. Then I'd return home to us, our unconscious lapses into habits punctuated by shared moments. If I had attempted to change the rituals of our days, would these tinkerings have made a difference?

As the taxi picked up speed, I turned in my seat to look for the woman again, for a glimpse of her face, her expression—would it be resolve or resignation? Or no expression at all? I had seen lives reduced to that. The street and its demolished houses had disappeared into dust.

The island of Srirangam marks the end of Andal's story. It was the temple city where she dreamed her wedding, and here I was freshly tumbled out of a plane, about to cross the Kavery River into its arms. Srivilliputtur, where Andal's story began, was still another half day by train. I added up the hours it would take, then counted out the petals of a brown velvet flower in the taxi's upholstery—he loves me, he loves me not—falling into the games my mind sometimes played in its attempt at icing everything into order when clearly the world rushing by outside my window was anything but. Another lone cow with a plastic bag hanging from its mouth ambled across four lanes of cars, motorbikes, and three wheelers. A bus careered into one-way traffic setting off a cacophony of horns. School children pedalled home oblivious to the cars swerving around them and December's sun shimmered the dust.

One night, that was all Marcus and I had spent in Srivilliputtur on our last trip, me holding tightly to the tattered pages of a poetry book found in Delhi a month and a half before. What were the odds in a country of more than twenty-five million people and twenty languages, and a hundred thousand gods, of then finding myself in the town where the poems had been written, three and a half days' train journey south? Was my path to the feet of a girl with a green parrot perched on her shoulder nothing more than serendipitous? It was as if I had been turned upside down, swung around in mid-air, then dropped into a myth that was not, in the eyes of Andal's devotees at least, a myth at all. Every day in Srivilliputtur they sang her songs and called her their mother. Andal, the goddess who refused everything except love.

I threaded my bangles up and down each arm, feeling their reassuring coolness, as the taxi braked, accelerated, and horned us on.

'A lady without bangles is undressed,' the old woman behind the counter had admonished as she slipped my hands through circlets of green and red glass. I had bought them on that one night in Srivilliputtur's temple arcade, then the next morning we were whisked off on an altogether different kind of pilgrimage. I kept those bangles like talismans. You will return, I had promised myself, watching the tall tower of Andal's temple grow smaller and smaller, as we sped toward a mountain called Chathuragiri.

I didn't know then that both these places were portents for me.

The towers of Srirangam's temple city came into view above the lush greens of coconut and banyan trees. 'Stop,' I said to the driver. 'Is there a ferry?' He turned to me with a look of alarm. 'But, madam, in two minutes I am delivering you.' He pointed to the wide river we were about to cross. 'It is dangerous for a foreign lady and the ferry stop is two miles upriver.'

'I will pay you.'

The Kavery is a river as sacred to the Tamils as the Ganges is to all of India. Once there was no bridge and all pilgrims, rich and poor, were ferried by boat. This was the very river Andal crossed on her way to the dark-skinned god she called Lord Ranganatha—her last recorded journey. I stepped into the small wooden boat and the ferry-wallah pushed us off. He was an old man, sinewy and weathered. I leaned into the rhythm of his oars as the river carried us, wondering if it might be ignorance, reducing life into a beginning, middle, and end, when these dynamics are happening in every moment. Downstream on Srirangam's banks, wood-smoke curled lazily into the haze. Silhouettes of pilgrims were turned toward the sun, three times submerging themselves for purification. Wherever a pilgrim steps into its water—at its source in the mountain ghats, where their god reclines in the temple's sanctum sanctorum, or where the Kavery is finally swallowed by the Indian Ocean—it is the same river, indiscriminately generous with its blessings.

We dipped and glided toward Srirangam's banks. It felt as if this passage across the river was somehow more of a separation from Marcus than the twelve hours of flight between Coolangatta and Tiruchirapalli. With each stroke of oar, I felt the division between us grow. What do you say to the man you fell in love with twenty-five years ago? What do you say to him when skeins of memories, of your love and despair, begin their unravelling? I trailed my fingers through the fast-flowing water, skimming small whirlpools of ash and marigold petals, of departed ones and pilgrims, and the intangibility of billowy clouds reflected all around us, banks of them building, shifting, and with each plunged oar, disappearing into ripples of molten silver.

What of this Tamil god Ranganatha known by a multitude of other names? He who has, as capriciously as this river, chosen to charge into my life along with all his incarnations—a boar, a tortoise, a baby floating on a banyan leaf, a dwarf, a lion, a blue-skinned flute-playing mischievous boy—none of it was logical. But that wasn't the point. They were all doors into the same house, elements of the same river flowing toward an infinite ocean of milk where a lord known universally throughout India as Vishnu floated on the sinuous body of a snake. On other occasions he might choose to stand with his feet on the earth, his head in a heaven called *Vaikuntha* and his body absolutely everywhere.

Tirumal, Narayana, Vatapatra sayee, Ranganatha … no Hindu I had met appeared to have a problem with their plethora of gods and it didn't seem to matter if a story mutated in the telling. The more the merrier. 'But Tirumal,' a priest said to me on that first night in Srivilliputtur, 'is the name you can be giving all of them.'

෧

I felt as if I had been coming to this ancient land forever, possibly even lifetimes. India was where I had first conceived. How close I had come, then, to my only child.

I was a wise twenty-one, unhinged from the trappings of the West. Returning home from my first adventure into the land of gods and goddesses and one lover whose face I cannot now recall, I clutched at the pain in my belly with a naive sort of disbelief. Blood started pouring from me for the first time in three months. Then I felt the slide of something whole as my body shivered waves of hot and cold. But in a few hours, I was diving into the sea telling myself all was well, it was meant to be. There would be other times. My life stretched from the small curve of my belly to the wide arc of the ocean's horizon. The thought anything different might await never occurred. It was a year before my falling into bed with Marcus and almost four before I stepped, dazed, from a consulting room, taunted by the red desert silt of a painting hanging on its wall.

I caught glimpses of my thinning face between the ripples of each oar stroke and, to the bemusement of the ferry-wallah, cupped my hands, filling them with water again and again until my face and hair were drenched and I was laughing out loud. I didn't mind what I saw, as I fell back into my reflection, the strands of soaked silver, the hint of a wilderness returning to those eyes. And then she asked me a question and I felt it like an uncoiling inside me. Who are you?

A long time ago I was content for hours combing a beach for perfect discs of stone. I'd skip them across the water, the more skips the better. Is that what I have been doing, only ever skipping the surface?

Chapter Two

I cooked sweet pudding for you
young paddy, pounded rice, sugarcane and jaggery

Nacciyar Tirumoli 1:7

Srivilliputtur was a town Marcus and I had never heard of before visiting our good friend the professor in Chennai. He had put a plan in place for us to meet him there, along with his entourage of pilgrims. Srivilliputtur was the closest train station to a village called Watrap in the foothills of the Western Ghats, and from there our ascent would begin.

'Gods willing, I want to make one last pilgrimage to Chathuragiri mountain,' the professor had said, cracking his knuckles and inching a stretch back into the cushions of his chair. 'You please come with us. In one month we go.'

Marcus's intrigue with everything alchemical and esoteric had led us to the professor's door. Whenever we were in Chennai, we visited him. Despite the aches and pains of old age and an ailing heart, his mind sparked at the mention of a Vedic text, the Puranas, the Upanishads, the Ramayana. And if Marcus asked about any ancient yogic teachings, the professor effervesced with stories, caves and shrines to visit, and *siddhars*, whether living or dead, we simply must seek out.

I had owned my book of Tamil poetry less than two weeks and my mind could not settle anywhere in the conversation he and Marcus were having. Ascetic practices of holy men paled against the aesthetics of one girl poet and the verses I had been reading ever since that day in Delhi.

If we come with flowers for you, if we chant with devotion and meditate, our self-delusion, past, present, and future, will burn like cotton in fire.

Hoping for a pause in the conversation, I took the book from my bag and placed it on the table between us. The professor stopped mid-sentence.

'Ah, the Azhwars. Have you been hearing their songs?'

I shook my head. The professor swivelled in his chair and pulled a leather-bound tome from a shelf. 'Four thousand verses,' he said. A whiff of moth, dust and the scent of yellowing paper filled the air as he opened it.

'*Iti iti*,' he read, stretching his arms out as if to hold the whole room. 'Meaning is: this too, that too.'

'*Neti neti*,' he chuckled, returning to the page. 'Not this, not that. Which one do you choose?'

He looked at Marcus. Long before I had discovered the downward dogs and shoulder stands of yoga, Marcus was walking his Marcus path, effortlessly folding his legs into lotus, eyes closed to the materiality of the world. His answer to the professor's question was obvious. *Neti neti.*

The professor looked at me and I squirmed. I had no idea what my path was, or even if I had one. I had dabbled that was all. Meditating here, chanting there. I was curious but never curious enough, or desperate enough, to leave my life behind and forge into the unknown with anything that might resemble a singular purpose. Did the professor really expect an answer from me? *Iti Iti. Neti neti.* I traced my fingers over the girl dancing on *For the Love of God*'s cover.

India had been in my blood from the beginning but in a dreamy kind of way. As a child I spent hours poring over a photograph album belonging to my grandmother. She had wrapped it in a piece of velvet studded with mirrors and slipped it into my mother's suitcase the day my father took leave from the navy to bring the two of us to Australia.

For Saisha, she had written in elegant loops and swirls of ink above the first photo, *so my granddaughter never forgets her home is also here.*

There she stood, a studio portrait, pressing her lips to my newborn forehead, one sepia mountain behind her. On the next page, my grandmother is kneeling, her head in the lap of a woman with *kajal* eyes, a diamante scarf covering her head.

'Who is this?' I asked my mother.

'That is another French lady who was living in India. Your grandmother took a steamboat all the way there to visit her. She was called The Mother.'

'And what does this say?' I pointed to more of my grandmother's handwriting on the opposite page.

'When you are older, I will tell you.'

I did not forget. 'Read to me, Mama,' I demanded when I was taller.

'It is something The Mother said to your grandmama. She has written it in Occitanian.'

My mother paused, as if remembering again the language of the life she had left behind, then slowly translated. 'Running away from difficulties is never a way of overcoming them. If you flee from them you won't be able to defeat them, and they have every chance of defeating you. That is why we are here in Pondicherry and not on some Himalayan peak. Although I admit being on a Himalayan peak would be delightful—but perhaps not so effective.'

'Where is cherry?'

I remember my mother's laughter. 'Pondicherry, sweet pea. A town by the ocean in South India, a very long way from Grandmama's house in the South of France.' I turned the album's page, to the stone cottage where I was born and behind it the mountain my mother often spoke about. On the opposite page, separated by a thin sheet of tissue paper, were sari-clad women, buffalo carts, and coconut palms. Two veiled lands shifting one to the other.

I felt Marcus nudge me under the table. Was the professor still waiting for an answer? His chin rested on his clasped hands, his eyes bouncing between the two of us.

Iti Iti. Neti neti. I wanted both, the pleasures of taste, touch, smell—but I wanted to be free from them too.

Drawing fingers through his white beard, the professor returned to the words in front of him. Flicking through page upon page of its swirling Tamil he said, 'This is the Vaishnavite book of books, their magnum opus, the *Nalayira Divya Prabandham.* All twelve Azhwars are here. Nammalvar, Tirumangai, Andal—or Kodai, as she was called by her father when he found her—he was an Azhwar too. His name was Visnucitta.'

The professor stopped and tapped a verse, considering its translation. '*I am like the flower emptied by the divine bee.* It is one of Nammalvar's songs. Some say he used to visit with Andal's father.' He sent a casual glance my way.

'Now,' he said, slapping the book shut, 'to our pilgrimage. All the necessary arrangements have been made.' He took a folder from a pile of papers and handed us an itinerary.

'We will make ourselves comfortable in three-tiered wooden sleeper class for the overnight train journey south,' he said. 'Breakfast parcels will be there when we arrive in Srivilliputtur. A minibus will take us to the foot of Chathuragiri and then we begin the eight-hour trek to its peak. You youngsters can walk it! I will have to be carried.' He gave a laugh as carefree as a child's.

I looked at Marcus and could tell he too was daunted by the sound of a twenty-four-hour marathon.

'Is it possible we can meet you in Srivilli …?' I chanced.

'Srivilliputtur!' The professor chuckled at my attempt. 'As you wish,' he said, 'but what will you be doing between now and then?'

He unfolded a map and proceeded to draw a plan of sacred sites and temples criss-crossing Tamil Nadu, and I wondered if one overnight train ride from Chennai to Srivilliputtur might not be an easier option. His pen moved south.

'After three weeks you will arrive here,' he said, circling the city of Madurai. We had visited its Meenakshi temple before and were happy to return—its labyrinth of halls and smoky shrines, its enormous resident elephant. 'And then you go to Palani,' the professor continued, marking the map with an asterisk. 'From there you take a bus and get off here.' He marked another asterisk. Ask for the siddhar called Mootai Swami, then you wait for a minibus to take you to a crossroads. From there it is walking distance only.'

We'll see, I thought, conjuring up a few rest houses away from the mayhem, a balcony and a sling-back chair, birdsong and the sound of wind in the trees. One book in my lap.

The professor returned my Azhwar paperback and walked us to the street. He hailed an auto and negotiated a fare with the driver. 'All of them rogues.' He shook his head. 'Even in heaven you will find them.'

As we waved goodbye, he said, as if an afterthought, 'Oh, and if you reach Srivilliputtur before us make sure you visit its temple. Very beautiful.'

Marcus left me at a tea stall in Meenakshi temple's marketplace, fortification for working my way through bolts of cottons before finding a tailor offering honest prices. After three weeks of travelling on passenger trains and antique buses, sleeping on ashram floors and scrambling over boulders in search of rumoured siddhars and their caves, I needed a fresh set of clothes. Marcus disappeared into the shadows of Meenakshi's thousand columned pavilion.

When we met later, there was a spring to his step, and over lunch at our favourite hotel, as we crumbled papadams over rice and made our way through the twelve little bowls on our *thali* trays, he said, 'I have found a place. I'll take you there tonight.'

'What, where?' Knowing, as I asked, not to expect an answer. Marcus, a man of few words, aloof to the chatterings of the world—still a mystery after all our years together. Maybe that was it. Without the mystery the magic would go. Or the challenge. What were the words my grandmother had written, *running away from difficulties* …? I swallowed them with a mouthful of vegetable sambar. Love, I thought, how do you make sense of something that is not black and white? The dhal was salty and sour with tamarind, the *rasaam*, spicy. Fresh corn and beans simmered in a coconut gravy.

As we ambled through the maze of motorbike-choked streets, I glanced up to see a crescent moon hovering behind the southern temple tower. It looked as if it had been caught in the arms of one of the tower's thousand sculpted gods, Hanuman, half-man, half-monkey. Police-frisked and bags checked, we strode over a high stone step into the domain of goddess Meenakshi. Marcus led the way through throngs of evening devotees to the steps of the temple's *teerthum* where the moon was again, this time a reflection in the centre of its sacred water, released from Hanuman's arms. Fountains sprang from the concrete lotus flowers at the teerthum's edge, rippling the moon into slivers of bright light. Past the main shrine with a notice saying Non-Hindus-Not-Allowed, past Ganesha, his golden body freshly decorated with marigold and jasmine, and into a dimly lit corridor blessedly empty but for a few of the devout briskly walking, prayer beads slipping through their fingers.

Marcus brushed the back of my hand, guiding me toward a dark alcove where four men and two women sat silently meditating before a small black granite Shiva lingam.

Lingams were everywhere—revered in temple shrines or the roots of a banyan tree on a street corner, worshipped beside holy rivers and in secret caves—these smooth oval rocks an ancient phallic symbol appearing miraculously out of the earth. I had found the whole concept bemusing at first, sacred stones so overtly sexual, openly worshipped by men, women, and children.

Marcus had a library of books at home about this elementary force—Shiva's subtle body in perfect union with Shakti—underlying every pulse of life. Books about *kundalini* and the serpent sleeping at the base of a human spine; what happens when it wakes and begins uncoiling through each of the seven chakras. Books about Tantra and the path to enlightenment; how to move from a world anchored in base desires to a finer, more pure awareness. Stories of yogis and yoginis living free from sexual entanglement and earthly attachments. I would run my fingers over the books' spines, curious on one hand, but reluctant to open their dense texts. How overwhelmingly far I was from understanding Marcus's resolve.

Evening eased into night. Except for the few ghee lamps lit by meditators, the temple alcove where we sat was dark. The man to my left was in full lotus, his eyelids open but both pupils disappeared toward his third eye. It was a rare sight in a temple, these singular bodies engaged in the channelling of breath and recitations of silent mantras, no hands out asking for favours, no grasping and pushing. To my right sat Marcus, serene and still, at home at last, the world left behind. Given the chance, I thought with a half-smile, he'd stay there forever.

In temples our paths often separated, Marcus staying put in

an alcove or shrine and me off searching its rooms for places where women gathered, smearing *kumkuman* powder on the pregnant belly of a statue, offering flowers at the stone feet of a boy god playfully playing his flute. So, it was on this night, a few days short of arriving in Srivilliputtur, I shook the pins and needles from my legs and walked toward the clouds of camphor and incense smoke filling Meenakshi temple's great hall. A sea of pilgrims were prostrating at the sanctum sanctorum's entrance. It was a sight as ancient as the temple itself and I stood mesmerised in the midst of their faith, the stones thrumming at my feet like some primaeval consciousness fighting its way into my body. Two decades. Was it really that long ago? I found myself questioning the renunciation of my sexuality, my body. What time had numbed rose up raw again.

§

If I was ever caught in the net of wanting more than Marcus was prepared to give, I attempted to think my way out of it. He was caught too, I rationalised, between one world and another, the wild lone eyes of Saivite ascetics who disappeared for years into remote caves only to appear in the world again needing nothing and no one. And yet Marcus lived the life of a householder with me.

'Choosing celibacy as a path liberates mind and body,' Marcus had said.

After meeting in India, we returned to Australia and began saving for our dream of an idyllic life in the country. Less than six years had gone by—it still felt like honeymoon days to me, wrapped in the mystery of him, beguiling as those clouds swirling Mt Warning's peak. I was only twenty-seven. I sat there, looking at him.

'Celibacy?'

'You will have more life force inside you, more energy for

meditation,' he said, before folding his legs into a half lotus and closing his eyes.

'But how can you love me and yet never make love with me?'

If my question was tinged with emotion he did not reply. He doesn't *do* emotion. I grew used to the strings of that net, despair and desire. Sometimes whole weeks slipped by without a tangle. There was flour to grind, bread to bake, a garden to weed, my three days of work in town. But I had no map, no way of understanding the serpent beneath the surface, coiled at my sacrum like the picture on the cover of one of his books. Mine slept on like the weight of a stone. Occasionally it might wake—if the whim took Marcus. I glowed for days, taking pleasure in the roundness and softness of my hips and breasts, the musk smell of Marcus's skin on mine, and I hankered for more. But more became less and less. Weeks turning into months, months into years.

There were nights I lay awake, my body burning to dissolve into his, the idea of a higher path to god distant as the Milky Way swirling outside our window—there for the sole purpose of mocking my attempts at his idea of love.

'I can't do this,' I moaned into the dark, squeezing a pillow between my legs or curling into foetus position and rocking myself to sleep. I was desperate in those early days; I clung to him, pleaded for a response, knowing all the while how pathetic it must look. And if Marcus did caress me, it was never enough; it only made me crave more. My body learned ways of survival. It knew touch meant eventual pain so it retracted from his touch, and that was a relief for Marcus.

Celibacy was his decision, not mine, and yet I chose to stay.

Away from the prostrating pilgrims, a young bride in cerise silk, arm in arm with her mother and grandmother, circled the image of a woman sculpted on a column, her ancient arms wrapped around her belly, her naked body glistening with sesame oil. The bride placed a red hibiscus at her feet, then offered a leaf-bowl of sweet rice.

There was no solace for me in the asceticism of sadhus, sitting on their cushions of stone, eyes turned inward away from the life pulsing all around them.

There was too much beauty in the world. Too much to love.

Chapter Three

Nacciyar Tirumoli *3:2*

We placed our trust in the auto driver, who drove us from Srivilliputtur's train station to the fluoro-blue steps of a hotel on the edge of town. Our room's air-conditioner worked, which was a plus, even though it sounded like a lawnmower. I unlaced my rucksack and took out *For the Love of God*. In the weeks since first setting eyes upon her, amongst the stacks of textbooks and trashy novels on the footpaths of Old Delhi, this copper-skinned girl dancing on the cover had taken up residence. She was the first to be unpacked and last to be packed. The book felt as permanent a travelling companion as did Marcus. It was an unsettling and inexplicable thought and I brushed it aside. The room was too tiny.

'A bed and a bathroom of any description,' Marcus rationalised with that endearing smile of his, never seeming to break free from its boundaries, 'is a luxury you and I deserve, Saisha, on the eve of our climb up Chathuragiri. And the advantage of the air-conditioner,' he went on, 'is it drowns the thump of music and shouts of men in the sleazy-lit bar on the floor below.'

I threw him one of my smiles across the few square metres of room before opening to a random page.

There is a saying that no matter how much a person searches for a teacher, a guide or a guru, in the end it is the teacher who finds the one who is seeking. I thought about this as I looked at Marcus. What destiny catapulted us into each other's arms all those years ago? We'd hardly exchanged names, and then we were living together. Sharing life with him was a kind of refuge, despite the challenges. He was my constant and he was kind, in his own quiet way. His mysteriousness drew me in like a magnet, but when he closed his eyes and lotus-crossed his legs, his presence felt more like an absence.

I returned to the opened page on my lap, scanning it for a verse to jump out. Who was this girl who composed these songs? And what was it about her longing and her despair that touched me so deeply? Was it as plain as that eternal conundrum, unrequited love, hers for a god and mine for this man I shared a bed with, but not my body? And why now, just as I am trying to read, does Marcus decide to banter away so uncharacteristically?

His sacred basil garland is all my heart desires. My mind grows wild.

Marcus and I did what we always do in the evening and set off for the local temple. But there were two temples, the hotel manager pointed out. The one he recommended was a temple to Shiva. 'Inside you will be seeing the famous Nataraja, the cosmic dancing god.' He stopped to light more incense for the small shrine on a shelf above his cash register.

'Which way is it?' Marcus asked. He had already decided.

'Is that the temple tower we could see from our train?' I interrupted.

As we curved one last time before the final stretch into Srivilliputtur, I had seen it rising above the town's trees and tiled roofs, like a rainbow-coloured beacon.

'No, madam, it is a different one. Twelve tiers this *gopuram* is having, the highest temple gateway in Tamil Nadu. Walkable distance, go left then left again near the bus stop.'

'I'm going there,' I said with a determination that surprised both of us.

Marcus turned right.

A coconut-wallah had set up his cart near a colonnade of trinket shops leading to the temple. I was thirsty. With a smile and a deft machete-whack, the wallah made a straw-sized opening. As I took long sips of its sweet, quenching water, a woman sidled up to me with garlands of green threaded on her arm. The scent of the leaves was pungent and spicy.

'For god,' the woman said, holding a garland to my face before the coconut-wallah had a chance to shoo her away.

He cut my coconut in half and carved out a primitive spoon from its husk to scoop out the slippery, transparent flesh. I turned to catch the garland seller, wishing I had followed my impulse to buy one for whoever the god inside was that I was about to meet. But there was another woman swaggering in her place with matted hair falling in thick dusty wads past her waist, her body swathed in faded red cloth hitched up to her knees. I caught a flash of the bangles covering her forearms and felt a kind of foreboding. She seemed out of context, too wild and unfettered for the quiet streets I had walked. Then she was gone —the scent of her heavy on the air for a moment, of sweat and smoke, earth and patchouli.

The temple was unlike the traditional square layout of others we had visited. Its walls were painted with the same red and white stripes, but it seemed more an L-shaped fusion of two temples, not one. I could see the top of its tall tower rising from another side and wondered which entrance to take. There was a sudden *rush-rush* of wings above me, a flock of white herons taking off from the sprawling branches overhanging the wall beside the coconut-wallah's cart. Velvet-black wings swirled across the pastel sky and descended, taking the herons' place. I traced my fingers across the wall's stones, still warm from the day's heat. A hush returned, once the fruit bats settled into their upside down roosts. A hush, unlike anything I had sensed in a long, long time.

I followed the length of the wall and came to another entrance. The gate was open. Inside, around an ancient low-ceilinged pavilion, was a garden hedged with jasmine, an oasis of perfumed shade, pomegranate and neem trees, hibiscus and roses. Before entering the pavilion, I glanced up into the quiet of the trees either side and noticed the silhouette of a small temple sculpted onto the pavilion's roof. Carved into its niche was a painted garden and the figure of a Brahmin priest, his arms outstretched to the baby girl lying in the earth at his feet.

Chapter Four

O lord of Villiputtur,
where graceful swans wander,
how I ache to gaze upon your golden feet

Nacciyar Tirumoli 5:5

On a night more than twelve hundred years ago, Visnucitta woke from a dreamless sleep. His wife, Varaji, slept soundly beside him, her arm pillowing his head. He was restless. Though there was just the two of them in their house, he felt the hovering of another. He slipped from his wife's embrace and stood at their bedroom window. Through lattice the shape of deer eyes he watched the moon appear, an arc of saffron light riding the mist. Clouds wrapped the mountains, zephyrs of wind from the west were coaxing them closer and closer each day. Visnucitta took a deep breath, smelling the portent of rain.

He tiptoed downstairs. There were enough hours before dawn to prepare a palm leaf, sharpen his stylus, and write a new song. He splashed his face with water from the well, lit a ghee lamp with the buried coals from last night's fire, prostrated in the direction of Lord Tirumal's sanctum, and then settled at his desk.

Closing his eyes, he pictured the cowherd chieftain's wife Yashoda rocking a cradle. He imagined the weight of her baby boy's rosy feet pressing into her hands. He heard the tinkling of Krishna's anklet bells and saw the affection shining through Yashoda's eyes. *Oh, moon if you desire to play with him, come out from behind the clouds.*

Visnucitta wrote until it was time to join the chanting of the temple's priests, singing in the dawn, waking up the gods. As he prepared to leave, he heard his dear wife Varaji opening the shutters of their house, filling their urn with water, the snaps of kindling as she prepared her cooking fire, the soft sound of her breath blowing the twigs alight. Star alignments had boded well for their arranged marriage and ten years had already passed. His future as priest of Villiputtur's temple was promising. A son, even a daughter, would perfect their happiness.

As for Varaji, the sound of children playing outside the walls of their house no longer pained her, but still she prayed, her palms together over her belly. Every year during the ninth month of Margazhi she joined the dawn procession of women down to the river. They bathed together and cupped their hands with water, raising them to the sun as they sang harvest songs then prayers to Lord Krishna and the goddess Katyayani riding her lion, each woman holding tight to private dreams of an auspicious marriage or a child to seal the union. But still, Varaji's body did not swell.

Visnucitta lost himself in the temple's garden. The fragrance of flowers and herbs when placed as garlands around his god were, he felt, more pleasing to Lord Tirumal than endless recitations of Vedas and Sastra texts. The trees he had planted in the year before his marriage to Varaji now towered over the temple walls offering protection for the new pond and a patch of earth where he had planted the bulbs of his favourite lily. If grown in shade its blue petals turned to deep indigo and when he placed a garland of these over Tirumal's sapphire-hued body it appeared as if his very skin absorbed them. Working in his garden was like painting, the colours of one flower brushing another. Visnucitta had already ploughed the earth around the pond, visualising how darkly beautiful the lilies would look circled with sacred basil. With rain imminent and the moon in the fifth day of the bright cycle, it was the perfect time to rake in his *tulasi* seeds.

In the smoky light of their courtyard Varaji, lifted sour-leav-ened rice cakes from the fire, then gave one last stir to the caramelising toddy-sugar. These were the scents that welcomed Visnucitta home from the temple, coaxing his mind from plans for his garden to the hunger in his belly. They ate together in silence, and over clay cups of ginger tea Varaji listened to some of the verses Visnucitta had written before dawn. Theirs was an unconventional Brahmin marriage. Visnucitta did not insist on eating first and was always eager to hear Varaji's thoughts on his poems.

He watched her moving from one chore to the next in an easy, contented rhythm, her whole body present and involved as if she were preparing for Krishna himself. To him, even though she was without child, her demeanour was in every way a moth-er's. But when Visnucitta wrote poems in the voice of Krishna's mother, Yashoda, it was the low velvet nuances of another woman he called upon for inspiration.

Sacred basil, fragrant and forest grown, a garland of wish-fulfilling flowers, gifts for you my king from lotus-born Lakshmi. Don't cry my gem-hued one, don't cry.

Varaji gave him an innocent smile of praise. Light was already dappling their courtyard and her eyes gestured toward their front gate; it was time he left for work. With a pot of tulasi seeds in one hand and a sickle for cutting flowers in the other, Visnucitta walked the short distance to the temple garden.

He wandered the length of his flower beds, bending low to see what buds had opened since yesterday, what colours to choose for Tirumal's garland today. He noticed bird prints in the furrows ploughed around the pond and took a handful of river sand to mix with the tiny tulasi seeds before planting them. As he ran his fingers through the sand, he felt the breeze suddenly drop and a shudder in the ground beneath his feet. The early morning chorus of birds stopped. Visnucitta's breath stopped.

A blaze of lightning electrified the sky, but there was no storm cloud in sight. A deafening crash of thunder split the air and again the earth tremored. The silence afterward was numinous. Visnucitta's heart thudded like a loud drum against his chest. Then he heard something else, like spring water bubbling from the earth into a pool of smooth pebbles.

He took tentative steps toward the sound. The air he inhaled was menthol and pungent. A cluster of last season's tulasi rustled at the centre of a bed, the husks of their seed pods shaking loose. He separated the tangle of leaves and stems, and a shower of seeds fell free. And there, where they fell, half covered in a crumbling of soil, Visnucitta found a small baby girl laughing at the tickle of seeds falling across her face. Her chubby arms and legs kicked up at the sky. He stood unblinking, jaw dropped in disbelief. She wore a smock of fine cotton, moon-white and edged with gold. Delicate bangles carved from conch shell clinked at her wrists.

'Oh! Krishna. Mukunda!' Visnucitta moved closer.

At the sound of his voice, the little girl turned toward him, wriggling her toes, shaking off the dirt. Then she held out her arms to him, and he heard two syllables sweeter than any song. 'Appa.'

The day Visnucitta found Andal her hair was straight, but by the time she learned to sit up it had curled into ringlets. Her skin, that had at first glowed red as gurivinda seeds, was now fair.

'Your face is bright as the moon,' Varaji cooed as she combed her daughter's hair.

'No,' Visnucitta joked, 'my daughter is the thief who stole the moon's light.'

'Ah, but you are wrong husband. The moon stole the light from Andal's face.'

Andal laughed in her high tinkling voice at the bantering of her mother and father.

As soon as she learned to walk, she ventured into the streets around their house, making friends, building sandcastles, and imagining, always imagining. In the evening, she climbed onto the laps of her aunties as they sat on their verandas cooling off and playing dice, blowing air into their right fist before throwing them for luck. The sound of their jingling bangles distracted the yogis walking past and the women laughed as they adjusted their breasts higher in their bodices.

Mango groves and rows of coconut trees, date palms, and areca nut shaded the streets and wells of Villiputtur. Jackfruit trees as old as the town grew by the river. When the fruit ripened and fell, the air was stinky and sweet, the ground soft and syrupy. Black bees swarmed all over the jackfruits' humped spiny skins so they looked like green elephants tied up with chains.

Every courtyard had a bathing pond and after the women washed, they sat on the steps massaging turmeric paste into their skin. At night, wild swans came to drink and sleep, safe from mountain lions. Their white feathers soaked up the leftover turmeric and when they flew into the dawn, the women said, 'Golden swans from heaven have been sleeping in our garden.'

Visnucitta had already joined the temple priests and musicians, their chants and instruments filtering over the temple walls and through the trees of its garden. Andal followed the eyes of her mother and aunties as they searched the colours of the sky for one last look at the golden swans.

'Lord Tirumal,' she heard them call from their long red beaks.

'Wake up,' they sang to the rhythm of their wingbeats.

Villiputtur's cows gave the creamiest milk, the juice from its sugar cane was the sweetest. The jasmine growing in her father's temple garden bloomed day and night. It was here, in this town where swans wandered, that Andal imagined herself a cowherd girl in love with the sapphire-skinned one. This was her secret.

When I come of age, she vowed, I am going to marry him.

Chapter Five

'A cowherder,' you say. 'A butter thief!'
Gossip mongers all of you.
He held Govardhana like an umbrella,
saved the world from torrential rains.
Take me to that mountain

Nacciyar Tirumoli 12:8

Leaving the ferry-wallah with a smile wide as the Kavery River, a fifty-rupee tip in his hand, I pulled my soaked hair into a knot, shouldered my pack, and walked into the scents of guava and roses, the tinkling of anklets and bicycle bells, and the tinny recordings of devotional CDs chanting Tirumal's names. Narayana, Krishna, Govinda. A herd of goats were sleeping away the heat nestled on a mound of sand dumped in the middle of East Chitra Street. Pilgrims dressed in red queued at a cart where a man dished out a *prasadam* of vegetable rice with pickles onto squares of newspaper.

'Hey!' One of the women tugged at the two uneven ends of

the *dupatta* draped down my back. With a welcoming grin, she evened my scarf and sent me on my way.

I locked my surprisingly spotless room and walked down the tiled corridor to the Pilgrim House's front counter. Flashing lights framed a print of Krishna as a roly poly toddler. He has tipped a pot full of freshly churned cream onto its side so he can reach into it with his hand. The feast has already begun and his delighted face is smeared with golden butter. Any moment his mother Yashoda will discover him, scold him, then again fall instantly under his spell.

The lady at the desk sizes me up. An old man had checked me in earlier, not bothering with the formalities. She was the owner. 'Passport! I am needing a photocopy.'

'Mrs Saisha,' she said, copying my details into the register, spelling each word out loud. 'S a y s h a. An Indian name you are having!'

Indian? No. Saisha was my grandmother's name and she was Occitanian. 'Excuse me, but that's not the same spelling as in my passport,' I said as she continued to write.

'Saysha,' she pinned me with twinkling eyes, 'is how we say it and how we spell it. My niece has same name. Meaning is giving the wish.'

Giving the wish? Wish-giving, wish-fulfilling? None of them seemed to fit me.

'I am Geetha,' she said. 'Meaning is song to Krishna.' She turned to the cheeky, buttery-smeared grin of the boy in the frame behind her.

Geetha tapped the kangaroo on my passport. 'Australia,' she said, sliding it back to me. 'My brother lives in Geneva.'

'Oh?'

'Wait. I'll call him.' She took out a phone from the folds of her sari.

I caught my breath, wanting to suggest there was no need, but the number was dialled and we waited for pick up.

He didn't.

Geetha smiled and tucked the phone back into her sari. 'Later,' she reassured, 'we can try again.'

Srirangam's streets had fallen quiet. The temple had closed, allowing the gods to take their lunch in peace, have a nap, then be readied by their priests for the evening lines of pilgrims eager for a *darshan*. Except for tea and *tiffin* shops, most doors were padlocked. A lone man sat under a blue tarpaulin strung up above a tiny alcove between a mobile phone store and a bangle emporium. His tools were simple and his spare parts many. Umbrella spokes lay in neat piles to his left, pieces of wire, lengths of string, patches of plastic. He is the one locals flock to with their nine-lives umbrellas when the rainy season comes, replacing broken spokes, tightening catches and reattaching the plastic with a few swift needle and threads. But it had not rained for months and the next real monsoon was due in July, at the earliest, depending, of course, on the gods. It made no sense, him sitting there, and yet the world he had created, the hessian sack floor, the tarpaulin roof over his head—it was a sanctuary of order. Order in life got a thumbs-up from me. When those monsoon clouds eventually came, he would be ready.

It seemed as if all Srirangam had retreated except for me and the umbrella man. We were the only ones left in the world. A world, the Vedas say, reeling from the misdeeds and greed born out of an age of plenty, such are the shallow minds of men. The sun was unforgiving. My head was pounding and my mouth parched. Was that Hanuman, the monkey god, flying through the sky, taped to the wall above the umbrella man's head? The more I read of Andal's verses extolling the triumphs of fantastical beings and the tricks of a blue-skinned boy, the easier it was to accept the role and reality of these stories for those who believed them. These divine and otherwise supernatural beings are as embedded in the minds and imaginations of the faithful now as they were a thousand years ago. However meagre an existence, a beneficent god could bestow a miracle. However full a politician's vault, the gods were the ones who, in the end, held the key. Tally or not, the gods had their reasons. There had been ages of great enlightenment in the past and hopefully in the future. Now, the Vedic scriptures decreed, was a period of darkness and desecration, the age of Kali Yuga.

An old man pedalled slowly past us, his eyes fixed on the road ahead. I watched him disappear, swallowed by the mirage of an ocean shimmering at the end of North Chitra Street. Saltwater or fresh, real or imagined, it didn't matter, my mouth flooded with saliva. I closed my eyes for just a second to steady myself and was assaulted by the crash of one of those waves played and replayed on television screens around the world, the tsunami that knew no boundary—India, Sri Lanka, Myanmar, Thailand. You never know when the waves of a cosmic sea might flood the earth again, breaking every dune and riverbank.

A long time ago the earth was deluged. Not a soul survived except for Tirumal. He incarnated into a gurgling baby boy, calling himself Vatapatra sayee. Taking refuge on a banyan leaf, he floated across the drowned world, falling fast asleep for an aeon before waking up to play with the light beams and rainbows skipping either side of his little raft. The wind took him wherever he wanted to go. He skimmed the tips of drowned mountain peaks and temple towers, then fell asleep again and another aeon passed until one bright morning the waters started receding. Light penetrated the depths where amoebas had drifted aimlessly for an eternity. Their cells began splitting into two, and two again, until the day came when creatures with webbed feet and wings flew from the sea. Others grew ten fingers and toes and made footprints for the first time on shores of fine pulverised coral. Their hearts began a kind of thinking. They built temples from stone. They weighed up right from wrong, always giving their god the final say. They took patterns of stars down from the sky and wove them into myths. It helped make sense of the world. Just like fairy tales, from imperfections. A prince from a frog. A god from a boar, and a goddess from a girl—Andal, whose father was a priest at the temple where Lord Vatapatra sayee lay. All those centuries ago her birthplace was called Villiputtur but now it is Srivilliputtur, the Sri added in honour of their queen.

The umbrella man's eyes fixed on mine, simple and consuming, and the world stopped its spin. He reached behind him into a small box then held out a necklace. Its beads were clear crystal interspersed with metallic-looking pearls and stranded together with twists of copper wire.

'Take it.'

'How much?'

He swam his head from side to side. 'Take it.'

Leaning over on his crossed legs he put it in my hand.

'Do not wear at night. Too powerful. If you do, the crystals will start shrinking and one day there will be nothing left.'

'What can I pay?'

'It is depending on you.'

He resumed work on an antique umbrella, unconcerned by the foreigner standing there, crazy in the midday sun.

I wondered how safe it was to wear. Maybe the gods would get it wrong and I'd be the one to disappear. There'd be a knock at our door. Sorry, sir, this is all she left. The black-suited bearer would pass Marcus an envelope and that'd be that.

The umbrella man paid no mind to the rupees I left at the edge of his hessian floor, and I continued on my way. More curious than superstitious I clasped the necklace at the back of my neck and tucked it into my shirt. It dawned on me that I might be jet-lagged. What's more, there was no Marcus, voice of reason and common sense, to suggest a walk at this hour was madness. I spotted a juice bar on the next corner, a dazzle of

Dulux yellow, and collapsed into the chair closest to the fan whirring at full speed above. A bare-chested boy with oil-slicked hair was rearranging fruit into mandalas of colour, triangles of Himalayan apples, Californian oranges, and Tamilian pineapples, their ripe scent overpowering the fumes of enamel paint. I pointed to the pomegranates, craving astringency. The boy whipped a towel over his shoulder, took a cleaver, and with uncontainable enthusiasm split the first pomegranate open. Severed seeds flew in every direction like bright jewels of fertility, their juices splashing dark against the boy's skin, splattering red across my white dupatta and making fluorescent purple stars on the freshly painted walls. He grinned ear to ear.

Safely back inside my Pilgrim House room, I collapsed on the bed under a stationary fan. 'Power cut,' Geetha had said. The heat was stultifying. I covered my body with a wet sheet and lay perfectly still, staring through the grilles of my window to the stone wall less than a foot away. Thoughts of Marcus wrenched at me from inside out. It was different being here alone. The world felt wider, and stranger. I had expected this, one more portal to go through, but I wasn't sure about the beat of butterflies in my stomach. I didn't want to be sick. And if it was trepidation, I didn't want that either.

I willed sleep, long hours of it, to wash my jet-lagged state away. I slipped the necklace off, just in case.

Chapter Six

What use is shame, all the village knows.
If I am to be cured … then take me to him

Nacciyar Tirumoli 12:2

'It is a vision of majesty, madam.'

I was standing in the shadow of Srirangam's largest temple tower, straining my neck back to take it all in. A vision indeed painted in technicolour. I nodded to the voice hovering at my ear.

'It is the raja gopuram madam. The first and largest tower through which the devotees will be entering on their way to the most sacred temple in all of India. You will be passing through six more towers, madam, before reaching the shrine of our Lord Ranganatha.'

It was early morning. I had slept through the night. Had it not been for the flip-flop of thongs up and down the Pilgrim House hallway and next door's guest—his snorts, guttural throat clearing and spitting—I would probably have slept some more.

But I felt rested and stretched long and slow across the space of my double bed. I could touch the stones of the wall outside my room's window, if I wanted to. It was, I realised, one of the temple's walls. If I was a crow looking down from above, there I would be in the arms of this ancient temple city's fourth enclosure. Each of the seven gateways, beginning at the Raja gopuram, mark the dropping away of earthly cares so by the time a devotee passes through the seventh and final gateway, she is ready to meet the god residing in its sanctum sanctorum—the *garbarigha* Tamils call it—womb chamber.

'Ha!' Marcus's voice entered my head. 'You don't have to tramp halfway round the world and through seven gateways. Meditate is all you need to do.' The sound of him, no matter he was thousands of miles away, made me grip the umbrella man's necklace. A defiant act that made no sense, really.

'Ha!' I replied out loud striding down the Pilgrim House corridor.

Geetha was on the phone and motioned me to stop. I waited at the front door watching school children bicycle past the same group of sleeping goats. She slid the phone back into the folds of her sari. 'For you,' she said, handing me a map. Then she took it back to proudly mark a cross where her Pilgrim House was so I would always be finding my way home. Her establishment, her pride and joy, built on a Brahmin street no less—for she was not a Brahmin and therefore a thorn in the side of a few of them. It had no view and no luxury either but it was clean and I felt safe and it was minutes from the main temple, so close I could leave my sandals behind and walk barefoot.

'Here is raja gopuram, then you go to Lord Ranganatha's temple,' she said, circling them, 'and here is best place for an *idli* breakfast.'

She marked a crossroads further along. 'This is small temple, we are calling it Veli Andal,'

'Yes, Andal, I know about her.'

Geetha gave me a pointed look. How could I, a foreigner,

know anything about Andal, least of all what happened to her in Srirangam? I needed to be set straight. She drew a line between the two temples. 'Sri Andal stayed here the night before her wedding to Lord Ranganatha.'

'Hundreds of thousands of years ago …' She sat her ample body down and told me to do the same. '*Ama*, yes,' she nodded with the air of an authority, 'you are needing to know the correct story.' She ordered tea and turned the fan on. 'See this?' she traced the curve of the Kavery River. 'In Andal's lifetime Srirangam was a small island only and the river came to where Veli Andal is.'

It looked like at least a kilometre of dry land now stretched from the river to the temple.

'Andal and her father, Visnucitta, crossed the river, got out from their boat, and stayed here.'

A ringtone Bollywooded into the story. 'Hello!'

It was a long conversation mostly in Tamil but then I heard 'foreigner' and 'Geneva'. I remembered her brother. The thought of talking to a stranger in Switzerland tongue-tied me. I finished my tea and pointed to the clock and to Veli Andal on the map. Have to go, I mouthed. Geetha smiled and waved me out the door. The first of the seven gateways and an idli breakfast were both on the way to Veli Andal.

It was Marghazhi, the month of early dew and purifying baths. To celebrate, every threshold was gaily decorated with coloured chalk mandalas called *kolams*. 'Morning is best time to see them,' Geetha had said. By evening they would be smudged beyond recognition as every guest's step through them into a home ensured blessings for all.

So enthusiastic were the early rising women of Srirangam that their kolams had spilled out onto the streets. Flute-playing Krishnas, birds, swirling *Aums* and entwining flowers. There was even a life-size Andal with a green parrot perched on her shoulder. It was like walking through the pages of a divine picture book. I was bewitched, free-falling into some parallel universe where the constraints of finite this and finite that were shattering into myriads of bright coloured fragments. I looked up from the mandalas at my feet into a kaleidoscope swirling across every inch of the seventh tower I was about to walk through.

'Will you be wanting a guide Madam?' His voice in my ear again. 'Every god, goddess, *aspara,* and demon, I can be telling you their story,' he said, following my gaze to the freshly painted deities sculpted across each tier. They were dancing, warring, meditating, coupling, eating, sleeping. Like us, I thought, but they never blink or perspire. Their feet never touch the ground. Such are the signifiers of the heavenly ones.

I turned to the pair of eager eyes still pinning me. 'Thank you, but no thank you.'

'Lord Ranganatha is the toppest,' he persisted. 'Without a guide you will not be getting permission to see him.'

'Not today,' I said. 'Maybe tomorrow.'

Geetha's voice played inside my head as I continued on my way. Hundreds of thousands of years! From what I read, it was more like one thousand years, give or take a century. Born in Srivilliputtur and disappeared in Srirangam. If the story was true and she did stop at Veli Andal, then that was where I wanted to be. I was not ready to disappear into the arms of any god, or man, for that matter.

Veli Andal's gate was open. The temple was long and window-less, one hall after another, deeper and deeper, into darkness and silence. I tip-toed to the end. Two wooden cradles hung from a ceiling beam like boats adrift at sea alongside clusters of bangles tied together with cloth. I pictured Andal arriving there as a young woman, and her yearning for Tirumal in the body of a cowherder called Krishna. *One word from your lips! You on your soft silk bed with ivory legs, reclining on Nappinai's scented breasts.*

An old woman shuffled in behind me. We stood together

outside the curtained shrine. A priest appeared from a room at the side. Back and forth he went. It's a busy time of day, waking a goddess. The brisk sweeping of a broom, filling lamps with ghee and bowls with sacred water from the Kavery River, sweetening the milk offering, incense, recitations—all done perfunctorily while silent prayers moved the lips of the old woman. She glanced my way through her thick-lensed spectacles and smiled before returning her eyes to the place where Andal was hidden until the appointed time. A bell clanged and the priest, his chants a barely audible mumble, drew back the curtain.

Silver-rimmed eyes shone out from the womb-like space before us. Her body was black stone and she wore a garland of pink lotus across her shoulders and another, of marigolds and tulasi, falling the length of her cobalt-blue sari. Rose incense burned at her feet. A diamond glinted in each palm of her hand, as did the bright jewel of her nose stud. But her eyes, I kept coming back to them. Pupils black as black. I felt them probing me, but my skull was an empty cave of bone.

The priest circled her with his *aarti* lamp and we bowed for the blessing from her flame-lit wide-open eyes. With a small ladle he poured the sweetened milk into our right palm, but it was more than milk now, it was nectar transformed by Andal and should not be spilled. We drank it quickly and I followed the old lady, patting the last precious drops over the top of my head. She leaned into her cane for a moment then slowly made her way outside.

My body felt suddenly leaden as if the four months of anticipation had now been sated and there was nowhere to go. This was where I wanted to be more than any place in the world, and yet … what was I thinking? I wanted her to see me, who I was. Maybe then I would know too. I wanted her parrot to spread its wings inside my heart.

Her dark primaeval pupils swirled the air between us. Just you sit, I told myself. This is what happens when you tumble off a plane into India. It's only day two. Take your time.

'Miss,' I heard from across the room. It was a high-pitched boyish voice and I really didn't want to be bothered.

'Miss!'

'*Miss!*

I opened my eyes. It was the priest standing near the door he had been scuttling to and from. He beckoned me over.

I stood up, ready for a launch into the telling of a tale followed by a request for money. 'Here is Lord Tirumal,' he pointed to the mural painted the length of the wall. I nodded like a good student, wondering if I would be getting a personalised rendition of his thousand names.

'Ananta Sesha,' the priest pointed to the seven cobra hoods shading Lord Tirumal's head and the seven serpent bodies rippled beneath him for a bed.'

'And Garuda, eagle head and man's body. Lord Tirumal's chariot,' we moved closer to the door.

'What country coming from?'

'Venezuala,' I said. As far as I knew they didn't play cricket there. It was inevitable if you came from Australia that that's what the next question would be about.

'Marriage?'

'No, I mean yes,' I said tripping over myself in an attempt to diffuse the personal.

'Children?'

I used to tell the truth but the looks of consternation or shock or pity made me even more uncomfortable.

'Three. Two girls and a boy.'

'Alone travelling?' He took a step closer. His moon-like round face unreadable.

'Are *you* married?' I asked and he swam his head.

'No children coming.'

'Oh,' I said, 'I'm sorr—' He grasped my breast and with his other arm pulled me, hard, against his body. I saw the open pores of his wide nose and felt the slick of the oily curl fallen across his forehead touching mine. He parted his mouth and tried for a kiss, his breath hot and stale like sickly-sweet milky tea.

I don't know what demoness I called upon but I used every bit of strength in me to loosen his grip. I snarled at him like a woman possessed. Then I ran. I ran from him. By the time I reached my room I was burning. I double-locked the door, threw myself on the bed and wept, all the tears I had been holding back, all the wasted years of my body's desiring mocked by the sting of a priest.

Chapter Seven

Hurry, cowherd girls of Ayarpadi,
shake off your worldly jewels.
Let's bathe in Margazhi's full moon dawn

Tiruppavai 1

The air-conditioner was silent. I had no idea how long the power had been cut; all I knew was the damp cling of bedsheets. I rolled into a ball listening to the distant sounds of a world waking up. A jangling of keys, the man in the adjoining room coughing up another night's worth of phlegm. The light filtering into my room through the frosted window glass was pale and lustreless. I lay there counting the hours back and forth. If I wanted to call Marcus, I needed to subtract six.

If I had dreamt, I didn't remember. I folded back the bed sheet, half-expecting the bruised imprint of the moon-faced priest's fingers on my breast, but there was nothing. What if I had played along? The dark confines of an inner temple room, the urgency of his body. What about the conflictions of mine, beneath the immediacy of my shock, beneath all my rationalisations? The idea of coupling with such a man disgusted me, and yet I still burned. And with Marcus, everything was turned upside down. After so many years of abstinence, even when I desired him my body felt unresponsive as stone, an unfathomable disconnect between my mind and what should have been happening. How effortless it used to be; how I had taken it all for granted.

It was not December anymore, I reminded myself; it was the month called Margazhi, beginning halfway through December. Seasons were another thing entirely. There was no winter, spring, summer, and autumn. Only heat, then the endless tease of clouds before the deluge. Margazhi's air, if the gods were disposed, was slightly chilled, a month of reprieve. Followed by Tai, dewdrops lingering on garlands long enough for a bee to sup. Then came Maasi, when the sun's flames were stoked again, and by the time Panguni arrived, brides-to-be rose from their beds feverish with its blazing.

All the years I had been coming to India felt like aimless wandering compared to this. A hundred thousand years, Geetha had said, or was it only a thousand? It was a mystery how a goddess born so long ago managed to pluck me from Delhi's streets and woo me with her songs. I didn't care about the why. I wanted to know her and for that I needed to step into every celebration of her short life.

Srirangam claims Andal for one of the songs she dreamed in her *Nacciyar Tirumoli,* and still today its eleven verses are sung by Vaisnavite brides. *My lion and I, we fed puffed rice to the flames. We rode in pageant on the back of an elephant, our bodies anointed with saffron and sandal paste. This vision I dreamed, my friend.*

But Andal lived most of her life in Srivilliputtur. I had only been there one night, but if I closed my eyes her garden was there, every tree, the scents of its flowers still vivid, and the sound of one woman's chanting, her voice as if potentised by a girl made divine. Not one month passes without a festival honouring each step Andal took toward love. And then there are the three months of Margazhi, Panguni, and Aadi, when excess leaps skyward into celebrations even the gods cannot ignore.

I turned onto my back and made a triangle with my thumbs and forefingers, holding this trinity up, reaching for the brave shaft of light brightening its way into my pilgrim room. In the four months I had waited to return, I learned that Margazhi was the month in which Andal wrote her *Tiruppavai* songs. In Panguni, she married the highest god of all. And in Aadi month, celebrating the day she was found born from the earth, she was carried through the temple streets in a giant chariot, thousands of her devotees taking turns to grip its pull-ropes and heave-ho. Ripe watermelons were thrown in the path of its huge wooden wheels and crushed like grapes.

I lay in my little room, knowing all of Srirangam was up. Margazhi preparations were in full swing. Arches made from tall banana stalks festooned with tinsel were set up in front of houses, halls, and temples. New colourful chalk kolams adorned the streets every morning. Each day, pilgrim numbers swelled through Srirangam's seven gates. Here, there was no time to waste because the time I was accustomed to in another world simply didn't exist in Tamil Nadu. The only thing to do was get up, bathe, and walk out the door. The rest, I knew, would be taken care of.

'Wait!' a woman's voice said.

In my months away, the sound of Bhavati's chanting voice had stayed with me, the clarity and steadiness of it visceral in my head.

'I am saying the thousand names of Tirumal,' she had told me. 'Vishnu, Narayana, Krishna, Ranganatha, Vatapatra sayee …'

But I had forgotten our conversation afterward as we sat together in the pavilion of Andal's garden. I had covered my face with my dupatta in an attempt to keep the clouds of mosquitoes away and opened my eyes with a start when I felt someone slipping it off.

'Ladies are not veiling inside Andal's temple,' she said, her smile like a mother's.

Now, I remembered. The last name Bhavati had called, as we watched twilight disappear into night to the hum of those mosquitoes, was *Bhooma Devi.* 'She is also here, Andal's sister, earth goddess. Every morning I say her name. Before leaving your bed, you do this also.' I followed her eyes into the branches above us where hundreds of black velvet wings were hanging.

'My mother would sing to Bhooma Devi whenever she oiled my hair.' Bhavati's voice shifted into the rhythm of a chant. *'Black bees look for honey left by your footsteps. Your hair covers the sky like dark rain clouds.'*

'There is a small book at my house telling her story, how she came here to Srivilliputtur and was born as Andal. I will show you,' she said.

'Oh! But my husband is waiting for me, and tomorrow we leave early in the morning.'

Bhavati swam her head. 'Then I will keep it for you. You will be coming again, yes?'

❦

Not a ripple disturbed the milky ocean where Tirumal lay absorbed in yoga nidra. Even the universe resting inside his belly slowed its spin round each of the twelve suns. On one side of Earth, the darkness of night lengthened into the days and birds did not leave their nests. The eggs underneath them grew heavy with embryos. Feathers formed viscous cocoons over soft skeletal wings. On the other side of Earth, children refused to come inside. Day followed sun-drenched day and the games they played exhausted all possibilities of evil triumphing over good or the conquest of good over evil.

Seeing Tirumal open his eyes, the king cobra, Ananta Sesha,

uncoiled his infinite body into a couch. He raised his seven hoods, swaying them slightly so his lord reclined in a shade as cool as the shadows thrown by wish-fulfilling Coromandel branches. Tirumal's consorts, Laksmi and Bhooma Devi, appeared in an instant and began to massage sandalwood paste over his chest and four arms. As they brushed against the lotus growing from his navel, their bodies assumed its fragrance and as they gazed into his eyes, they slowly disappeared into him. But Bhooma Devi stood back at the last minute. She bathed for a moment in the sapphire glow of his skin; hers was dark as the loam of paddy fields after a storm. Bhooma Devi's spacious mind and light-filled body, at ease in the playfulness of heavenly realms, had begun to feel weighed down. She had a question.

'My lord, who do you love most on Earth?'

Tirumal twirled the discus in his fourth hand, considering the way it sliced the air into prisms of rainbows. With this sharpest of weapons, one touch was all that was needed to sever an ego. How else, he mused, can a mortal mind petrified in the illusion of separate self-existence experience truth? But there was one other way.

He replied, 'Those who are desireless, constantly thinking of me without selfishness.'

Bhooma Devi retreated to her home in the Mandhava Mountains where the white-pebbled shores of its lake lapped the edge of their cosmos. She looked into the crystalline water, deep as Mount Meru, and watched how the reflection of its peak shimmered across her own. A strange emptiness swirled inside her. A comet crashed to the bed of the lake and through to the other side leaving, for an instant, a tail of fire. In its burning, she heard cries from men and women, of their separation. As goddess and consort to Tirumal, she was one with him, but her body ached for all those on Earth who were not. She prayed.

Tirumal hushed the waves of his ocean to listen.

'Lord, let me take birth on Earth as your greatest devotee. And only then let me be one with you.'

'Bhooma Devi, you are stubborn as the Earth itself! As you wish, be born as a girl-child. You will then know the bliss of longing for the divine. And there you will find me again.'

I put my fingers to the floor and called Bhooma Devi's name, then took my first step into the day. I poured tumbler after tumbler of water over my head, letting the moon-faced priest wash away for good. It was an odd feeling having nobody in the room to answer to, to confer with, about the hours ahead. I wrapped my hair in a towel and glanced in the bathroom mirror. I would visit Lord Ranganatha's temple before leaving Srirangam, but it was the intimacy of Srivilliputtur I wanted, its temple garden, and to meet with Bhavati again. Most of all I yearned for the girl born there, from a patch of red soil. Andal, incarnation of the Earth goddess, Bhooma Devi. Myth or fanciful tale, I didn't care. Srivilliputtur was where I needed to be. It was my beginning too.

Chapter Eight

Nacciyar Tirumoli. 2:9

Every morning when her father returned home from his garden, Andal joined him in their courtyard. She watched Vishnucitta intently as he wove flowers for her dark-skinned god reclined on his serpent bed in the temple next door. Never had a day passed where Visnucitta did not enter the temple's innermost shrine, hold high the garlands he had made, and whisper gratitude into the ears of Lord Tirumal for the gift of his daughter.

Mounds of marigold and roses, sacred basil, lotus and kuvalai lilies lay in piles all around them. In the summer, Andal brought her father thalampoo flowers fallen from high branches in the night. They looked like little white trumpets and smelled sweet for days.

'Do not pick them from the tree,' Visnucitta said. 'Take only ones the gods let fall.'

Andal helped her father choose colours and perfumes, but she was not allowed to touch the garlands once they were made —they were offerings for the divine and must not be polluted by any human hand. Bud by bud Visnucitta twined, stopping to measure one length against the other, sprinkling them with water and laying them in a silk-lined basket. Lost in the rhythm of his work, Visnucitta's mind began its wanderings through all the myths and songs he had been sung by his father and his grandfather. He would gauge the expression on his daughter's face and choose one for her. That is, unless she had not already begun pleading for a particular story. Andal knew all of Lord Tirumal's *avatars* and consorts—Vamana the dwarf and Varaha the boar, Kamadeva with his love arrows. But it was one blue-skinned boy who persisted with his visits to her dreams. Again and again he came, taking her hand, leading her to the village where he had been born, Vrindavan, far away to the north.

He grew up in the simple daub house of a cowherder. He was adopted too. Krishna! It was the first word Visnucitta had uttered the morning he found his miracle daughter, and Krishna's stories were the first ones he sang to her. Even before Andal could walk she knew the name Krishna. By the time she was running wild, pretending to be a *gopika*, a cowherd girl, with her friends Marali and Sarvani, she knew everything there was to tell.

'Appa, sing me the one about naughty Krishna and his mother at wit's end.' Or, 'Can we have the one about him stealing the gopika girls' clothes?'

Visnucitta indulged her with whatever tale she wished, having no idea in those early days how deep was the stirring in his daughter's heart. Sometimes Krishna was so mischievous he secretly climbed inside Andal's skin—and she had no idea. Using her arms, he would pluck a river reed, fashion it into a flute, and begin to trill. Marali and Sarvani played along, making a circle around her, kicking up clouds of dust with their feet, mimicking the dances of their mothers. They clapped sticks together above their heads, whirled, then bent low brushing the ground, all the while keeping rhythm with the flute he held to her lips.

It had started so innocently, playing the usual games of little girls, throwing *molucca* beans, drawing circles in the sand, making dolls out of *korai* grass, and then every morning and evening insisting on another story from her father. If Varaji so much as hinted doubts about the existence of this cheeky cowherd boy, with her give-away raise of an eyebrow or a 'tsch' and a pull of her daughter's braid, Andal folded her arms, squeezed her eyes tight, and refused to eat. Andal was as tenacious as Krishna was precocious. It was unnerving for Varaji, seeing Andal step into her imagined worlds, more and more mistaking dreams for reality.

'Amma, we have to practise making sandcastles down by the river. Soon it will be the month of Tai and the castles we build in the streets need to have windows and doors and bridges over the moats, otherwise how will Krishna get in?'

It was useless to argue. Varaji wrapped a lunch of green gram balls and mango pickle in a banana leaf, tied the parcel into the end of Andal's shawl, then stood at the gate of their house, her arms heavy at her sides, watching her daughter skip down the street, only to return at the end of most days with tears tracked down her dusty face.

Rushing inside, she would grab at the folds of Varaji's skirt. 'He has done it again, Amma. I built a castle for him. But as soon as I turned my back, he came out of hiding and smashed it. Why does he keep teasing me like this?'

'It's just a game, my darling.' Varaji stroked her daughter's hair, untangling the peacock feather caught in its curls. 'Probably one of your friends pretending to be Krishna.'

Varaji sometimes blamed her husband for Andal's wayward behaviour. 'You are feeding her head with too many stories, Visnucitta. She moons about the house and then disappears for hours with her friends. One aunty at the well yesterday accused her of being the ringleader. "Girls should be at home learning from their mothers," she said, "helping with cooking and house-keeping."'

But she was torn too. There were days when Andal returned home from the riverbank as dishevelled as ever but bright-eyed and singing at the top of her voice. Hers was the happiest daughter in Villiputtur. What mother did not want this for her child? Did it really matter, Andal's infatuations, Krishna this and Krishna that? There was time yet, a year, maybe two, for her to grow out of it.

But still she worried, until Visnucitta suggested a solution. He had been given the role of chief acharya in Villiputtur for a new school launched in Tamil country. It was called Pancaratra. For the first time, non-Brahmins sat with acharyas, and women too. It had upturned a few milk-vessels in more conservative households, but that was always going to happen.

'What is the harm?' Visnucitta had said. 'We all bleed the same colour. Why don't we enrol Andal? It would be an honour for our family and an opportunity for our daughter.'

'She has only just turned eleven, husband. You don't think this too young?'

'We will wait a few months then,' he said to placate her. 'If there is any girl ripe for these teachings, it is our Andal. Her mind is sharp. We know she has devotion in her, but too much of this she channels into dreams and make-believe.'

Varaji kept her eyes downcast, picking fallen grains of rice from the hearth, unwilling to meet Visnucitta's eyes.

'Three years it will take and by then, trust me, she will be ready to marry and settle down.'

It was in Varaji's nature to doubt. But she held her tongue.

'She will study the ways of temple rituals until she can prac-tise them blindfolded.' Visnucitta kept on as if, Varaji thought, he was trying to convince himself it would work. 'Learn the intricacies of mandalas and how to travel inside them with her mind. With her hands she will dance the language of *mudras*. She will practise the yogas and find the wisdom to navigate her five senses. All these desires and fantasies she is having will fall away.'

It was worth a try, Varaji thought. She would let her husband have his way. Andal already knew every avatar's name and all of the gods residing in Vaikuntha. She had a head-start there. And at the same time, she would continue preparing Andal for marriage, passing on to her the ways of a good Brahmin wife, from the grinding stone in their kitchen to the porch of their house. The art of drawing kolams on their doorstep.

'These designs come from your grandmothers and their grandmothers,' she said in their first lesson. Varaji sprinkled a line of rice powder into a perfect circle. 'For the palace of the heart. See how delicately it is done?'

'Amma, Marali and Sarvani are waiting. Can I go now?'

Months were passing and nothing was changing. Outside the hours of her Pancaratra schooling, Andal seized every chance to return to the paddy fields and riverbank on the outskirts of Villiputtur. Alone or with her friends, she continued her trysts with Krishna, the one who had stolen her heart.

Varaji was never sure if all the other girls Andal mentioned were real or imagined, but once the house chores were finished, she had no choice but to let her go. The consequence of making her stay for an extra hour of stitching or the pounding of fresh rice was a lifeless lump of a girl incapable of threading a needle let alone lifting a pestle.

It was often dusk, or later, before Andal returned home. Varaji wrinkled her nose as she stepped Andal out from her petticoat. A scent like the grassy heat of milk-cows and the sour-sweet of churned curd pervaded her daughter's skin. Andal's time of first blood was nearing, but this was not the perfume of a girl's ripening, she thought as she lowered a bucket into the well. And neither did she know of any friend Andal had from a cowherding family—the closest farms were on the other side of the river.

'Where have you been? A good Brahmin girl spending days in the fields! Look at you, all covered in dust, the hem of your skirt soaked in mud.'

All of this passion she is having, Varaji despaired, what will happen if it is never returned? God bless Visnucitta, but my doubt is turning true. The hours her father has invested are coming to nought. If anything, Andal's feet are further from the ground.

Soon enough the earth felt Andal's first drops of blood. She was kept in a room for six days, away from the eyes of men, and fed fruit, milk, puffed rice, and molasses. Her hair stayed uncombed and without oil, her body unwashed. On the seventh day, Villiputtur's chief temple dancer led a procession of women arm in arm, Andal hidden in the centre of them, down to the river for her ritual bath. Wrapped in new clothes, shining bangles at her wrists, Andal returned home a woman accompanied by hula-huluing voices and drums and flutes. A feast awaited them, dishes Varaji had been preparing for days.

Before putting the first grain to Andal's lips, Visnucitta covered their heads with a cloth. Three times he whispered a secret mantra into her ear and three times she repeated it.

'My daughter with lovely long tresses, now you are purified, god can take shelter in you.'

'Tomorrow is the first day of Margazhi.' Varaji held Andal in her arms like a fragile gift. 'Your body has blossomed. You can join us now, your aunties and grandmothers, and all the Vaishnavite ladies of Villiputtur.'

Andal had counted the moons since her first blood, impatient for this day to come. She felt the budding of her breasts in those four months with a kind of wonder. When the sound of her mother's footsteps disappeared down the stairs, she climbed out of bed and drew back the shutters Varaji had just closed. The moon looked as if it were caught in the branches of the old neem tree outside her window, white as a pearl. She watched its perfectly round body drift from the neem's branches into the sky above Villiputtur, silvering the town's tiled roofs, embroidering its streets with shadows. The rains had come from over the mountains tempering the heat and washing everything clean. On the edge of town where the three sacred rivers meet, Thirumukkulam's temple teerthum was full.

'It is so full,' the most beautiful of all temple dancers had told her when they passed each other on the street. 'Even though you have grown tall as a ripe sugar cane, if you wade into the middle the water will cover your head.'

Andal counted lamp wicks until the hour before dawn. Sleep was impossible.

'Leave your hair loose,' Varaji said, choosing not to scold Andal for another sleepless night. Not a crease marked her bed, the shutters wide open.

She stepped Andal into her new cotton skirt specially dyed with marigolds, then threaded her arms into the matching bodice.

'Breathe in.'

Varaji laced it up at the back and turned her around. She clicked her tongue and gave each of Andal's cheeks a little pinch. 'Suitors will soon be knocking at our door.'

Andal laughed and pulled away, pretending it was just a game. But it was not.

Chapter Nine

If you hear him playing
in the lush groves where cows graze
bring the droplets from his flute's mouth
anoint my face, revive me

Nacciyar Thiumozhi 13:5

The train to Srivilliputtur was running late. 'Forty-five minutes only,' the lady at Srirangam's ticket counter said with one of those unconvincing yes-no nods. None of the other passengers appeared particularly perturbed. I paced the platform feeling like a puppet dangled on strings at the whim of some impish god.

One and a half hours. The sun rose and rose, uncharacteristically hot for Margazhi. Two hours. I resorted to the fizz of a GoldiSpot orangeade and scanned the list of stations my train, when it eventually arrived, would then be passing through. It was a passenger service, the opposite of express, and the only train scheduled that day for the Srivilliputtur line. I was too impatient to wait another twenty-four hours just to catch a faster train. Now I was being rewarded. I felt the sugary rush from my bottle of GoldiSpot and smiled to myself. I was in India; it was working its magic.

Passenger trains stop at every station, that's one of the reasons they take twice the time. I sing-songed my way through the long list of stops between Srirangam and Srivilliputtur listed on the sign above my head—Ponmalai, Kolatur, Samudram, Manaparai, Vayampatti, Tamaraipadi, Dindigul …

Dindigul Junction. Marcus and I had taken a train there on our way to Palani, our last stop before meeting the professor in Srivilliputtur. Aside from the siddhar spirits we might see on our Chathuragiri pilgrimage—'Like shooting stars from mountain to mountain,' the professor had said with a twinkle in his eye— there was a living siddhar he wanted us to meet. Not a visit with the professor passed without a mention of one siddhar or another. They were becoming as endangered as India's forests. We learned from him that some siddhars are buried in temple grounds, lowered into the earth upright and in lotus position. The air around their tombs is electric and the siddhars will speak if necessary. 'You only have to listen,' he said. Their bodies remain intact and if the skull of a buried siddhar is split open, blood gushes from it like a river.

Mootai Swami was the name of the siddhar near Palani. I put my half-empty bottle of orangeade down. It was too sweet. As I wiped its stickiness from my mouth with a corner of my dupatta, I felt something else, something rough at my lips. A grainy sensation, like earth—a memory—the rim of a terracotta cup.

❦

It was a long walk on a narrow track across fields of ploughed black soil. We came to a small thatched house, a stable and one shade tree where a gathering of people were seated and there he was, a green-checked towel wrapped around his head, a faded green lunghi hitched above his knees, and a green blanket folded over his shoulder. He was pacing back and forth, clasping an empty plastic water bottle behind his back, looking at nothing and apparently seeing everything. We found a small pocket of shade to sit, and waited. After a while, the Swami roused us all to move down the track and into a field. The crumbles of black soil were larger than tennis balls and baked hard as rock. I spotted a discarded fertiliser bag and claimed it to sit on. Luxury is a relative word. The Swami continued his pacing, then waved his hand and all but a few of the women stood to attention. I stayed seated.

The ways to enlightenment are mysterious. Short of cracking a skull open and letting all of its attachments spill out, fertiliser bags included, Mootai Swami had devised his own way. Those who were brave enough to stand up began, at the Swami's instruction, picking up the stones and rocks scattered over the track. They carried them ten metres or so, then put them in neat lines either side before returning for more. Back and forth they went. The Swami paced too, with his empty water bottle. He pointed to a group of men and then to a pile of huge boulders on the other side of the track. Three men were needed to move one, and they were big men too. The biggest, a giant with a gentle face, seemed to catch the eye of the Swami. The minute he paused for breath or to wipe the sweat from his eyes, the Swami took to him with his bottle, shouting and berating in Tamil.

'What is he saying?' I asked the woman beside me.

'No Engleesh.' She shrugged.

All this time, Marcus was doing his best finding rocks of manageable size and keeping a wide berth. He looked very hot and a bit bewildered. I didn't know whether to be shocked, to giggle, or to join the cries of a child who seemed put out by the whole charade. But maybe it wasn't. Marcus had once told me about a teacher instructing students to take nail scissors into his garden to cut the grass.

It was a strange afternoon, sitting those hours under the sun, guilty one minute for not picking up rocks and thinking in the next how ridiculous it all was. The woman beside me asked for my water bottle. She took a long swig, then passed it to the woman beside her. That was the last I saw of it. Back and forth they plied their rocks. Desperate for water, I took the fertiliser bag from beneath me and used it as a sun shield. One sip was all I asked, if anyone up there was listening.

A man leading a cow appeared from nowhere, the rope attached to the ring in the cow's nose loose in his hand. I watched him weave through the rock carriers, his upper body long and lean and dark, a checked lunghi tied at his waist. Oblivious to the devotees' sweaty brows, slow as you like, he ambled toward the thatched house we had come from and the only tree for miles with its lovely pool of shade. They disappeared into the stable. I took it as a sign, an invitation, and got up to follow, my legs like jelly, mouth dry and gritty with black dust, my head spinning.

That's when I saw her—Andal—leaving the same stable and stepping toward me through the waves of heat across the black earth, her bare feet not touching the ground. Her hair was loose and she wore a long slip of silk the colour of sunflowers. She looked through me to the mountains in the distance. *A breeze is over there*, she said, *in the coconut palms. If you listen, it is a song to Krishna.* Instinctively I turned around, believing I would hear it, but instead the air swelled with cicadas like electric drills, and I was met by the eyes of the Swami. He was looking at me, looking through me. Did he see her too? Then he waved me away. I was dismissed. I turned back to the stable, but Andal had disappeared.

I stopped at the stable door, curious as much as anything. The man was squatting beside his cow, resting his forehead against her flank as he milked. He looked over to me without pausing; each rhythmic spurt into the iron bucket a cooling staccato. The air smelled of hay and engine oil, animal and man.

'The Swami, they call him their Jesus,' he said in perfect English, taking his hands from the cow's udder and readjusting his position. The cow turned and gave his shoulder a nudge and the man replied with an affectionate slap to her haunch. 'Wait just one minute,' he said, and to me he motioned to the shelf at the back of the stable. 'Bring me a cup.'

My eyes adjusted to the dark. I took one from the neat row of stacked terracotta cups. He dipped it into the pail.

'You looked thirsty,' he said. 'It's thirsty work, watching rocks being hauled from one place to another.' A hint of a smile flirted with the corners of his mouth as he offered me the milk, his fingers hesitating for the briefest of moments on mine. 'Drink it.'

Milk, any kind of unflavoured milk, turns my stomach. But I was thirsty. So thirsty! I put the clay rim to my lips and tipped my head back. I felt him watching me as I drank. I felt the reflexes of my throat closing in but willed the milk down. It was warm and layered with cream. It was good.

'Thank you,' I said. I wanted to know who he was, what he was doing here milking a cow miles from anywhere. Tamil farmers don't usually speak such impeccable English.

'Throw the cup,' he said. 'Wait under the tree. They'll be back soon.' The cow lowed with pleasure as he rested his head against her again and resumed milking.

The troupe of rock movers staggered in, Marcus among them, weary, thirsty, and sunburned. Was it some kind of penance, or a surrendering of ego? There was no idle chatter as they passed a pitcher of water for hand washing before settling down under the tree. We were each given a banana leaf and a feast appeared. Light plumped rice, dhal, vegetables, pickles, and cold buttermilk fragrant with coriander and green chillies. As much as we liked. It was a scene akin to the loaves and fishes. A bench was brought out for the Swami and made soft with a pile of hessian bags. He sat and watched us eat as one of the women massaged his legs.

Every now and then I'd cast a quick glance to the stable door, but nobody entered, and nobody left.

Walking back to the crossroads, our stomachs full, thirst quenched, the sun set behind the ghats, it all seemed clear to me in that moment. The mysterious methods of the Swami. Andal appearing. How Marcus and I could travel together and yet be shown different paths.

We waited for the minibus, in silence mostly, that comfort of silence you can have with another. Insects hovered in a small cloud near a tree across the road then flew above our heads. Dragonflies. We heard the faint glistened whispering of their wings. There was something else too, unhinged inside me—how I had swallowed that milk. The taste of it, still on my tongue.

Chapter Ten

Wrapped in a crimson shawl, Andal reached high to lift the latch of their gate. She stepped out into the chilly air with her mother and they joined the women gathered at the temple's gopuram. For the next thirty days, they would chant through town in the last hour of night leaving Villiputturians to sleep until cries from their she-buffaloes heavy with milk pierced their dreams. For Andal, it was as if they walked into the fertile dark of Lord Tiru-mal's belly where time and space hummed. Will he recognise my voice? Surely he will, she thought, now I am a woman. She imagined their singing coaxing his eyes open, his body rising from his serpent bed, resting one of his lovely long-lobed ears on one hand, leaning the other ear toward them.

Linking arms with her mother, they walked to the large

stone teerthum of Thirumukkulam. Andal took off her shawl, loosened her bodice, and untied her skirt. Stepping into its water was like entering a vast mirror of soft cerulean sky. Her petticoat clung to her legs, and with each step down the ripples grew wider and the water colder. She waded in until waist deep, then dipped her whole body three times before raising cupped hands to the coming light, to the sounds of water merging into water as it spilled in tiny cascades through her fingers. Trills of black kuyils filled the air. She sang with the women, their songs to Katyayani and to Krishna. She felt her face blush at each mention of his name.

'These songs are more ancient than the banyan trees shading us,' an aunty told her. 'Listen,' she said, 'to the sound of the Malaya wind heralding rain. In its breezes you can find the scent of the kurunci flowers growing in the forests of the mountains. Breathe it in, child, long and deep. In their fragrance lie the memories of your ancestors. This same wind gave your great, great grandmothers' prayers their melody.'

Andal listened.

She knew each woman wove her own secret wish into the prayers she sang. Girls her age prayed for a good and gentle husband; their mothers prayed for a son-in-law to provide for them. New brides asked for a child and if their husband was a paddy farmer, a bountiful rice harvest.

As for her wish, she knew by the thirtieth day, when the Winter solstice moon was set, the seeds of her vow would be stitched into the stars. She was sure of it. And he would have no choice but to reply.

Chapter Eleven

Waist deep in water,
we remember Purusha's story.
In three strides he measured the world

Tiruppavai 3

Andal's temple entrance was awash with water and milky disinfectant, a sure sign a festival was imminent. In the stables by the first *mandapam* hall, old women stooped back and forth with brooms and buckets, slushing the stones until water the colour of cow dung spilled onto the thoroughfare. I left my sandals at the entrance and followed the line of pilgrims, tip-toeing through the puddles wondering what strength of bleach had been used while everyone else sloshed through, oblivious to all but the goddess awaiting them. Perhaps they thought, as they entered her temple, everything here is transformed into the sacred.

'You are entering god,' a voice said. It sounded an odd thing to say but it made sense too, as if the woman straightening up beneath the second gateway was answering my thoughts. She held a bowl of white rice powder and stood back from the kolam she had drawn with her fingers, a mandala of lotus petals covering the flagstones leading in. The giant stone Yali on the column behind her, rearing its lion body and grasping the elephant trunk swinging from its fanged mouth, seemed almost a warning: this was not a woman to be tampered with. She looked me up and down, placing the other hand on her ample hip, taking note of my new toe rings, my clothes, the messy way I had pulled my hair back, the red *tilak* on my forehead. But then she smiled.

'You coming from?'

'Srirangam.'

'Staying?'

She didn't wait for my reply.

'Come to my house later.' She pointed back to the temple entrance and to the right. 'Ask for Kartika.' Then she waved me on over her lotus mandala and through the dark corridor to the next mandapam. A shaft of light beamed down through an opening in the temple's roof, bathing the golden flagpole towering through the centre of it. Hundreds of tiny flames from ghee lamps flickered at its base. The golden pole reminded me of an antenna, a sort of cosmic connector, between earth and heaven, if heaven existed. Quite possibly Kartika was right: something godly was here. The pilgrims in front of me were already prostrated around it.

The man from the ticket desk got up from his chair. He was tall and lanky. He looked down at me, squinting through the glasses perched on his nose. They didn't have any lenses in them. 'This is the purifying place,' he said, suggesting none too subtly with a tilt of his chin that I should join them, the pilgrims on the stones.

'All bad karmas you will be leaving here.'

Hurry, cowherd girls of Ayarpadi ... begins Andal's *Tiruppavai*. I had no idea what to expect on Margazhi's first morning, how many women would gather and where we would go. We didn't strip down to our petticoats and wade into a river or a temple teerthum. An *acharaya* led our procession accompanied by his young apprentices, one holding a flag, one an umbrella, and the third a lamp. Without fanfare, and blessedly no loudspeakers, just the delicate tings of finger cymbals and the pad of our bare feet through the pre-dawn, we began our small procession, chanting the words of Andal in a re-enactment of a thousand years ago ... *shake off your worldly jewels, bathe with me in Margazhi's full moon dawn, dip into water dark as Tirumal's rain-cloud coloured skin.* It was all in Tamil, of course, but I knew the refrain at the end of each verse, *El or empavai.* It was a thrill to chant at least this and I didn't have to imagine Andal's words— *like dewdrops at sunrise our separation is dispelled*—I was a dewdrop with them. Srivilliputtur's women welcomed me into their fold without any questions, not even a quizzical look. We circumambulated the Brahmin streets hugging the temple walls, chanting the *Tiruppavai's* thirty verses, and then it was time for coffee. I felt blushed as the sky with gratitude. I had come home.

'What is the meaning of *El or empavai?*' I had asked Kartika later that morning on my first visit to her house. These three words were never translated in my copy of *For the Love of God.*

'He gives everything,' she said, putting another idli on my banana leaf. 'What can we do?' She added a spoonful of coconut chutney, clearly not expecting any answer from me.

Kartika leaned over and looked me in the eye. 'Sri Andal is making a vow. You keep reading the *Tiruppavai* and you will be knowing it.'

We ate in silence, then folded our leaves and rinsed our hands at the well in her courtyard.

'Three things you do,' she said. 'Offer flowers, and his favourite, tulasi, the sacred basil. Second, daily chant the one thousand and eight names of the lord. Third, listen to the stories of god. You do these with a pure heart, Saisha. Simple. Everything else will be taken care of.'

But I was complicated, my mind catapulted in. Couldn't she see that? And I didn't think it was just me. Doesn't every girl struggle into her woman's body? And every woman, no matter what culture, surely, sometimes, questions her place in the cycles of keeping house and earning her keep, of lovemaking and child-bearing? And what about these when they are turned upside down? And when best to speak her mind, or is it better to not?

Kartika began readying herself for the day. She was the wife of a priest and her life was busy. 'You come again tomorrow, early morning.'

&

Come, the water is cool and deep, Andal says in her *Tiruppavai.* I thought of the ocean minutes from my other home, thousands of miles away, taking into itself whatever colour the sky. I used to dive beneath its waves and breast-stroke underwater for as long as my breath allowed. In that submerging, something of me disappeared and yet, I was held. These thousand and eight god names, Kartika was telling me to chant, and every one of them with a story. Is that what happens? If you chant them, you eventually disappear into the sound of them, are held by them. Simple, she says, everything else will be taken care of.

Simple as Purusha, whose divine consciousness propagated an entire universe. One of his incarnations was Vamana the dwarf. Andal loved this young man's story so much he appears a dozen times in her songs. He asked the King, Mahabali, for just enough land to sit and meditate—three strides long was all he needed. Mahabali puffed up and said to the little figure, why of course I can give it. In front of the king's court, Vamana put down his staff and umbrella, his deerskin and water gourd, ready to take his first step. There was a collective gasp as Vamana's body grew and grew and grew. One stride. Two. Three. The whole world became his.

What does it all mean? I wondered over a second glass of sweet South Indian coffee. Customers bustled in and out of the tiffin house where I stood, buses roared in and out of the depot across the road. The world was awake and going about its business, while behind closed doors priests were attending their goddess, and on the other side women sat, all of time theirs, as they called her name and the names of the ones she loves. Krishna, Tirumal, Narayana, Vamana, Ranganatha. In this wide-awake world where merchants trade and bullocks haul, where children parrot arithmetic and an old man wonders about time wasted, where a lover waits and another weeps, where myths are played out true as truth. *Give us the fan, free us from ourselves. Give us the mirror, so we can see,* Andal says.

Days rolled one into the other for the first half of Margazhi. Then, as the moon began to wax so too did the crowds. Every morning, Andal was elaborately dressed and taken in procession around the same streets we had walked before dawn. Fancy dress is too trite a word for the visions of her carried in a different chariot each day, on the shoulders of men. A golden swan, a golden horse, a serpent, a mountain sheltering her like an umbrella. One morning, she appeared as Krishna, complete with a ball of fresh white butter in her hand. The next day she gripped a silver staff and was churning the ocean, and on another she was cross-dressed as the lord himself, Tirumal, holding a conch, discus, lotus, and chakra in each of his—or was it her—four hands. She was seated some days and standing others, dressed as queen one day and a cowherd girl on another. Garlands fell to her feet, thick and lush, her necklaces, anklets, and bangles studded with precious stones, golden and staggering.

Priests followed her chariot, chanting the songs of the Azhwars, and I stayed with the women who followed behind them. Families waited outside their homes with offerings of bananas and grapes, coconuts and camphor, and the chariot paused for every exchange of gift and blessing. The procession stopped each day at the temple tower and the chariot was turned so the eyes of Andal saw through to the other side. One of Srivilliputtur's three *Araiyers* arrived and stood to her left. Grandfather, father, and son—they were servants of Andal and answerable only to her. Their lineage dated back to the tenth century and they called each of their ancestors by name. Everybody fell quiet when the Araiyer placed the blue conical hat on his head and took the red tasseled cymbals from his dhoti. My gaze shifted from Andal to the Araiyer to the place where their eyes were focused. One breath taken might break the spell. But it didn't and we were there, listening to the Araiyer become the voice of Andal speaking to the god inside, Lord Tirumal.

Each hypnotic note, long and slow, nuanced and deep-felt, echoed through the stone gateway into the sanctum sanctorum where Andal's lord reclined on his serpent bed.

Chapter Twelve

Hiding among kurundai flowers, your desire is ours too—
but if our mothers see! We must leave before they do.
Please, give us our clothes

Nacciyar Tirumoli 3:3

Andal felt the warmth of her mother's hand around hers as they walked home from Thirumukkulam that first Margazhi morning. She pulled at the damp ringlet of hair falling across her face and tucked it behind her ears. She played with the rhythms of the women's chants under her breath, weaving her own words into them. She felt grown up, taller, and took pleasure in the way her body tingled in the places it was changing, the way her hips swayed from one side to the other, like those white swans come to nest every early dew month. She pushed her small breasts out and lifted her head high; she was a cowherding girl free to roam where she pleased. Yes, she promised herself, I will write a song for each of the Margazhi dawns and I will sing them in the voice of a cowherd girl. All my gopika friends will join me. The streets of Villiputtur will become the streets of Vrindavan and we will make our procession. One by one, I will wake my friends and together we will go to Krishna's house. We will beat at his door.

Noble lion in a mountain cave, rain falling, his fire-filled eyes opening. Rolling, stretching, shaking his scented mane, he comes out fiercely roaring. And you, dark-complexioned lord, deep blue as a pavai flower, won't you rise from your bed?

Visnucitta's stories flooded Andal's mind like pieces of a puzzle, the pieces as infinite as the gods. She started to skip, impatient to tell her father, the best storyteller in all of Tamil country, that there were stories spinning inside her too. Varaji laughed with joy at the sight of her Andal, so carefree, racing ahead. How could she know this was the morning her daughter began composing songs that one day would bring men to tears? She watched Andal unlatching the gate to their house. How brief and precious childhood is. And, as the gate swung shut behind her, how quickly its innocence fades.

Sunlight was already streaming through their courtyard. Andal shook her hair out to dry, beside herself with everything she had to tell but knowing she must wait for her father to speak first. Visnucitta looked up from his prayers, pressed the beads to his forehead, then wrapped them into the fold of his dhoti. Scents of cardamom and ginger filled the air as Varaji began preparing their breakfast *payasam*.

'You have made your first Margazhi procession, Andal. This is a day to remember.'

'Appa! We offered marigolds to Katyayani, then floated them on the water. We stood waist deep and chanted our *pavai* vow,' her words tumbled out, 'and as Grandmother Bhittika sang a song about Damodara—how Krishna grew inside his mother and brightened her womb—a baby kuyil bird flew down and pecked a grain of rice from my hands. Grandmother said it was a good omen for all of us. I wanted to stay there forever.'

Visnucitta smiled and patted the mat beside him. 'Sit. Pass me the bowl of flowers.'

They sorted them into colours. Purple lilies, crimson roses, white jasmine. Varaji rolled her pestle back and forth on a stone grinding fresh coconut to a paste.

'Tell me about Lord Krishna and the gopika girls,' Andal pleaded, her mind feverish now the eyes of the world deemed her ready for marriage. It was a story she had heard a thousand times, but how she loved to sit with her father every morning and lose herself in the palaces and forests he described and in the eyes of that boy with the bluest of skin.

Visnucitta feigned a frown and handed her a spool of twine. 'Cut it long enough for a garland. Double the length from your waist to the top of your head.'

They settled into the task and he began.

Krishna's real mother was Princess Devaki, the sister of King Kamsa. His father was Vasudeva. A soothsayer's prophecy shadowed King Kamsa like a vulture: the eighth son of his sister would murder him. He threw Devaki and Vasudeva into a dungeon, swearing to kill every son they conceived.

Tears rolled down Princess Devaki's cheeks as she suckled her newborn prince. It was midnight and the prison guard's snores grated the air. Vasudeva found the padlock to their cell door open. Had the gods slipped arrack into the guard's water? They quickly swaddled their son and Vasudeva disappeared into the night with him, taking the forest path down to the river. He carried their baby high as he waded across the Yamuna to the cowherd village of Vrindavan. There the chieftain's wife, Yashoda, had just given birth to a daughter. Krishna's father secretly exchanged the two babies and returned to Devaki.

Yashoda woke the next morning in her simple daub house to find a son, not a daughter, in the cot by their bed. She gasped at the sapphire hue of his skin, iridescent as a peacock's feathers and, as if a charm was cast, accepted the baby boy as her own.

All of Vrindavan was entranced with Krishna, his chortling laugh and chubby arms, full of mischief, playing havoc around the house. Again and again, Yashoda found him in her kitchen surrounded by upturned pots of curd, butter smeared over his face and honey dripping down his fingers. Krishna grew into a handsome young man, more and more spirited, more and more bewitching.

&

Visnucitta paused at the sound of Andal's laughter. He looked across at his daughter. She was swaying, eyes partly shut. Her hands lay open and empty in her lap. He needed more twine cut for the next garland but could not bring himself to disturb her. How deep her recognition was. She was a child no longer. He remembered the day he found her, the way she looked at him and then, the first word she uttered. 'Appa.' Perhaps she never was a child, the way she bowed at the feet of Tirumal, pressing her forehead into the uncoiled tip of his serpent bed. The way she drew stories from him like the breath of some goddess teasing clouds from a mountain. He felt as incapable of hiding the truth from her as he did from himself. He thought of a temple sculptor visualising the grace of a dancer in a pillar of stone. The tiny waist, hands unfolding like wings into mudras, breasts like the sun and the moon. All he need do was chisel the way to her. And what of us? Visnucitta wondered. I am a sculptor of stories but Andal already *is* the story. There is nothing I can keep from her. How then can I protect her?

He cut more twine and continued.

&

'Vrindavan's cowherd girls were so enchanted by the sound of Krishna's flute that they vied to be the prettiest, weaving flowers through their hair, tying drapes of transparent silk round their hips, pencilling dark kohl under their eyes, and pinching their turmeric pasted cheeks.'

Andal heard her father's voice. She smelled the crush of each petal and tulasi leaf as he threaded them onto the twine. Every sense in her body sharpened when she entered his stories. The gaze of her half-closed eyes flickered, then moved up toward her crown. Her legs became heavy as stone, then her arms, then her torso. She felt them like an anchor as they swelled larger and larger, filling the room. The heavier her body turned, the lighter her mind became until it drifted free. The voice of her father faded into the leaf songs of a forest. She saw a faint trace of footprints where the long grass was parted and followed them, listening for the voices of her friends.

'I will be his mistress!'

'No, it will be me. He came in a dream last night and told me so!'

'What are dreams?' another girl scoffed. She twirled three times, swaying her hips, her arms raised high, hands sinuous as a snake. 'Krishna can never resist me.'

'But when his eyes are closed, how can he see you?' another said, holding a make-believe flute to her lips like some ecstatic bard, as if she were Krishna himself.

They ventured along the path he had made to a hidden pool, far from their village and the eyes of their mothers. Their imaginary games turned more and more audacious. One girl pretended she was Krishna as the others began unplaiting her hair and shaking it loose, as if to shake out the dust kicked up by his cattle after a day in the fields. They stroked her body as if it were his, rubbing their thighs against hers, circling her and tickling her back and front with the slightest touch of their small, firm breasts. She half closed her eyes and parted her lips as if waiting for a kiss. They took turns to be the one until all of them were undressed and breathless and giggling.

Little did they know, as they entered the water, Krishna himself was sitting high on a tree branch looking down at them. Choosing first this one, then that one, his skin glowed as if charged by lightning. While they splashed about, swimming out of their depth, diving under lily pads and taking fingerfuls of lotus pollen to mark the parts of their hair, Krishna climbed down from the tree and stole their clothes.

The girls waded to the edge of the pool to mould an image from wet sand of their goddess Katyayani. They spread sandal paste across her breasts and belly, offered lilies and lotus and small cakes of sweet coconut rice wrapped in banana leaves. Facing toward the morning sun, they prayed, 'O supreme eternal one, mystic goddess, make the son of the cowherd Nanda our husband.'

As if Katyayani herself had heard their request, the unmistakable sound of a bamboo flute lilted across the water. The girls looked up, delighted to discover it was Krishna, until they realised the trick he had played. All their clothes were draped over the branches either side of him.

'Gopika girls,' he said with a rascally smile, 'your prayers to Katyayani were so sweetly sung. Now, if you want your silks you must come and get them. Come one by one so I can measure your tender heartedness with my eyes.'

'Lord Krishna! Put down your flute and throw down our clothes,' they cried all at once, their high bell-like voices a mix of thrill and panic. 'This minute! Give them back to us.'

'How can you ask Katyayani for my hand then deny me this? I do not joke when I ask you to stand before me.'

'If our mothers find out we will be in big trouble. Krishna please! Can't you see we are shivering? Lotus stems are prickling us like scorpion stings. Fish are nibbling our toes.'

Krishna simply smiled. He put the flute to his lips and continued playing as if he didn't care whether they came or not.

He had won. Covering themselves with their hands, the girls took turns climbing onto the bank. Seeing him so close, his skin dark as storm clouds, his eyes like slow-opening lotus buds, they forgot their nakedness and raised their hands high in *namaha*. One by one they lost control of their limbs, collapsed to the ground, their foreheads sinking into the mossy earth.

Krishna threw their colourful silks into the air and watched them drift down, covering each girl in turn like the transparent wings of new butterflies awakened from their chrysalis. Free from worldly desires, liberated.

'I accept you,' he said. 'Go back to Nandagopa's village. Praise Katyayani with dancing and drums. Worship me and indeed you will have me.'

Andal heard her father's voice as if from far away. The sweetness of the plumped raisins in her mother's payasam filled the air of their courtyard. She knew she should be helping her father, but her eyelids were too heavy to open and there was more to imagine. Praising Katyayani was the end of her father's story. There were days when Andal ventured further, when it was just the two of them. Krishna took her places Visnucitta had never mentioned. Side by side they herded his cows, holding noose ropes over their shoulders, playfully wielding sugarcane stalks across the cows' backs as they whistled them on. Further and further into the forest.

They played hide-and-seek among the giant roots of fig trees, and in the shade of its branches they made swings from vines. As they rocked back and forth for idle hours, his arm against hers felt cool and smooth as polished lapis and yet, when she woke up in her Villiputtur bed, her sheets were damp with perspiration and there was that milky taste on her tongue again, warm and fertile and sweet.

Chapter Thirteen

Kuyils and peacocks, clusters of karuvai flowers,
luscious bilberries, purple kaya blossoms—five sinners
at loose in this spacious grove—why torment me so?

Nacciyar Tirumoli 9:4

Priests and pilgrims, dignitaries and troubadours, came from far and wide to hear Visnucitta's songs. 'But I am only a gardener tending flowers for Lord Tirumal,' he protested, passing the tamboura to the bard beside him, its strings now expertly tuned. 'Look at my hands,' he opened his palms, 'weathered and blistered from ploughs and rakes.'

When news spread about Visnucitta reciting more songs, the front room of their house quickly filled. People crowded onto the *tinai* benches of their porch and squatted beneath the windows straining to hear every word. Into the early hours of morning the men accompanied his recitations, drank tea, then played music again and Visnucitta sang some more. But it was god who heard Visnucitta's poems first. Every day after offering freshly made garlands and chanting the Vedas, he sat alone at the feet of Lord Vatapatra sayee and sang his new songs.

If Lord Vatapatra sayee approved then Visnucitta's voice rang like a perfectly forged bell, his words vibrating off the walls; but if the verses were not ready for the ears of the all-knowing one, the stones did not resonate and Visnucitta found words caught in his throat. He knew then he must return home, smooth a clean palm leaf, and sharpen his stylus.

Devotees listening to Visnucitta's songs found themselves effortlessly carried into the realms of the gods and if a song was about the world in which Krishna played, grown men listened with the rapt attention of a child. Women swooned as if they were holding the toddler Krishna in their very own arms. And Andal, wide awake no matter what the hour of night her father sang, closed her eyes and rocked side to side, the pulse of her wrists and temples falling into the rhythms of each line and her mind into the magic of his words. She took her father's verses and kept them like seeds in her heart.

Andal stepped into each story her father sang. She stood waist deep in that forest pool, forgetting that any minute Krishna would again climb down from his hiding place. She was Yashoda, Krishna's mother, hands on her hips attempting to scold her son. 'Stop gobbling butter, you naughty boy, or I'll have to tie you to a post.'

'Why do you pretend you are the voice of Yashoda?' Andal asked her father one morning after a night of songs.

Visnucitta put down his tamboura. 'Ah, my little daughter in love with Krishna.' He laughed affectionately. 'You of all infatuated girls should know. Of course, everyone is capable of loving the divine but in daily life, tell me, what love is strongest?'

Andal thought about the facets of her father's love. How he entertained guests until dawn experimenting with different ragas for his own compositions and singing ancient songs from the Sangam Age, every verse suffused with nature. His role as a *Veyar* of the Brahmins, setting Vedic scriptures to music. Tending his garden, weaving its flowers into garlands for god.

What does he mean, Andal asked herself, calling *me* infatuated? He may as well call me a raven eyeing crumbs. No, she thought, my heart is spoken for and it will be forever. When our house fills with my father's music, all of me is lost in the divine world he invokes. Just one mention of any bird or flower or fruit —kuyils and peacocks, bilberries, karuvai, and kaya flowers— and I will never forget their names. They are the language of love. Love? Oh yes, Appa's question. Seems to me he is happiest of all on these nights, but is this the kind of love he is talking about? Sometimes I catch him, his arms curled around Amma, and there is a look on his face I do not see any other time. As for my mother, her face turns liquid as honey on a Panguni night.

'Is it the love between a man and wife, Appa?' she asked.

Visnucitta swam his head. No, it was not.

Perhaps it is a trick question, Andal thought. Love is love. She glued her eyes to the floor on which they sat, tracing the straight lines of the tiles between them. How can such an emotion be contained by anyone? Other than a god, that is. Andal pursed her lips tight.

'Imagine how Yashoda felt seeing baby Krishna in the cradle beside her bed. So instantly did she fall in love she forgot she had just given birth to a daughter! Or the distress of a mother crying Krishna's name. "Give me back my girl, she is betrothed to a good man. I know what you are doing! Stop bewitching her with those eyes of yours and the sound of your flute!" By entering a woman's heart,' Visnucitta explained, 'and speaking with her tongue, the path toward god becomes swift as the course of an arrow. It is through a woman's body we are born. Think of the tenderness in a mother's love. She can be fierce as a lioness too, in the safekeeping of her daughter.' He stroked Andal's hair then lifted her chin. 'And then there is the intensity of a gopika girl's love-struck heart.'

Andal felt the lines of the floor tiles beneath her begin to ripple. A sound of rushing water filled her ears. She was there again at the river, dipping her toes, then wading in. How could her father possibly know the warmth of the breath she felt at the nape of her neck and the soft cajoling voice in her ear?

'Dive in,' it said.

She turned red as kumkuman powder—the sound of his voice—the tickle of the peacock feather tracing her arm. But no matter how many times and how quickly she turned to see his face …

Visnucitta had picked up his tamboura again, remembering the words of Nammalvar, a poet who had visited the night before. '*I am like the flower emptied by the divine bee,*' he sang, closing his eyes.

Andal knew he would not open them again anytime soon, so she left him there, strumming the gourd's four strings over and over.

Chapter Fourteen

Dates and times were decipherable enough inside the glossy covers of the temple's festival booklet, but everything else was in Tamil. Kartika might volunteer some information if we happened to meet, but then again, she might not. The hours of each day melded one into the other until they didn't matter—as long as I woke in time for the morning's *Tiruppavai* chanting around the temple, and I always did because a little bird *kol-kolled* outside my window at the exact same time in the hour before first light. I had read about a bird who fed on moon-beams and wondered, are you the one?

For three weeks, I had fumbled from one place to another, to the celebrations and rituals particular to each of Margazhi's thirty days, and these on top of the temple's normal timetable, which was busy enough, waking all the gods and goddesses who lived there, bathing and feeding them, attending to their adornments. In a week, Margazhi's moon would be full. The anticipation was building. Rather than return to the fluoro-blue steps of my hotel and its claustrophobic room, I stayed on in the shade of Andal's garden until its gates closed for lunch, stopping for a coconut before retreating to the fan-cooled rooms of Pennington's library, a few minutes' walk from the temple. Mid-afternoons are usually sleepy in Srivilliputtur and the streets deserted, but on this day the sharp beats of wooden thimbles on the tight skins of a drum signalled a procession. Through the library's windows, I heard the faint voices of women, the drone of priests, and the slow rolling of a chariot's wooden wheels. There was nothing to do but get up and join them.

'Where are we going?' I asked the woman next to me.

'Sri Andal,' she replied. But where? And what was going to happen? In those early days, I survived on a kind of faith that this was the place I was supposed to be and usually Kartika's advice was right: everything will be taken care of.

'We are going to Thirumukkulam,' a voice behind me said.

'Tiru…mu' was all I managed to pronounce. I turned to see whose voice it was.

'Bhavati, it's you!' Her smiling brown eyes were framed by eyebrows lightly meeting at the bridge of her nose. Eyes full of light, but deep too, as if coming from faraway.

'We are going to Sri Andal's bathing place. Come, walk with me. I heard telling there was a foreigner lady here.' She laughed, waving her hands about her face. 'Saisha and the mosquitoes.'

I laughed, too, at how my Western idiosyncrasies must mark me and how that first night in Andal's temple garden she had gently slipped the dupatta from my head—*we leave our hair loose and free of flowers*—leaving me no choice but to let the mosquitoes feast.

Bhavati pinched my cheeks affectionately. Every day since my arrival, I had looked for her, even though that first night in the temple garden we had hardly spoken.

'I have been at my daughter's house in Sivakasi,' she said. 'Soon she will be having her first baby.'

She linked her arm into mine and we joined the chanting. '*Margazhi thingal* …' I knew enough now to sing the *Tiruppavai's* first lines—*mathi niraintha nannalal.*

On this full moon day this month of *Margazhi.*

Fringed with sprawling banyan trees stretched the enormous teerthum, Thirumukkulam, its stone walls whitewashed and striped red, the sign of a sacred place. Here, the myth says, India's holiest rivers, Ganga, Yamuna, and Saraswati, mingle. I had wondered about this phenomenon, the miracle of three great rivers flowing underground for thousands of miles in order to bubble up in Srivilliputtur. Marooned on a dried-up section of mud flat near the middle was a small pavilion. There was not a lot of water. But I didn't care. I took the myth and swallowed it whole. My beliefs were becoming as suspended as my body felt, picked up at less than a moment's notice, taken hither then thither, into another time, another world. The chariot lurched over rutted ground to the steps of a larger blue pavilion at the edge. Ropes were unknotted and Andal's palanquin lifted onto the shoulders of eight men. Peeking out from her veil of gold organza, I caught a glimpse of the bright jewel adorning her nose.

Like a flock of birds of paradise, women jostled for position on the pavilion's floor close to a dais where, behind a curtain, Andal was already seated. Bhavati led me to a column at the side with room to stretch our legs if needed, but we were soon as crushed as the women at the front. The air shimmered with silks and polyesters of every colour imaginable. Arms, legs, and bottoms rustled into every inch of space. The stones took all of the chattering and echoed it back like an amplifier. The lady next to us made a nest of her lap for a basket and began threading white buds of fragrant flowers into garlands, others took out fans to ease the heat of anticipation building in the fuse of elbows, knees, and hearts. Finger cymbals percussed bell-like rhythms into the chants and songs overlapping each other, until there was nothing but a sea of voices and bells and smiles and flowers gathering like a monsoon cloud filled with promise. Painted on the ceiling above us were the petals of a multi-coloured lotus spread out like a mandala. A mix of *mullai* flowers and coconut, rose and tulasi, and the thick purifying smoke of benzoin pervaded the air, and yes, in all this there was a hint of rain.

A conch trumpeted, the curtain was flourished aside, and a murmur of awe rippled through the room. A turbaned priest, his midriff wrapped in silver brocade, approached the lady seated on her throne. He drew close, as if nearing a wild bird, and we watched with bated breath as one by one he removed her veils. First the gold organza, then a wrap of diaphanous green, and a third veil of lace. Andal's eyes swept over us and out through the pavilion's blue columns to the expanse of Thirumukkulam's teerthum, her golden body swathed in white satin. With a tulasi leaf, the priest simulated the massaging of her body, but never was she touched. A *nadaswaram* accompanied him, the flautist working his breath so each nasally note sounded like the calling of a swan. The brushing of her teeth is ritualised, the cleaning of her tongue, the priest's hand never venturing closer than a millimetre. He offered her water from a golden cup and betel leaf to sweeten her mouth. Every act repeated three times. So mesmerised was I, I could not move. If I took a breath, it was not mine to take. I was caught, utterly and completely, in the aura of a queen.

A woman began to sing as the priest took off the gold chain circling Andal's head. If the air held a portent before, now it was truly charged. He loosened her hair, shaking it free, teasing it, letting it fall down her back to the ground. The conch trumpeted again and a vessel of dark unctuous oil was brought.

'*Sanandhi thalam*,' Bhavati whispered, touching her hand to her heart.

'Sixty-four herbs boiled in forty-two litres of milk for twenty-four hours till reduced to one litre,' Kartika had told me later with her usual jovial authority. The perfect priest's wife. What would I do without her?

The priest dipped his fingers into it. The conch was blown again. With long, adoring strokes, he saturated Andal's hair, then gathered her glossed locks, twirling and wrapping them into a bell-like bun at the back of her head. The garlands of white buds my neighbour had been threading since the ritual began more than three hours ago were given to the priest. With a silent prayer on his lips, he circled them round and round her raven hair.

'Like a beehive,' Bhavati murmured with a dreamy smile as the curtains were drawn.

The ritual was over, and chaos descended. An Araiyer stood at the front, holding the vessel of oil high above his head with one hand and taking smears of it with the other to spread on the palms of Andal's devotees, their voices beseeching, their arms outstretched, desperation on every face, bodies pushing and shoving.

'Saisha!' I heard Bhavati calling from the edge of the melee and squeezed my way toward her. She held my head steady and drew a perfumed line of sanandhi thalam from my brow to my crown, then pressed a small vial of the oil into my hand.

'Come,' she said. 'We wait outside.'

There is more? I staggered behind her like some drunken woman, legs like jelly, head still swimming with the visions of a myth come to life, the line on my forehead cool and velvety.

The teerthum's pools of water looked a little more cheery in evening light. The tease of clouds gone, one bright star and the hint of a moon. It made sense to me then, how a moon's phase and the patterning of stars determined timings for the rituals marking Andal's life. I'd be given the time for a procession or special *puja* and arrive as punctual as someone in a business suit only to spend the next hour, or more, waiting. I learned some markings of the clock were more a British throwback, not necessarily in keeping with a thousand years of temple tradition, of zeniths and the revolutions of stars. It seemed a more reasonable way of living, in tune with the elements rather than fixing ourselves on top of them—it was not mercurial at all!

There had been a short miraculous time in my life, pre-Marcus, when I took a lover. We lived in a forest cabin with no power or phone-line. Off-grid it's called these days, but back then it wasn't called anything. Sometimes we fire-gazed at night-fall, but more often we'd go to bed, easing ourselves into a love-making that was less about doing and more about the darkness and its night creatures, the babbling of water over rock at the bottom of our valley, the wingbeats of an owl, the howl of a dingo, the way all of it entered our bloodstreams as our four limbs moved as one body.

It was a long-ago memory and there was nothing to hold onto, like waking halfway through a dream you knew was good but couldn't remember and what remained was a numbed sort of sadness. I followed Bhavati into the blanket of a Margazhi night, leaving the aura of a goddess for the smoke of open fires and tempering spices, of cow dung and jasmine. The stone steps to the teerthum's edge were uneven. I stumbled, and Bhavati took my elbow with a firm hand.

We wove through the mayhem past a second dais where Andal had been newly ensconced behind makeshift curtains, the busy shadows of priests moving back and forth around her. 'For her bathing,' Bhavati said, 'the *abhishekam*. It will be soon, maybe two hours. Or three.'

We strolled the length of the teerthum talking like sisters catching up after a long separation. How good the cool air felt, my legs tingling back to life after sitting for so long.

'In a few days I have to return to Australia,' I said.

'What is this? Every time we are meeting and then you are going!'

I didn't know what to say, how to explain, how to tell her every cell of my body wanted to stay.

'Next time you come to my house. I am having a small room

on the rooftop. Everything you will be needing is there. I am keeping it for you, if you promise to come back,' she said, squeezing my hand.

'I promise.'

Two men scuttled past carrying a huge cauldron of prasadam. Bhavati quickened our steps back into the pavilion and we joined the queue. Steaming mounds of *pongal,* glistening with ghee and studded with black peppercorns, cashews, and charred slivers of green chilli were dished into our hands.

'Bhavati,' I said, the silky rice warm and fragrant in my cupped palm, 'I'm so happy to be here, and to have met you.'

She pinched my cheek again. 'Taste this prasadam from Andal, Saisha. She will be sealing our promise, and when you stay in my house, I will make you pongal for breakfast.'

O Govinda, Sublime One, all come to you, no matter how contrary. Cool and comfortable we sit together, receive bowls of milk rice pudding. Melted ghee drips down to our elbows.

We found a place to sit among the fancy silks and jewellery of Srivilliputtur's ladies, their chattering as animated as a flock of parakeets round a bowl of sugar water. Bhavati's sari was one colour, like the last blue of a twilight, and without brocade. She was different, not so caught up in adornment. A single bangle threaded on each arm, her wedding necklace tucked out of sight in her blouse. The devotion in her was quiet and contained. Rows of fluorescent tubes hummed on, calling to them the moths of the night. I watched them dive-bombing the light and it struck me how they knew what was real and what was not, and that the light's reflections on the teerthum's water shimmered on, prettily, without incident.

A conch was blown. The beats of a *mridangam* drum reverberated through us. This time Andal was standing, her beehive of thick roped hair wrapped in white cloth, her body swathed in green and a newly made parrot perched on her shoulder. A priest unwrapped Andal's hair. He massaged lemon juice through its long thick lengths, then tender coconut water.

A second priest approached. 'He is descended from Visnucitta, Andal's father,' Bhavati said, 'two hundred and twenty-five generations back.' I believed her. We watched him take three purifying sips of tulasi and camphor water.

The elder Araiyer stepped to the front of the dais and turned to face Andal. To the slow rhythm of his red tasselled cymbals, her abhishekam began. Water dipped with mango leaves was poured from a vessel beginning at Andal's feet and moving up to the crown of her head. She was bathed with turmeric paste and next with sandalwood paste, then milk, honey, and sesame oil. A silver sieved tray was held above her. Two priests approached with elephant-spouted pots balanced on their heads. Holding the pots high, they poured long streams of water into the tray.

'Sacred water,' Bhavati whispered. We held our breath as this infusion of herbs and flowers fell through the sieve in a fine shower over Andal's head. Hundreds of adoring eyes looked on as her radiant soaked body was garlanded with crimson flowers and again the curtains were whisked closed. We waited, attentive to every billow as the priests bustled about inside preparing Andal for her final appearance.

My heart was jumping all over the place. More than five hours had passed since the first of three veils was slipped from her body. A queen intimately attended by her assembly of priests. It was pure theatre, every choreographed movement demanding, sometimes teasing, my complete attention. Erotic one moment and then in the next, honeyed with devotion. I felt elated, light, satiated, as if her bath might also have been mine. There was a glow inside me, deep and from a long time ago. Was this love? I glanced up to the fluorescent tube above our heads— still the moths came.

When she is revealed again, she is dressed in saffron silk and garlanded with vetiver grass, her green parrot poised on one hand. She looked over us. We stood, and bowed, our palms pressed together. She looked inside our hearts, her fragrance enfolding our world.

Chapter Fifteen

Look how loose my shell bangles.
Little kuyil fly to him from your grove
of laurel, wild poppy, nalal and pear,
make him come quickly to me

Nacciyar Tirumoli 5:1

And so the month of Tai followed Marghazhi, then came Maci. Soon it would be Panguni. Andal was in her second year of Pancaratra schooling. Despite her errant ways she was one of her father's best students, her mind matured beyond her twelve years. She asked questions, even challenging some of the principles he taught, but always outside of class. She was a girl after all —soon to be someone's wife, her parents continued to think— and therefore must show deference. Andal tried her best but it was hard, so many constraints. Temple courtesans, on the other hand, lived independent lives practising their worldly skills and temple arts. Andal watched the way they walked Villiputtur's streets, so self-assured, only beholden, it was said, to the gods they served. But she noticed the way some of them toyed with the wandering eyes of men and she wondered what kind of love they practised after putting their gods to bed.

Visnucitta had once explained how originally there were just three pursuits of man—morality, love, and wealth. But in Pancaratra there was a fourth pursuit: liberation.

Andal thought about this, then came to her father after class insisting, 'But Appa, there's no need for any fourth pursuit. My love for Krishna *is* my liberation.'

It was becoming more and more difficult for Visnucitta to set his daughter straight, and as her body changed neither could he brush her behaviour off as girlish playfulness. On that same day, she returned home at nightfall dishevelled as ever but bright as the moon. Refusing a bath and all but a handful of rice, she entered the gathering of troubadours and poets settling in for an evening of music at their house. She waited impatiently for the musicians to tune their instruments, her eyes imploring her father. She put her hand to her throat. Visnucitta knew what she was asking. He had listened to the verses she had composed, but it had only ever been just the two of them.

'I am calling them *Tiruppavai*, Appa, a garland of thirty songs.'

Anyone was free to contribute their songs to these night gatherings, but never had a girl. It was a bold request, and to have her thrust it on him like this! But he knew her songs were worthy and the price of saying no did not bear thinking about. He turned to the musicians, gesturing toward Andal. Let my daughter be the first to sing.

Verse after verse, her voice filled the room, her words swallowing the hearts and minds of Visnucitta's guests. They sat up on their cushions, murmuring acknowledgements at the end of each refrain. When she finished, they were speechless.

Varaji held the kettle high, watching the tea splash and froth into their clay cups. She heard the sound of bullocks' bells and the voice of their driver as they trundled past the door. They were the timekeepers of dawn and dusk, coming and going from work. This evening it was a mournful sound.

'Well, husband?' she said, placing a cup in front of him. He glanced up to the arching of one of her eyebrows, knowing well where his wife was headed.

'Villiputtur is too small a town.' He shook his head. 'Everyone knows our daughter. No amount of dowry will make any difference.'

'Andal is almost thirteen, Visnucitta. Time is running out. You must go to Rajapalayam and Sivakasi. Even Madurai if you have to.'

'Varaji, you know it is not so simple. If I travelled to the Himalayas and found a prince for our daughter, what then? Do you think she will circle the marriage fire a demure and blushing bride?'

Her eyebrow arched a second time. It was maddening, but he knew she understood. Whenever Visnucitta insisted it was time Andal settle on a husband, her stubbornness sucked the very air from their house so none of them could properly breathe.

'Appa, if you force me to marry a mortal man, I will use the very same yogic powers you have been teaching me and leave my body … for good!'

Before tears had a chance, Andal's eyelids would start their uncontrollable fluttering, her dark irises rolling up and out of sight as she fell into another trance. The more they broached this question, the less she ate. The bangles around her forearms began slipping from her wrists and the waists of her skirts needed constant tightening.

But it had to be done, even if the suitors knocking at their door had whittled to the desperate ones. On the days Andal was presentable, she was paraded in front of them. She hated it.

What girl wants to be chained to the earth with some nose-picking boy for the rest of her life? All Varaji could do was serve tea and make polite references to the auspicious star alignments of such a marriage while wringing her hands beneath the veil of her sari, silently calling on the powers of Sri Laksmi.

On the days Andal refused to come down, she sat by her window humming Tirumal's name, looking through the branches of the neem tree for a glimmer of him. But still he refused to appear. She let her eyes float up into the world where he lived, dark and teasing as a monsoon cloud; she searched in every direction while downstairs prospective mothers-in-law settled into the plumped cushions of their front room scoffing sweets. Andal heard the sounds of an expectant husband clearing his throat as he waited for her arrival and the apologetic tones of her mother making up excuses. Late from music class. Such a devout daughter, she has probably stayed on at the temple. Or Aunty is ill and Andal will not leave her side. When the guests eventually left, Varaji shut the door on another proposal and seethed up the stairs. Such a nice boy too, she would say. But Andal peeked through the lattice as each one departed and all she ever saw was a string of pudgy, pimply, lanky, and lack-lustre.

One night after evening puja, Visnucitta stayed on at the temple weighing the growing disgrace of his unmarried daughter against the unerring devotion he saw in her for the very lord he himself was serving. Another monsoon had come and gone. They should have been happy months, the gods stoking their sun then the miracle of a rain-soaked earth, but as paddy shoots turned ploughed fields into seas of iridescent green, all his soul felt was fallow. He poured his anxiety into a poem.

My daughter, I raised her free as she pleases. How perplexed I

*am, her love for Govinda, and her breasts not yet ripened. She falls
into a trance calling his name.*

He put his stylus down and sat long after the last oil lamp
had burned dry. He needed guidance, a sign, a dream.

Long before the birth of Andal, Lord Tirumal had come to
him, so why not again?

'Go to Madurai,' he had said. That was the night everything
had changed.

When the king of Madurai overheard a Brahmin priest say the
body is like a water bubble, he looked around his pleasure palace
with shock. Life is transitory, he thought, how can any of this
bring lasting happiness? He commanded a sack of gold coins be
tied to the ceiling, then summoned priests, pundits, and
siddhars.

'Whomsoever names the god who can rescue me from
endless cycles of life and death will have this gold.' For days the
debate continued between well-meaning but delusional men, the
greedy, and the pompous.

Lord Tirumal whispered into Visnucitta's dream, 'Stop these
graspings of straws by desire-filled minds.'

'Why me?' Visnucitta asked, but how can you argue
with god?

Visnucitta went to the palace. He patiently listened to the
debates, then stood in front of King Vallabhadeva. 'The paths to
liberation are three,' he said, 'wisdom, devotion, and action
without expectation. Begin by practising the eight limbs of yoga.
Continue every waking moment. Concentrate your mind on
Tirumal, his red-lotus eyes and beautiful cheeks, his three-folded
belly and deep navel, four arms stretching to his knees and
thighs like the trunk of an elephant, his tasty calves and leaf-like
feet. Limb by limb meditate on them and his matchless ocean of
wisdom will flow into you. There is nothing else to say.'

The coins fell until Visnucitta stood knee-deep in gold. The King changed his pleasure-seeking ways and Visnucitta returned to Villiputtur. He built a temple tower and mandapam hall. He planted a temple garden with pomegranate trees, rows of tulasi, and one hundred and eight kinds of flowers. The garden flourished and Villiputtur prospered. He was given a daughter. Songs rolled from his tongue. As for Andal, the verses she composed were surpassing even his, each one profound yet suffused with an innocence the likes of which he had never heard, not in his lifetime nor in any Sangam text from the age of poets ten centuries ago.

Visnucitta lay down beside his sleeping wife. Andal's behaviour was becoming more and more worrying. He knew too well how their neighbours liked to gossip, these women sitting on their tinai benches with nothing better to do than whisper behind hennaed hands.

And now … what to speak of his daughter's latest antic? It was unforgivable. Even as he prayed for an answer, Visnucitta could feel the dread of what he knew growing inside him. He cocooned Varaji's body in an attempt to sleep.

An answer did eventually come—in a dream, from Tirumal —and he woke with a mix of wonder for what Tirumal had asked, and foreboding for what this meant for his family.

Chapter Sixteen

I have kept my vow—I bathe before dawn,
offer kindling without thorns or insects to the holy fire.
Now take from your quiver one flower arrow
shoot it for me from your sugarcane bow

Nacciyar Tirumoli 1:2

All night Andal had smarted from her father's anger: her life finished.

Visnucitta brushed a ringlet of hair from her bloodshot eyes. 'Lord Tirumal came to me in a dream,' he said, 'and spoke of you.'

He leaned close and whispered, *'Choodi K Kodutta.'*

'This is how he described you, my daughter.'

Andal felt the heat of her father's breath on her cheek. The remorse and doubt she had harboured until dawn, all the tears— they were for nothing. Her whole body flushed at the sound of Tirumal's name.

'These six syllables we must keep secret,' Visnucitta said, 'as secret as the flowers of his garland.'

A shiver ran up her spine, bright sparks flared at the base of her neck. She felt the fire of Tirumal's spear-like eyes. They were the same as Villiputtur's Lord Vatapatra sayee, as Krishna's, as Narayana's, but each body told a different story. She loved him, in whatever form he showed himself, and she felt his penetrating gaze, now, as clear as his clearest reflection.

Andal braved a glance at her father.

&

Every morning after Visnucitta had woven Lord Vatapatra sayee's garland, he placed it in the same silk-lined willow basket then put it in the shrine room of their house. Here it stayed cool so the lotus and rose buds remained half-closed until the time of offering at the temple's evening puja. With the garland safely kept, Visnucitta returned to his plough. Varaji left for the market, on Monday for buttermilk, on Tuesday for jaggery and tamarind, a visit to the tailor every Wednesday. Every day she had an errand, leaving Andal alone in the house.

Whatever room Andal was in, if she closed her eyes and kept perfectly still, the garland's perfume filled her body. Kamadeva teased her with his nonsensical whisperings. That mischievous god of love with his sugarcane bow poised and quiver slung over his shoulder. She felt the whoosh of his flower-tipped arrows into her heart, each thwack stranger and more powerful than the last, until she found herself propelled toward her parents' room.

Andal slipped behind the curtain hung at its entrance. She reached under their bed to quietly slide out the wooden trunk in which Varaji kept her wedding sari. She stripped down to her petticoat and wrapped herself in its nine yards of red brocade. She tied a gold linked belt round her hips and draped a string of her mother's pearls across her little breasts. From Varaji's paintbox she always chose the same small pot of colour to paint her lips coral.

Thwack thwack went Kamadeva's arrows. Andal tip-toed to the shrine room where the garland was kept. She drew aside the damp cloth and carefully lifted the flowers up over her head, letting them circle her shoulders and fall soft, scented and heavy, cool as dew, down her body. Then she walked to the stone rim of the well in their courtyard. By now the morning sun was three quarters high, enough to illuminate the silhouette looking down into the well's circle of dark water. Most days Andal saw herself and she said, 'Yes, I am beautiful enough for you. I am ready to be your bride.' But there were some days the face in the mirror was not hers. It was his!

She put the garland back exactly as she had found it and did the same with her mother's sari. She washed the colour from her mouth and brushed the flowers' perfume from her skin, but never all of it. She would leave traces of fragrance hidden beneath her bodice, of sacred basil, rose, lotus. By the time Andal left the house in search of her friends, her hands had stopped trembling and she could walk straight as a blackbird flies. No one, except Kamadeva, knew her secret. On her tongue new songs unfurled, just like the buds of the garland she had worn, each petal soon to be coaxed open by the warmth of Lord Vatapatra sayee's indigo body.

These were Andal's pleasures until the night she heard the slamming of their front gate. Visnucitta had returned home earlier than usual from his temple duties. Gruffly, he called Andal to his room. Varaji brought in his evening tiffin but he waved her away.

'Do you know what they do to people who touch flowers prepared for the lord?'

What reply could Andal possibly give?

'No?' he said in a low voice, more threatening than any shout. Rarely had Andal seen this kind of anger visiting her father.

'How is it possible, my very own daughter forsaking this law for nothing but foolish daydreams? Do you not remember the story of the King who severed his wife's hand for taking a flower meant for an offering to Lord Shiva? And the saint who cut off her own nose for unwittingly smelling a garland made for Krishna?'

'Tell me, is this yours?' He unfolded a palm leaf and took from it a long strand of hair. It was raven-black and curled and the exact length of Andal's. She blushed and smiled, she could not help it. How especially sweet the flowers were that morning and today, oh today, it had been his face with a flute at his lips, not hers, looking back from the circle of water at the bottom of the well.

'No god can receive polluted flowers. What you have done is unpardonable. Your behaviour causing gossip, your refusal to accept a husband and now ...' Visnucitta slammed his hand on the floor in desperation. 'How long has this been happening? I had to burn the garland. All I could offer our lord was incense.'

'Go! Go to bed and tomorrow our family fasts as penance. No games, no singing, and no more arguing. You will marry the man we choose, and it will be done within three moons.'

Cicadas shredded the night, the air thick and too hot. Andal dared not close her eyes. She tossed and turned, praying for the balm of her lord's breath. But there was nothing. He too was angry and had deserted her. Not even the hint of a breeze, not one star visible in the sky outside her window, only the suffocation of clouds dense with rain but unyielding. Her father's threats, the consequences she would have to face, and yet ... Andal's cheeks flushed; now their trysts had been discovered, she felt something new and bright burning inside her.

At dawn, she heard the familiar pad of her father's feet, the stairs creaking, a splashing of water from the well as he washed his face, the crackle of kindling and metal against clay as he ladled water into a pot. But she did not hear him pull up a stool, nor the familiar rustling of his palm leaf pages and the sound of him sharpening his stylus. Andal left her bed and tip-toed through the silence to find her father.

She knelt in front of him, touching her forehead to his feet.

'Sit up, daughter,' he said, his voice velvet as churned milk, his eyes full of light.

'I could not sleep, Appa. Please, will you ever forgive me? I promise never ever to …'

'Shhh,' he said, putting his fingers to her lips. 'I am thirsty. Bring me my tea and we will drink together.'

Andal made it sweet with jaggery and poured two clay cups. They drank without speaking, enveloped in the curls of its spiced steam. The first call of a kuyil came in through the window.

Visnucitta put down his empty cup. 'Lord Tirumal asked why I did not bring flowers yesterday.'

Andal kept her eyes downcast for shame even though her whole body trembled at the sound of his words.

'Child … look at me. Do you know what he said when I told him why?'

She felt the tickling of hair rising on her limbs. He knew, then. Lord Tirumal knew it was her! She listened to her father as if it was the lord himself talking.

'"I stand on a lotus of one thousand and eight petals," he said to me. "I am the source of all perfumes yet not ensnared by them. They are mine to give and to withhold, but …"' Visnucitta paused to swallow, '"… but the garlands you have been bringing me are especially sweet and I can no longer wear any flowers but these."'

Andal blushed head to toe, too afraid to look at her father. What Lord Tirumal had asked was taboo. What will the other priests say? How can her father do this without risking their lives?

'Remember, Andal, when I told you the dream I had before you were born? How my life changed because I trusted the words of Tirumal. If we do not listen to the divine when it comes to us, then what to speak of our destiny? Who knows, would I have even found you?' Visnucitta gently lifted her chin. Their eyes met. 'I have no choice but to do as he desires,' he said.

This is the devotion of my father, Andal thought, as she prostrated in front of him.

'From now on, my daughter, every morning after I have woven his flowers, you must wear them. Wind the jasmine buds around your hair. Take the thickest garland made for his chest; keep the twined tulasi at the nape of your neck and let its flowers drape your body so the lotus buds brush close but do not touch the tops of your feet. I will tell your mother but no one else must know.'

'Come close, you whom I have loved as my only child.' Visnucitta took his daughter's face between his hands, gently kissing her above the place where her eyebrows met.

'Choodi K Kodutta,' he whispered into her ear a second time. 'The lady who offers the lord garlands first worn by herself.'

Chapter Seventeen

Playful one. Prince of cow herds—
come! O kutal bless this circle

Nacciyar Tirumoli 4:8

Besotted was how Marcus described my state of mind. If a question arose, I turned to Andal's songs, opening a random page of *For the Love of God* for an answer. It might be veiled one day and sweet as honey on another. Sometimes she gave nothing. *I am weak, parched as an erukku leaf in summer heat. Will he not send one word to me?* That was the first verse I opened to after returning to Australia. I had stayed in Srivilliputtur for Margazhi. It was the compromise we had made, not one day more.

I flew into a heat wave. I felt brittle as a fallen leaf.

'You will settle down, Saisha,' Marcus said. 'Just give it some time.'

Settle down into what?

I worked as many night-shifts as I could, overtime and weekends, saving every penny. I swam in the ocean, diving under its waves, surfing them, but all I felt from its vastness was distance. All I tasted was brine. If I was stung by a blue-bottle I didn't bother with vinegar. I let it burn. It was better than feeling nothing.

'Marcus, it will be Panguni next month. I want to go back,' I said, sitting in the same chair, looking out the same window of our kitchen to that crooked peaked mountain. He just shook his head and walked out the door. I sat there and cried.

The airport bus pulled up at our gate, its engine blowing clouds of exhaust into the eucalypt air. I stepped into the cool of dawn, down the rickety steps of our house, and turned a final time to look up at Marcus. There he stood, and above him, one star left in the sky.

'Safe journey,' he said, 'and remember, you are walking into wedding fever so be careful.'

It was his idea of a joke.

Bhavati welcomed me home like a long-lost sister. The little room she had prepared on the rooftop of her house was my refuge. It was within walking distance to the temple; I could come and go any time. Andal's garden, her *Thiruppoora nandavanam,* became my sanctuary. I sometimes played with these words, and others, as I sat in the shade of its trees, accustoming the contours of my mouth to the sing-song staccatos of Tamil, feeling their foreignness vibrate my lips like the tang of some exotic fruit. Returning home, Bhavati would listen to my attempts at pronunciation with endless patience, and we would laugh and I would try again between mouthfuls of delicious tiffin, of her *dosas* or *uthappams* or *puthu*.

Most mornings I spent in Andal's garden. My days and nights felt cyclic, perpetual as a rose-bud to flower to rose-hip, the life of a red hibiscus unfolding in the morning, withering in the evening, the sleeping shadows of upside down bats chequering the soil from which all of this life grew. I listened to the sounds of a hoe splitting earth above the nasal voices of priests parading through on very important business. Squirrels scampered light as light along the temple walls, and all the while *Aum Namah Narayana* droned assuredly from a hidden cassette player. The same priest was always there, the hint of a shy smile on his lips. The Andal he attended in the small alcove at the end of the pavilion was more primitive than the golden Andal of the main temple. Except for silver-rimmed eyes she was black stone and featureless, as if rooted into the ground of her birthplace. In front of her was a stone pedestal sculpted into an opened lotus and filled with the dark crumbled earth from her garden.

If I arrived early enough, the same man in a white dhoti, the string of a Brahmin across his chest, would be weaving his way through trees and hedges carrying scissors and a shallow basket, collecting leaves and flowers for the parrots he made every day, just as his father did and his before him. A pomegranate flower for the beak, tapioca leaves for its body and wings. They were the parrots I saw every evening newly alighted on Andal's shoulder until the next night when a new parrot took its place.

It was Rani who told me these charmed parrots were then purchased by devotees, VIPs and VVIPs. Brides-to-be coveted the blessings of this love messenger and in the marriage month of Panguni daily migrations of parcelled parrots were flown all over India, even America, to ensure auspicious unions.

Kartika had introduced me to Rani one morning in the temple garden. Rani folded me in her ample arms like an old friend and insisted I come to her house for tiffin. She was too young to be a widow.

'Look, not even one grey hair! But this is my fate,' she said.

Her husband had died suddenly, leaving her with an unmarried daughter, a falling down house, and a motorbike, which she insisted on learning to ride, to the mortification of her neighbours. Her house was close to the temple. Here, widows wore white and didn't work. Rani worked and wore colourful saris. How was she to provide a dowry for her second daughter if she gave up teaching? I liked Rani.

It was in her house I saw my first migrating parrot. 'See!' she said, opening the two bell-studded doors to their family shrine where a statue of Andal stood surrounded by prints of Tirumal's avatars. The parrot attached to her shoulder was bought by her husband for their first daughter's wedding. 'She is married to an engineer,' Rani said with pride, 'living in Chennai.'

The parrot's leaf feathers and pomegranate petal beak were faded but the whites of his shell eyes gleamed.

'Every day this parrot is chanting Tirumal's thousand names into Andal's ear,' she said.

Rani's youngest daughter looked up from her homework. 'He also tells Andal her favourite stories about Krishna.' She paused for a minute, chewing the tip of her pencil over an intricate diagram—the mechanics of a screw gauge—before turning to the television in the corner of the room where a villain dragged a maiden by her hair into the maw of a cave. Stepping from one world into another, easy as that.

Rani slipped a booklet into my hands as I left. 'Andal's *Nacciyar Tirumoli*,' she said. 'Fourteen songs, one hundred and forty-three verses, in English, so you can read them. These we don't chant, only the sixth song for marriages, but now it is Panguni you need to be knowing,' she said, fixing me with eyes stern as a mother's.

She took the booklet back and flipped through its pages. '*Govinda, Govinda, my parrot calls from its cage …*' she recited, '*if I refuse him food, more loudly he shrieks.*'

'Wait one minute!' Rani disappeared into the kitchen and

returned with a piece of sweet *palkolva* on a leaf plate. She offered the palkolva to the statue of Andal for her blessing then placed it in my hand. 'My youngest daughter wants to be an engineer too,' she said with pride as she adjusted the parrot on Andal's shoulder, 'but I will also be needing to find her a good husband.' Her daughter flicked her long braids to her back, pretending not to hear.

I walked to the temple garden, chose a column dappled in shade and let the booklet fall open on my lap. Persistent squawks cut into the silence and I looked up to see flashes of a green parrot darting through the trees. I followed her flights back and forth to a nest built into a crevice of the temple's stone wall. Her tiny babies were crying out for all the world to hear until their mama dropped an insect into their wide-open beaks. Talking parrots, drunken bees disappeared inside kuvalai lilies, she-buffaloes with heavy udders—Andal's songs were steeped in a bucolic world. I could have stayed in her garden the whole day swooning in the beauty of it. I rested against my column and looked down to the open page—*Ocean! He entered your depths and churned you, that illusive one. He took your nectar. He entered me too and stirred my soul, stole my being.*

Just as I was settling into the timelessness and ease of my return to Srivilliputtur, the peace of my little rooftop room, of nowhere to go and everything was going to be perfect, I was landed into the heart of a question I had safely packed away. Once upon a time I had cried out too, my hungry body.

I turned to the next page and read, *Why is it Lord Ranga reclines on that fire-spitting serpent's bed, and not a glance for me?*

'You will need to be knowing,' Rani had said. Did she realise what she was saying?

For a girl stepping into the body of a woman, hips swaying a new language, nipples darkening, womb ripening, there is nothing more profound, more consuming, than the yearning for a love—when it eventually presents itself—that is more mysterious than it is straight forward. My desire for a man could never be compared to Andal's desire for a god but I had known the anguish burning on the page in my hands. It had anchored me like a stake to the ground when all I wanted was to give myself away.

I looked back to find that hunger, to feel it again.

ﺂ

I walked barefoot down his path in the middle of one spring day. He had planted marigolds and red poppies either side but I took no notice. I did not know his name, had barely brushed past him in the street, only once caught myself in his eyes, and now all I wanted was him. How strange the day I saw him drive past the gate of our house and turn into the farm next door. It was predestined.

Here I was living, if living was the word for it, in the middle of nowhere, sharing a bed with Marcus. There were nights I lay awake, and if I lay awake too long, I might quietly run my hands down my body just to feel its yielding to touch. And in the morning as the mooing of milk-heavy jerseys echoed up the valley, Marcus might hold me and I would press into him, my body aching like one of those cows. He knew this. He knew the wildness growing in me but did nothing.

The soles of my feet did not touch the ground as I entered the stranger's house, so incorporeal my body had become. He showed no surprise, made a pot of tea. Did we talk? I can't remember. And where did we fall? That I do, the bed of flowers he made for me.

ﺂ

Had I been born a woman in the Sangam Age of Tamil country, ten centuries before the birth of Andal, and had my husband preferred the arms of some harlot, an acceptable practice appar-ently, I would have *dried up and rotted within like an abandoned tortoise egg.* Imagine my flush of recognition coming across this phrase in Pennington's library one hot Srivilliputtur afternoon. There were dog-eared volumes of poetry and ancient treatises on Tamil culture groaning on the shelves of what had become my favourite room when the temple gates were closed. Once past the security check, the shoe counter, the bag counter, then the interrogation of a conscientious junior as to my reasons for needing their establishment—I said poetry and she was satisfied —I followed her up a spiral staircase and was offered a desk with a view to the mountains and, above me, one of those single-speed ceiling fans powerful enough to tear a loose page from its hand-stitched spine.

'Tea or coffee, madam? Sugar?'

Married women were chaste creatures in traditional Tamil society. Men, on the other hand, flitted from blossom to blossom like honey bees, their golden bodies pleasured, nectar dripping from their mouths. The list of fine qualities, I read in one tissue-paper paged volume called *Glimpses of Tamil Culture,* was impressive for a man: he should be strong like an elephant, bold as a tiger, intelligent as a swan, regular as a rooster. The aspirations for a woman seemed positively coquettish in compar-ison: she should be like a parrot in speech, a peacock in her beauty, swan in gait, and have eyes demure as a deer. Good cook and child bearer were implied perhaps, as these tasks, by nature, were invisible to men. Was it just the hot air whirling like a tornado above my head making me cynical or the concurrence of my dried-up eggs and brittle insides? I looked across to the mountains and wondered about the fates of women and really, has much changed in twenty-four centuries?

Was my acquiescence to Marcus's statement of celibacy an aberration unique to me? Would any other woman have simply checked out, the holy ground of her body too precious to waste? Or was my response a virtuous one? In staying, I chose a path untainted by a desire as base as sex. I stirred in the layer of sugar granules at the bottom of my teacup. There were chinks of higher ground in my rationale. I had made a choice, passive as it was, but was I kidding myself? My body stayed independent of the arguments I conjured and no matter how noble my thoughts it just kept on fanning the flames. And what about love? Was love our even keel?

I don't think love even had a chance in the heat whipped up through those first years of our celibacy. I fell into the arms of a secret stranger or two, my body allowed to wake and glow temporarily, my mind numbed by the comfort of it and my heart never sure of its place. Everything changes, that's one certainty at least, and my body did, eventually. It began to need less and less until even if I desired sex, I was unsure if it would be physically possible. My vagina felt like it had petrified into a channel of stone and no amount of flower offerings or incense smoke was going to wake it up.

My lord in virtuous Srirangam on his serpent couch, robbing everything, leaving me with nothing.

A woman's lot was a life of quiet duty and adornments, in these ancient texts, while the list of qualities for a man continued: he should be industrious as an ant, hard working as a bull, selfless as a cow, patient as a donkey, chaste as a monkey—the sip of tea I had just taken spluttered across the desk, wrinkling that last phrase. My guffaw earned the eyes of one of the newspaper readers. Should I ask him for an interpretation? But he had swivelled his chair away from me. I wiped the page and read, last but not least, a man should be faithful as a dog. I, Saisha, of Western disposition and with inestimable patience for the fickleness of men and the playfulness of the gods was buoyed by this contradiction. Or was it a joke? Or did men simply get everything they desired then saunter home, king of their castle?

Coming to Srivilliputtur alone, and this time without a fixed return date, I could take as long as I liked wherever I was. In the evenings, the creamy pink skies above Andal's garden were a migration of herons and geese. The soft pad-pads of devotees' feet were constant as they came for blessings and left with a pinch of earth in their hands. And in the mornings if the leafy serenity of Andal's garden was blown asunder by the throb of a generator, nobody seemed to mind—except me. But then, something might come of that, the din and the fumes might fade into another world altogether. One day it was a tinkling of anklet bells and the skips of three girls. I swear their skirts brushed my knee. They sat in a triangle under the pavilion's lotus painted ceiling and began their game of *Kutal*, a game Andal used to play, taking turns to be blindfolded then drawing a circle on the stones. If the circle joined, there were shrieks of joy, their wish for a handsome prince would come true. Even the old man cross-legged behind his stacks of terracotta lamps turned to see what all the fuss was about. Were they real or a dream? Camouflaged in the leaves of a tree laden with long pendulous fruits, one of the garden's parrots spread its wings, readying for flight to a quieter branch. As it took to the air I saw beneath its tail feathers an iridescent flash of turquoise. The girls looked up too, from their perfect circles, and we laughed with delight.

And then one evening, after Bhavati had finished chanting Tirumal's thousand names and left for home, I stayed on for the last hour before the garden's gate was closed. Eight months had passed since my first step into Andal's temple, a few short days after sitting in that field of black earth watching men and women toil back and forth with their rocks. I closed my eyes, letting the sounds of nightfall wash through me, god's thousand names lingering. When I opened them, there he was, as if he had been there forever, his long perfectly straight torso unflinchingly still amid the comings and goings of pilgrims. Even in shadow I knew.

'You look thirsty,' he had said. I remembered the hint of playfulness in his voice, the way he leaned into the cow he was milking and the heat I had felt, standing there at the stable entrance, as if mine was the skin being touched.

I could not recall one feature of his face; we had barely spent five minutes in each other's company. Yet I was stricken with panic, couldn't get up, couldn't sit still, ricocheting between wanting to race out the temple gates, for the safety of Bhavati's house and my rooftop room, to willing him to turn around. To see me.

Of course, I didn't run. That would have been foolish, and I had stopped foolishness, I told myself, a long time ago. I stayed until the rasp of a key turned in the lock of Andal's shrine, until *Aum Namah Narayana* clunked to a stop and all but one of the pavilion's lights were switched off, leaving two shadows, his and mine, sitting on the pavilion floor. The priest's exit seemed more perfunctory than usual as he walked between us rattling the keys tied at his waist. How I wished my limbs were as brisk and lithe as the priest's, but standing up and retracing my steps into the world outside felt as impossible as fixing my head onto my body, securing my heart back into its case.

'It's you, isn't it,' I heard as I slipped my toes into the loops of my sandals.

It wasn't a question.

How was I to feign surprise when his voice felt so familiar? I did my best, turning to look at him, hesitating, grasping for the right words. Something cleverer than yes. Or no. But this wasn't a game of snakes and ladders, or chess, or pick up sticks—all my strategies disappeared into the mouths of insects calling up their night.

'Would you like tea,' he said, a second question that wasn't.

'Your shoes?' was all I asked as he took off.

'Bare feet are the two things in life I cannot give up.' I heard my laughter alongside his, and that was that.

We strolled through the side gate of the temple, turned left then straight, to the main road where buses plied back and forth day and night to the next village and on to the four corners of

India. We stood at the edge of that world waiting for a chance to cross.

We found a table at the back of a crowded tiffin house. He ordered uthappams for two and strong tea sweetened with condensed milk and sugar.

Chapter Eighteen

O clouds! Drench Venkata with your calming water,
tell Narayana who entered me, who burgled my soul,
I am empty as a wood-apple sucked dry by a gnat

Nacciyar Tirumoli 8:6

His name was Vasur. We were discreet, the days we met in Srivil-liputtur, because eyes were in the walls of houses attached to the temple and it was common knowledge by then that this white woman coming to their town had a husband. Tongues, I imagined, were already wagging about what I was doing here alone. No Tamil wife ventured anywhere without her husband, and if not him she had a chaperone. If the chaperone was a man, it was her brother or uncle, and if it was a woman—well, women were the very best at keeping each other in check.

Vasur, it turned out, knew Srivilliputtur well. He had come here as a boy with his mother on her visits to Andal's temple. They lived in Madurai, his father was a teacher, and he was an only child. He was vague about detail—it was irrelevant, he said

—preferring to steep our days in the lores of whatever temple or mountain or cave we visited.

I had resisted at first, the places he wanted to take me. So much of myself was invested in Srivilliputtur, the circular path I took every day from Andal's garden to her temple and then to the shrine of the one she loved. Marcus sent me messages like a kind of metronome, details of his life without me, simple accounts and some of them cryptic, to keep me close, I supposed, and yet none of them espousing love. It's a given he replied if ever I asked. Even in letters he'd never sign off with *love*.

I was holding tight to the pages of Andal's verses, as if hidden in her songs was a thread and all I need do was find the end of it, hold on, and follow it in. But how do you hold tight to anything in India where nothing seems fixed and everything is pre-destined? It was an order of chaotic dimensions—then into this comes conviction in the eyes of a stranger. Was he just an apparition? I asked myself as I lay awake in my rooftop room the night of our meeting in her temple garden. All we'd done was share a meal. Our arms had barely touched, but the ripple through my body then, infused me now like an embrace, silent, non-conditional, and entirely unsolicited.

Vasur turning up in Srivilliputtur was about as mysterious as my path here in the first place and I knew better than to brush our encounter off as mere coincidence. Every cell in my body thrummed like a tuning fork struck by some god looking down on us.

'Why are *you* here?' I asked him the night we met.

Had it not been for the tea's caffeine coursing through my blood, I would have fallen into his eyes because they were all that existed in the crowded tiffin house where we sat.

'Eat,' he said when the uthappams were brought to our table. With our fingers we tore off pieces laced with red onion and green chilli. I did as he did, mopping up the spiced watery sambar running to the edge of my leaf plate.

'Mootai Swami told me to leave. I had been there eight years already, sometimes driver, sometimes rock moving, other times cow herder, doing whatever he wanted until there was nothing more for me to do. It was the week after you left, funnily enough. Swami said to me, "One more mountain you will be climbing." So that was that. I walked to the closest station, took the first train to pull in, and when it came to Srivilliputtur I knew the mountain Swami meant was near. Chathuragiri. So I got off.'

It was a shock to hear him say Chathuragiri because that was where Marcus and I had gone after our very first night in Srivilliputtur. My mind flashed through the tangle of months since then, to the broken shoes and sandals littering the eight hours of path we climbed, and the ghostly footprints left behind from the hundreds of thousands of pilgrims who had recently flocked to Chathuragiri for the Aadi month's full moon. It was the almightiest of human traffic jams going up and coming down the entire length of the mountain.

'You have been there ever since?' was all I mustered, and he swam his head side to side.

'When you think you have reached the top of the mountain, where the temples are and the pilgrims congregate, you are only halfway. You can climb some more through thick forest to a plateau where rare herbs and flowers grow and a tribe lives, but you know this already I think because that's where I heard about a foreigner woman who had just visited, a few days before I arrived. Her face was coated with white ash, they said.'

He leaned in close as if to count the lines furrowing my forehead. 'They thought you were some kind of visitation, and you know what happens to a whisper if it gets whispered enough. You're quite the legend now.' He laughed. 'Somehow I knew it was you.'

Vasur folded his banana leaf. 'Like this,' he said. 'If the food was good then you fold the leaf toward you before throwing it. If it was not tasty you fold it the other way.'

'But what do you mean, *you knew*?' I asked. He had this habit of changing a subject mid-sentence, from the surreal to the mundane, as if the two were perfectly connected. 'How could you have known it was me?'

'That's how I saw you, sitting in Swami's field the day I walked by. It was probably just dust and sweat, but your forehead looked smudged with ash then and I thought to myself, she doesn't know what she wants. In the heat of that day the air was shimmering like a mirage and there you were treading its waters.'

The air in the tiffin house suddenly felt suffocating even though every fan in the room was spinning full speed. My cheeks felt burned to scarlet, that this man beside me seemed to think he knew me better than I knew myself. I didn't know what to feel. Affronted, embarrassed. Grateful? He had no right to talk like this. He was a charlatan and I should be careful.

'I need to go,' I said, standing up.

He stayed seated. 'Tomorrow we will meet.'

'Tomorrow?' I hesitated.

'All right then,' I muttered, when what I wanted to ask was what time, and where, but I played the game I knew, of pride and safe distance, of catch me if you can. I walked the two blocks to Bhavati's house and climbed the stairs, two by two, to my rooftop refuge. I poured bucket after bucket of cold water over my body until the concrete floor of the bathroom felt solid again beneath my feet. Whenever I closed my eyes, the scent of musk filled my nostrils floating its way down to the back of my throat, sweet and slightly bitter. It was the same smell as the *vibhuti*, the sacred ash the priest had put into my hand at Chathuragiri.

❧

Marcus and I had woken before dawn to attend the day's first puja, an hour of bells and elaborate bathing of the temple's auspicious lingam rising crookedly from Chathuragiri's ground. Milk, yoghurt, ghee, and honey. A cow pushed past me, her pink tongue dripping at the sight. The priest gave her a friendly slap, sending her back. Pongal rice was offered to us and then the sacred ash. Whether it was the power of a ritual performed this way for thousands of years, the altitude, the wet nose of the hungry cow nudging into me, or just a lack of sleep—we had stayed up half the night looking for the lights of siddhars zipping through the sky—I took the vibhuti in my palm and without thinking streaked all of it across my forehead. Meanwhile Marcus, like the professor and his pilgrims, was carefully applying the three horizontal lines of a Saivite across his.

&

Of course, I looked for Vasur the next day. By noon, when the gates to Andal's temple were closed, I began to panic. He had gone. I had amused him, that was all. He'd met the *legend* and looked through her to find nothing on the other side. I was just another foreigner caught in her entirely fabricated world.

I stopped at the coconut seller's cart, squatting in the sliver of shade thrown by the temple wall. The tiers of the temple tower were being spruced up with fresh paint, hot-pink and lime-greens, sky-blue and electric-violets, looking ludicrous as a Bollywood wedding cake. After drinking the coconut water, I felt a little better and pulled from my bag the second book of Andal's verses Rani had given me.

When will I hear the conch that touches his coral lips, the great twang of his saranga bow?

Perhaps I was too tired for a properly attuned divination. The line read like more of a mockery. I closed the book and returned to my room, bathed the heat in my body away, slept, woke to the cool of an evening breeze, then set off for the temple through streets I now knew well enough to walk blindfolded. It was a Friday night.

It struck me, as I entered the last corridor before Andal's inner sanctum, that her words from a few hours before were nothing compared to what I was about to drink in. Mohini stood at the very end of the corridor two metres high, looking down at everyone about to enter, her stone fingers poised as if to pluck whomever she deemed unfit for the vision inside. I took in Mohini's tiny waist, the tight swell of her belly above an array of brocaded belts and girdles, the see-through wisp of cloth clinging to her hips, thick sculpted bangles and anklets, her elaborate headdress, long circlets threaded through her earlobes like plumes of an exotic bird, the jewelled chokers and the tease of a four-petalled ornament at the cleavage of her impossibly perfect breasts. Those arched eyebrows so finely sculpted, the long regal nose, and lusciously plumped lips. But she was an illusion, she wasn't a woman at all. She was Tirumal assuming the body of an enchantress, his incarnation. His to call upon whenever he wished to step into her lovely femaleness. The fluorescent tube above her head flickered and I saw the wink of one kohl-lined eye. She waved me through.

Andal's inner sanctum stands on a pavilioned platform built, some say, on the foundations of the house where she lived. The door was open. Soft light and the scent of incense filtered out. Before climbing the stairs, I circumambulated the pavilion, passing the small corner shrine to Laksmi and the panels of paintings along each of the three corridors. Tirumal and his avatars, all the stories Andal had loved, were there. I heard hushed murmurings through the high stone latticed windows of her sanctum, the strikes of a match, the tinkling of anklets. She had been brought out from her shrine to a dais at the front and was sitting with her lord on a golden swing decorated with flowers. A priest gently swayed them back and forth, suffusing the air with perfume and reverence. Nobody would think of disturbing the Friday night pleasures of a goddess and her divine lover—it was a tableau too intimate. Every time, I swooned in the visual beauty of it, I fell into the fairy tale. Their gazes skimmed the tops of our heads. What did they see? And what kind of love had they accomplished?

But there was an emptiness inside me on this particular night and the voice of reason, like a slow and deliberate oar through water, decried the lengths taken to ornament a goddess made of precious metals. And how credulous was I, the romanticisms of a girl in the body of a woman old enough to know better. I fought these conflicting thoughts and they disappeared, like they mostly do. The priest handed me a sprig of sacred basil and I put it on my tongue then turned to leave, taking a moment to peer down the well on my way out. It was the very one Andal had gazed into, people said, whenever she tried on the garland meant for god.

'What is it you see?' a voice asked.

I concentrated down into the well's dark square, the smile at the corners of my mouth threatening to stretch ear to ear.

A small girl pushed in between us. Vasur stood back for the girl's father to lift her up. She threw a coin and from far, far away we heard the sound of it go *plink* as it hit the water. I caught the faint glimmer of silver discs but no sign of any face, mine or the little girl's. My heart raced all the same. I felt Vasur's eyes and turned around. He gestured the way out. A large mirror, its glass mottled with age, hangs tilted outside the entrance so you can see the garbarigha behind you as you leave. I risked a glance of us, walking side by side, with the eyes of Andal and her lover, steadfast at our backs until we turned to the left and climbed down the stairs. Through the corridor of gods we walked, past Mohini, and Rati astride her peacock claiming the eyes of Kamadeva standing opposite her, one sculpted foot forward, his sugarcane bow poised and a quiver of flower arrows at the ready.

'There's an hour of light left,' he said. 'Shall we walk? I can take you to a small temple on the edge of town, not far. It's quiet there.'

'I'd like that.'

We strolled in an easy silence past Srivilliputur's main road, down the last few streets of houses to a narrow lane with fields either side, clumps of bamboo and gnarled trees shading the occasional farmer's hut. From a herd of grazing cows, one lifted her head to watch us; a peacock's call shrilled the air. We turned into a dirt track and at the end were the tell-tale red and white striped walls surrounding a temple. Its painted dome was small, compared to those over Andal and Lord Vatapatra sayee's inner sanctums, with not a gold leaf in sight.

'This is a temple to Krishna,' Vasur said. 'Not nearly as visited but once a year Sri Andal comes, and the rest of the world follows. They queue for hours just to glimpse her in a pose with Ranganatha.'

Vasur took the shawl from his shoulders and left it folded at the gate. He was as I had first seen him—months, or was it life-times ago?—a cotton lunghi tied at his waist, his skin dark burnished brown, limbs moving fluid as water, no resistance and never in a hurry.

We walked through an aisle of columns sculpted into larger-than-life figures similar to those inside Andal's temple, each of them stepping forward, agile, alive, vigilant. Krishna was there, a ball of butter in each of his hands, and two bewitched gopika girls either side of him.

'*Om Navanita Viliptangaya Namah,*' Vasur chanted, '*Om Navanita Nataya Namaha.*'

'To the lord whose body is smeared with butter,' he said, 'to the one who dances to receive its taste.'

I followed him to the end of the aisle.

'Can you feel it?' Vasur asked as we stood in the shadow of Hanuman the monkey god, his arm raised in a victory dance, the crown on his head proclaiming him king of monkeys, for he had saved Sita from the villain Ravanna in the greatest epic of all: the Ramayana. Sita, like Andal, born from the earth. All these myths of gods and goddesses, their stories shape-shifting around me, one incarnation slipping into the body of another. But Vasur was not looking at Hanuman or Sugriva or Arjuna or the stone courtesans dancing between them. He was staring at the dais in front of us.

'For one night, Sri Andal stays here. She is holding court, Lord Ranganatha reclining beside her, his head resting in her lap. Their eyes sometimes closed. Like this ...' he said, taking my shoulders and turning me to face the empty dais. He floated my eyelids down with his fingers, then placed the soft pad of his thumbs into the bony hollow between my eyes and nose, gently pressing upwards.

'Closed but never sleeping,' I heard him say from a far-off place, 'and all-seeing.'

A sensation of fingertips brushed the crown of my head, and then light. I couldn't see a colour to name it but I could feel one, like pressing my cheek to a window warmed by the sun. A sunflower. The same colour Andal had worn in the Swami's field. I heard humming in the air, like bees gathering pollen from deep in a forest, and then I saw her. She was listening to them too. She shook the knot of her hair free, then jumped lightly from the dais. I, if there was an I, felt each subtle touch of her toes to the ground, a soft dapple of footprints dreamlike and other-worldly and outside of time, as if she and the earth were playing, as a lover might trace the body of her beloved, as she wove through the columns of the temple where we stood.

I don't know how long I was there, if it was a minute or half the night.

Inside my bones and skin again, I felt the weight of my body on the ground, the stones of the temple wall supporting my back, and I looked up into the thousands of stars you can see when there are no streetlights or moon.

'So, you decided to join us?' Vasur's voice broke into the silence. He had wrapped his shawl around me.

'All I know, Vasur ...' I turned to him, searching for words, 'is ... I don't really know anything at all, except that I am here in Srivilliputtur because of Andal and, somehow, you are now also part of the reason.'

'There is a line in her Nacciyar Tirumoli, *I am empty as a wood-apple sucked dry by a gnat,*' he said. 'We wander from place to place seeking truths and happiness. But who is the wood-apple and who is the gnat? It is an endless cycle. When you step out from your house you will eventually come to the edge of the land you know. There will be a river, a lake, or an ocean, it is depending on your circumstance, but a boat will be there, waiting for you, ready to take you across. It happened to me and I think the same is for you. Every journey is different but the destination is the same.

'Do you remember halfway between the temple and the plateau on Chathuragiri, there is a giant lingam rock in the forest, tall as ten men? Near there is a cave where an old siddhar lives. I used to visit him. He let me collect wood for his fire, bring him water. Then one day, some restlessness came over me and he said to stop whatever it was I was doing. I wasn't sure what he meant—the half-filled basket of kindling I'd collected or the path I had been on ever since my wife died.'

Vasur paused, tracing a spiral in the sand between us with his fingers. 'I had wanted to renounce everything, and it was Mootai Swami who did his best to make sure it happened, but what if this wanting remains even after everything is stripped away? There was a great poet, Adi Shankara, who lived as long ago as Andal. He said, "Day and night, winter and spring, time passes, life ebbs to nothing. But the storm of desire never disappears." It turned out the old siddhar did not mean the fire I was about to build for him. It was time to leave an ascetic life. I'd reached another river and he was steadying the boat I needed to get across. And who should be on the other side less than a day's walk but Andal. *The nourishment of serving you extinguishes desire,* she says, *sorrow and exhaustion turn to bliss, only love is left.*'

Vasur's shawl felt prickly against my skin, but it was warm and I was shivering. He pulled it closer around me.

"All the knowledge in the world is useless tinsel if it is not integrated into life," the siddhar told me. They were the words that his close friend Rajaji had written after reading Adi Shankara. "*Jnaana* and *bhakti*, knowledge and devotion, are two paths but they are not different. When wisdom comes alive in your heart and flows out as action, it becomes devotion."'

I followed Vasur's eyes up into the sky. What star was he seeing, and what were the odds of us sitting here together, light years below?

Chapter Nineteen

Black sparrows at dawn announce the Dark One
I hear them chant his sacred names. Is this true?
Lord of Tirumaliruncolai, King of Dwaraka,
Vatapatra sayee asleep on a banyan leaf

Nacciyar Tirumoli 9:8

Visnucitta returned home from the temple garden to find Varaji squatting in the kitchen grinding coconut and green chilli back and forth with her stone pestle. All of her strength was concentrated in the task, as if the infusion of the chillis' fiery heat into the sweetness of a fresh coconut was life. Back and forth, back and forth, until the paste forming in her mortar was the colour of lime flesh. But life was not always a simple matter of two ingredients, two points of view. Truth felt like that sometimes; it needed pounding again and again before its many lessons could be realised and the way forward revealed. She added a little tamarind juice for balance and then some salt.

'Where is our daughter?'

'You are asking me?' Varaji stopped and looked up at him. 'You seem to know her whereabouts better than I!'

'Varaji, please, we have argued enough.'

He watched her spoon ghee then mustard seeds into the *kadhai* hanging over the fire. They spat and spluttered into the air.

'Husband, do you think your dreaming of a god's request for garlands worn by our daughter is going to solve anything? That your dream means an end to our problems?'

He sat down beside her, took the spoon from her hand and the pot off the fire.

'But don't you see my dream was a blessing? Now Andal has the ear of Lord Vatapatra sayee. I am certain this will appease her long enough for us to find a match. She will see the sense in Valluvar's words, "Women who honour their husbands will be honoured by the gods."'

Varaji looked him in the eye, shaking her head. 'Forgive me, husband, but if you think you can placate me with a soothsayer's tongue, you are the fool. Quote poets and sages if you like, but we both know the wilfulness of our daughter. She has a river inside her running deeper than any plumbed by them.

'Remember when you found her in the garden, you said she was a gift from god?' Varaji took both his hands in her trembling ones. 'I think she is more than this. Consider it, how the night before you brought her home, I had to poultice my breasts to quell the pain in them. And then when you walked through the door with her in your arms, milk started to stream from me. Is this even possible? This was not of my doing, it was hers. Don't you ask yourself how a young girl is able to compose such verses? You have seen a room full of pundits made speechless by her songs. And when she practises the mudras you teach, she brings to them subtleties only elder temple dancers have attained. Her friend Marali was telling me only yesterday how Andal had walked fearlessly into a field of bulls and all they did was low, and whenever cows refuse to give milk the herders call our daughter. Just one touch to their udders and milk flows. Tell me how a child brought up as a good Brahmin girl can do these things? Marali said if a calf is there, bleating with hunger, she will hold it in her arms, soothing it with one of her songs to Krishna, before putting its little mouth to the cow's teat, insisting the farmer wait until her calf has drunk its fill. Our daughter, Visnucitta! Have you not seen the red glow of her body when she returns home? Doesn't this make you think of Bhooma Devi?'

'Come now, Varaji, these sound like farmers' tales, and as for Andal's skin, what do you expect when she spends half her days kicking up clouds of ochred dust with her friends?'

Varaji took a breath, dismissing his argument, and returned the pot to the fire, adding the ginger she had chopped and a pinch of hing, then cumin and a sprig of curry leaves, tossing them till they sizzled. She spooned in a bowl of fine chopped beetroot and covered it quickly so it steamed. There was more she had to say.

'As if these were not signs enough, my husband, what about the owl roosting outside Andal's window?' Varaji put her beet-stained fingers together in prayer, turning to face the shrine on the shelf above them.

'*Aum Srim Hrim Maha Lakshmayai Namaha.*' Three times she chanted to a small clay image of Laksmi draped in silk. 'I bow to you, Great Goddess.'

Visnucitta followed her gaze. They had been hearing the owl's call every dawn and dusk for a year now, *povaa-aa, pova-aa.*

Varaji removed the kadhai's lid and stirred in the coconut paste. 'Munnu, the tribesman who delivers our wood, told me this is a call to the spirit world. It frightens me, Visnucitta. You know how they sacrifice owls to Laksmi during Deepavali, with all their toddy drinking and fire-dancing. I know Andal is already on their tongues. Too much of their reckless talk can turn a grain of millet into a palm fruit.'

Taking the tulasi prayer beads from his wrist, Visnucitta let them slide through his fingers, one bead for each silently breathed mantra to Laksmi, a thread of fear caught in his throat.

'But, Varaji, this is nothing but the superstition of mountain people. Uluka, the owl, is Laksmi's chariot. Such a bird outside our daughter's window is auspicious.'

Varaji's eyes brightened. She had skilfully coaxed her husband into the palm of her hand. 'Yes! Don't you see? All the signs are here. Bhooma Devi and Sri Laksmi. Lord Tirumal's consorts are revealing themselves through our Andal.'

Varaji spread a mat in the shade of their courtyard. She scooped out warm tamarind rice, then ladled sambar and a spoonful of the beetroot *poriyal* onto their leaves. They ate in silence, their fingers deftly popping food into their mouths without defiling their lips. They drank a spicy pepper rasaam for digestion, then buttermilk for cooling. Visnucitta stretched out onto the cushions Varaji had arranged for him. He watched her mix bitter slivers of areca nut with sugar crystals and anise seed before wrapping them into two bite-size betel leaf envelopes. They chewed, releasing the tastes of astringent and sweet, the juices turning their tongues bright red.

'I agree with you, husband, we must keep your dream and this garland-wearing a secret. But you can see, can't you, how compromised we are every time a suitor's family comes knocking at our door? There is more to Andal's stubborn nature than the fickleness of ordinary lovesick girls. Ever since she began to talk, all her babbling and prattling has been Krishna this and Krishna that.' She thought better of adding that his daily storytelling had not helped.

'We have to think of a plan. You must ask for another dream, but until it comes, we need to keep Andal safe from prying eyes and the *snip-snip* of ears curved like scissor handles. She needs to be protected from herself too. Her arms are starting to look like blades of paddy grass. She must eat!'

Varaji raked the fire's coals into a heap. 'I am praying daily to Sri Laksmi for her to send a man worthy of our daughter.

Marriages of love are rare. They must be nourished, like the seeds you plant, Visnucitta. Like us.'

Visnucitta leaned back, his belly too full. Now who is placating whom in this game of man and wife? he thought, the dream hovering above him no longer as sweet as it had been sitting across from his daughter that morning. He took the vessel Varaji handed him and spat out the juices filling his mouth.

Chapter Twenty

Shining, slender,
swaying hips like serpent coils
rising to the hood of a king cobra.
Wild peacock dancing before the storm

Tiruppavai 11

Why tonight? Visnucitta thought, crossing his legs on the floor at the entrance to Tirumal's shrine. Every full moon they made obeisance together. Why this one? He touched the cylinder of Sirimai's palm leaf message, checking it was secure in the folds of his dhoti. Her servant had passed it to him in the dark of the passage leading to the temple gates. His heart beat thick and fast when he heard the ringing of kin-kini bells. He did not look up to catch a glimpse of her face for fear of giving himself away. Sirimai knew him inside out, every intimation, any hint of desire trapped at the corners of his mouth. Her slender feet moved past him, her painted toes tracing circles mid-air. The rows of tiny golden bells on her anklets rang out each time she stamped her feet. Visnucitta held his breath, half-expecting the bells' echoes to pit his skin as they staccatoed off the stones.

The head priest walked past them, through to the inner sanctum, closing the curtains behind him. The drummer opposite Visnucitta started beating his kettle.

Tā tey tey tat ta tām, takre tā tey tey tat ta tām.

Visnucitta began to chant, forgetting the heat rising in him. Sirimai began to dance. She opened the palms of her prayer hands and covered her eyes. Night has come, divine ones, it is time to sleep. Between the beats of the kettle drum they heard the priest inside offering sweet saffron milk to Vatapatra sayee. Splashing it high from cup to cup, frothing it light as a cloud, so when the god sipped he drifted into dream. Wooden wheels revolved across the stones as the priest moved a cot in front of the shrine, a sound etched into the ritual of every night. The flickering of a lamp's flame threw shadows across the drapes as the priest prepared Vatapatra sayee's bed. Sirimai's hands spoke the ancient language of mudras as she danced her lord's body from the couch of the cobra Ananta Sesha to his banyan leaf bed, massaging his limbs, making a pillow for his head, guiding his passage into sleep. Opening her arms wide then moving them over the curves of her body, she described what heaven was, Vaikuntha, a place where gods dream, keeping safe inside them those who love them. Her body was snake then bird then leopard, but most of all woman. Her wide kohl-blackened eyes, graceful as a long-tailed fish, nuanced every emotion. Every word Visnucitta sang she threaded with life.

The priest made one last circle of flames clockwise over the reclining Vatapatra sayee. He stepped back over the threshold and Sirimai stepped in. She let her shawl of dark mulberry silk slip from her shoulders to the ground and took the yak tail fan lying across the end of Vatapatra sayee's bed. Visnucitta watched her shadow grow tall in the steady light of the ghee lamps— flashes of the silver girdle low on her hips, the voile skirt clinging to her legs, and the shape of her bare breasts wavering as she, the chosen consort, lifted then let fall the fan across the body of their god.

≈

Visnucitta left by the north gate, then turned right into the street of the dancers. Vines of night jasmine framed every window, terracotta pots of tulasi flanked each front door. But more than this it was the perfume of women he breathed in, of languishing, of hair soaked in coconut oil and plaited long with sprays of *kurunci* blossom. The serpent coils traced on their skin with sandalwood paste, red saffron painted on their breasts, and the smoke from Arabic resins used to smudge their secret places.

The turquoise door to her house was slightly open. His feet knew every grain and polished knot of the stairs he climbed. At the second arch of her hallway he drew back its beaded curtain.

≈

Four moons had passed since the death of Sirimai's patron. Any of the temple's courtesans would have taken another immediately, for the keep he gave, the jewels and the little luxuries life was so colourless without. But Sirimai had no need of such. She had enough for another ten lives, so generous had her last patron been. There was not a dancer who matched her artistry within a month of journeying on an elephant's back in any of the four directions. Her body was as supple now as twenty years ago when, at the age of nine, she was bequeathed to the temple. Pilgrims still clamoured for a pinch of dust from under her feet. She entertained kings when they visited Villiputtur, but she knew by the end of the night it would be the king entertaining her.

Sirimai had just turned twelve and was newly initiated when she and Visnucitta first brushed one against the other in their ritual communion with the gods. She danced for them and he sang. It was unordained delicious play until the moment Tirumal absorbed both of them. Sirimai's hands were no longer her own, she was god's servant, her worldly life left behind. Visnucitta's eyes rolled to the back of his head, a whole universe swirling inside. Words poured from him—he was the mind of Yashoda distraught at having to wean Govinda from her breast. She was the peacock unfurling its feathers in a dance at their lord's feet.

Visnucitta watched Sirimai grow for one cycle of seasons. Then he married Varaji, their stars foretelling a perfect alignment. She was a good and loving wife. But still he watched. Their first tryst was not planned, it just happened, as mysteriously as the moment their mortal play dissolved into the gods. Perhaps the gods had decided to play with them.

After the birth of Andal, Visnucitta's visits were less. Three months, sometimes six. His last visit had been almost a year. He trembled as he crossed the room. How well they knew each other. How far apart, now, they lived. He curved one hand around the back of her neck, let it rest there long enough to feel her warmth and her yielding, before following the contour of her shoulder down to the small hollow grazed by the line of her bodice. Rising and falling.

'Do you think time cheats us?' Sirimai rolled over, circling Visnucitta's naval with kisses, whispering into it.

The wicks in the lanterns had burned down to nothing. They lay in darkness by the window catching last glimpses of as many stars as possible before they disappeared. It was a race, this game they still played at the end of night, one they never tired of.

'Sirimai, look.' Visnucitta pointed to the hint of light arcing over the thatched and tiled roofs of town, over fields of sugarcane and sunflowers. A lone swan flew west, as if in slow motion, its wings washing the sky white, readying it for the colours of the day. 'There is your answer,' he said, turning to face her. 'Do seasons ever cheat the migrations of a swan?' With his fingers he traced the small conch shell tattooed on her left shoulder, kissed it, then did the same to the discus imprinted on her right.

'But where is its mate?' Sirimai spreadeagled him with her legs. How she cajoled him with her questions one minute, then teased him with her body in the next.

'Still asleep in its bed, soft as the down of two mating swans.' He cupped her breasts then tussled her down.

'Sing me one last song, Visnucitta,' Sirimai pleaded, shaking the bedcovers off so the morning's light gilded their bodies.

He half sat, leaning on an elbow, twirling the strand of hair fallen across her face.

... virtuous lady, with your vats of curd and fresh churned butter ...

'The dance of Senkeerai!' Sirimai laughed, curling and uncurling her hands so the bangles around her wrists percussed a rhythm. She shimmied herself up to sit opposite him, telling the story he sang with mischief in her eyes; of a mother coaxing her toddler's butter-smeared face away from the upturned pot he held, holding him steady, swaying his body to the melody of her song. She matched her whole being to Visnucitta's words till the last verse.

Visnucitta opened his eyes to find Sirimai waiting, still as the core of earth. She knew about Andal. Of course, she knew. Most twilights, Andal accompanied Visnucitta to the temple. As Sirimai danced, from the corner of her eyes she could not help but mark each inch the little girl grew. The way she had first crawled toward Tirumal's feet and screamed when pulled away.

She had listened to Andal singing her first songs and saw beyond their innocence. It was almost two years since she had accepted Varaji's invitation to dance the morning of Andal's first blood ceremony and to lead the procession of hula-huling women afterward. Their celebratory cries filled Villiputtur's streets, letting every prospective in-law know her time had come.

And soon she would be turning fourteen, older by two monsoons than Sirimai when she first danced in the sanctum of the temple, and on the same night entered the king's bedchamber. Her life was a privileged one, highest of mortal consorts to god and king, but she would not wish it on any girl, especially the daughter of the man she loved. She knew there was whispering among the women in the temple—the priest's girl's reckless behaviour, rumours of marriage proposals denied—as if a silk veil over their malicious lips hid their talk. What was to become of her?

Visnucitta began slow humming an *alap*, improvising on its first notes. Sirimai recognised his raga of dawn and drew a shawl around her shoulders. There was sorrow in his voice. She felt his same yearning, pale as the shafts of sunlight moving across their bed.

Before the east is lit, my daughter wakes. That red-eyed lotus one, will he command her to churn the thick white curds? He treats her so disparagingly. Is she strong enough for him?

'There is time yet,' Sirimai said, resting a hand on his knee. 'Do not let the idle talk of ignorant people bother you. What do they know of love? Let the suitors come. Feed them sweets, make the dowry offerings. If a proposal is accepted, then request first the advice of Manu, my astrologer. Tell him you need to delay the wedding. I will talk to him—he owes me. Let the stalling come from his mouth, not yours.

'And don't worry, no priest or temple authority will be able to corral Andal into any service unworthy of her with me standing at the gate. For all the wisdom they espouse, they are nothing more than self-serving bureaucrats. I have the ear of the king, and of Lord Tirumal too.' She winked. 'Isn't it so?'

She piled her hair in a knot on top of her head, a picture of authority.

'But what then, Sirimai? Every moon, Andal grows more uncontrollable. For too long now, if marriage to a man is even mentioned she rages about the house, crashing into walls like a stunned bird. If one word of betrothal slips from our mouths, it's as if all the air is knocked from her body. She doesn't sleep or eat. Some days she barely has the strength to walk across a room. One year, maybe two, of this, and then? A woman destined for life as a *nityasumangali,* forever bound to a god—I cannot imagine Andal's discontent if she were shackled with a ritual husband, let alone a mortal one. As sacred as your role is, Siri-mai, each night waving the lighted lamp and dancing our god to sleep, my daughter desires more than a nityasumangali does, she wants nothing less than his lap to lie in and is prepared—'

Visnucitta drew in a deep breath, remembering Andal's threat to use the yogic powers he himself had taught her. He dared not tell Sirimai about the secret wearing of Vatapatra sayee's garland. But Andal's ultimate desire, she at least knew. Sirimai's lips were pursed as she gazed out the window with that faraway look of hers. Her mind, he could tell, was scheming.

The day had broken. He did not want to leave the bed of this woman who had always released him from the constraints of worldly life, but the weight of this morning, he felt, was also inside her.

'And if she does not marry,' he said, 'her life will be worth less than a widow's.'

'In whose eyes?' Sirimai leaned close to him, fierce for a moment. 'Listen to yourself, like a trapped lion round and round with your thoughts. Be fearless, be the man I know! If you doubt your daughter, then every song you make is a lie. Be patient.' She took his hands in hers, shaking them as if to shake sense into him, her voice softening. 'Show me a girl her age who has composed verses of such devotion. Trust me. Tirumal has come to you before in your dreams and he will again.'

Sirimai watched Visnucitta from her window as he made his way to the temple gates. Only when he had disappeared did she go to her courtyard to draw water from the well. She took time to wash; she had the whole day to herself. She massaged sesame oil into her skin and coconut oil through her hair, letting it fall loose past her waist. For perfume all she wanted was memory. The liquorice taste remembered on her tongue, the sour-sweet scent of him still swimming inside her. She tied a long skirt at her hips and criss-crossed a silk shawl tight over her breasts. She filled two terracotta pots with ghee and floated a wick in them, lit them, then placed them at the base of the shrine built into a fork of her beloved *ashoka* tree. Tiny buds were appearing on its branches. She kicked the tree's trunk so they would open. The tree desired her and if it was to flower it needed to feel her feet, to hear the tinkling of her anklet bells each time she hit its thick-as-elephant-hide bark. She had first done this in the last days of her own pregnancy and had continued to do so for thirteen springs—every Aadi moon.

'Sorrow-less tree,' Sirimai chanted as she took the bowl of water from the shrine. All night it had infused under the moon. Three times she stirred the ashoka buds floating on its surface, then drank long and deep every drop of the water. She scattered the buds at the base of their mother and said a prayer to Kamadeva, the god of love. 'Take from your quiver your ashoka arrow and aim it at the heart of the lord. Tell him there is a girl who will have no other. Who else but he can turn this bud into a flower?

'And god speed to the dreams of her father,' she added, kicking the tree once more for good measure.

Chapter Twenty-One

Young elephants spar in Tirumaliruncolai,
in every jasmine blossom I see his smile,
whole clusters of dark Pata flowers mock me.
O friend to whom can I complain? This garland he wears

Nacciyar Tirumoli 9:2

There were mornings I made my way to the temple before dawn and it was deserted, the bell-studded doors to Andal's inner shrine still locked, so I sat. The same old lady, haggard and hunched, came with her broom and her mutterings, giving me a remote look before starting to sweep—the dust, the rat droppings, the remnants of sunbeams from the day before, a sweet wrapper carelessly dropped by a child, the contents of my mind —all these she swept down the stairs, clearing the way for the cow and her calf, for Jaya Malika and the women who followed.

Jaya Malika is the temple's resident elephant. Every day she comes, her mahout by her side. He has no need of a stick; she knows the way, loping up the stairs in the early morning light, rotund and wrinkled, her four legs circled in bells, bright designs painted between her eyes. She waits at the door for the cow and her hungry calf to enter first. At the feet of Andal, the cow is milked, a brass bell clangs, then Jaya Malika makes her entrance, greeting her garlanded goddess with a low bow.

There are sculpted reliefs on the platform's columns and walls either side of the garbarigha's doors: stories of Tirumal and his avatars, of guardians, consorts, hermits, demons. An elephant is carved on one of the columns, standing docile as a pet, letting four-armed Tirumal stroke his back. It was Gajendra, the elephant who had struggled for a thousand years, his leg gripped in the jaws of a crocodile, until the day Tirumal saved him. I would run my fingers over them as if this might help make sense of the story.

The place I claimed to sit was always the same, opposite the carving of a young woman. She is black as black in the forever half-light filtering through the slats of stone above. Her body relaxed and naked. Cross-legged, she clasps her hands in her lap as if above them, in a belly round as a ripened moon, she holds the whole world. I would close my eyes and rest in her. She was as ancient as the beginning of time and yet I felt completely present in her company. Sorrow would sometimes fill me, and longing. It was deep and its reason nameless, swelling in the core of me like a river filling with the tide of a sea. When I left her and walked back through the temple, the world was different, my pace slower, my mind more subdued instead of racing this way and that. The sounds of a town waking—steel shutters rolling up, motorbike horns, calls of the flower sellers—an indistinguishable hum until the spell of other-worldliness pervading the womb of Andal's temple and the calm of that naked black stone girl dissolved into the ordinariness of daily life.

I watched the slow ease of Vasur walking toward me. We had planned to meet for breakfast and I was early, standing at the corner tea shop next door. I ordered a cup for him, cleaving my eyes away, back to the tea-wallah pouring from glass to glass at arm's length until all the sugar had dissolved. Maybe that's what it was about Vasur; he was casting a spell just like the cross-legged girl's, only more complicated.

'Have you eaten yet?'

'No, I was waiting for you.'

'Today I am going to Kattalagar Temple. Come with me, Saisha.'

I had heard of Kattalagar, not far from Srivilliputtur, but it was a walk into the ghats and I had been advised against going alone. 'Dangerous, madam, you would be needing a guide,' etcetera etcetera. Marcus's warnings, to take every precaution, hovered in the background too. We had seen the scat of a panther one trek into a forest and our guide said in a spooked garbling of Tamil-English that we should turn back. This was where the trail ended, he said, when clearly it didn't. We kept going, believing his fear was superstition. So much of Indian life was disconnected from wilderness, a far cry from the songs of the Sangam Age I had discovered on the shelves of Pennington's library. I doubt if there is any poetry as steeped in nature as these songs written ten centuries before Andal's appearance.

I hesitated, and drank from my cup, surveying Vasur chatting with the tea-wallah, his invitation hanging in the air. I pictured him living those eight months on Chathuragiri and the tribespeople he would have encountered. They wandered naked until a few decades ago, the professor had told us, adding with a twinkle in his eye, 'Before the religious and the righteous moved in.' He had suggested one of the tribe's young men guide us further into the forest to their plateau home above the temples. I can still remember that nimble boy, disappearing then appearing out of nowhere, as if by magic, free from the confines of the time and space anchoring us. The smile lighting his face was without content, without thought. It was there as naturally as a play of sunlight on water, wild grasses dancing in the wind.

What first compelled me about Vasur when I saw him leading a cow through the Swami's fields—his steadiness and ease—had now amplified. Wilderness became him. Sipping the last of our tea, I fell into absolute trust. To the moon and back, I wanted to say out loud, but didn't, which was probably just as well.

We smashed our clay cups to the ground—Srivilliputtur being late to the modernity of plastic meant a community of potters were still making their sun-dried vessels. Shards of red earth disintegrated under our feet as we left the tea shop for breakfast at Kathiravams. Over leaf plates of idlis and sambar, Vasur explained some more about Kattalagar Temple as if I had agreed to go with him, when I'd said nothing.

'It is not the same place Andal speaks about, the forest of Tirumaliruncolai, near Madurai,' Vasur said. 'Another temple is there called Kallalagar. Similar name but it is different. Same god though.'

'I'm looking forward to whatever story you'll be unravelling for me,' I said, a little too flirtatiously.

Vasur called the waiter to bring a parcel of idlis.

'Will do my best. So many temples you are needing to see and each one has its own reason for existence.' He either didn't hear the flippancy in my voice or pretended not to notice. I ticked myself off.

'First, we will stop where I am living, then catch a bus from there. It's on the way.'

We walked through town, taking the same path to Thirumukkulam where I had spent the hours watching Sri Andal's ritual bath. There was even less water in the teerthum, but the clouds above us were rolling in from the west, teasing. Rain would surely come soon. Behind the pavilion was a thick grove of banyan trees and a cluster of stables and sheds in various states of disrepair, a scent of cows and the occasional clang of metal buckets. I followed Vasur through the gate to the sprawling branches of a tree where a tarp was strung across its pendulous roots.

'Welcome to my palace,' he said, ushering me past a fire pit. I left my sandals outside and stepped into a small dappled space, its smooth dirt floor swept of leaves. A thin bed of hessian bags was laid out in one corner, an iron pot and a kerosene stove opposite.

'You live here?'

'I inherited it. Good until the rains come, then maybe I will move in with the cows, or move on. Who knows?' He lifted the lid of the pot and took out an orange and two bananas. 'Prasadam from yesterday, we can take with us.' He unknotted a cloth bundle hanging from a branch, took a lunghi out and tied the idli parcel and fruit into it, then threaded the knot onto the end of a wooden staff. 'Are you ready?'

Was I? In the West if I was preparing for a trek there'd be provision calculations, energy snacks, all-weather gear, and a good set of boots. But this wasn't the West. I'd seen Indian women in immaculate saris and fancy sandals set off into the jungle with not a hair out of place, just their dear husbands at their side, and faith. But I had more than that; I had trust, complete trust in this man standing at the entrance of his house waiting for my reply. I looked down at my feet, already calloused from days of rubber thongs on dusty streets and the flagstones trod barefoot every day in Andal's temple. A hint of wood-smoke hung in the air from the fire pit outside. No traffic bedlam, at all. The stillness was surreal. I wondered if a trek to anywhere else but here was even necessary.

Vasur broke through my wandering mind with a chant-like song.

'One of Andal's songs, a favourite of my mother's. When I was a small boy, she would urge me on with it as we climbed to the other Kallalagar temple. I'll translate for you when we are on our way, assuming, that is, you still want to go.'

An ancient bus jolted us down a corrugated road to where the Kattalagar Temple track began. It took a while of walking over stony ground, through thorn trees and scrub forest, before the heat of the bus passengers' eyes boring into our backs dissipated—we must have looked an odd couple.

Vasur led the way and we walked in silence, into wildflowers and weeds, the calls of tiny birds darting through brittle branches and hints of cooler air as the path began its ascent. I had forgotten how thoughts can fall away when civilisation is left behind, when there is no judgment, only an evolving into the spaces between trees self-seeded from the beginning of time. No grand plan beyond roots seeking water, and leaves reaching for the light, tall and taller, deep and deeper—we become wanderers in their world.

It felt like the turning of a page entering this country and that there was no turning back. But before the forest eventually closed in around us, there was evidence of pillaging for fodder and firewood. I sensed Vasur's body stiffening when we passed stumps of trees recently felled, the sap like coagulated blood around each primitive cut. He saw it as much of a desecration as I did and it pleased me to know he did not approve, that this was not a place of dark and evil to be wounded into the harsh light of an Indian sun; it was as precious as any deity in a temple. I watched his bare feet fall light and sensitive, whether on rocks or river sand, his long legs sinewy yet fluid.

I lagged a little, enjoying the solitude and the quiet. Vasur was waiting for me at the first riverbed. It was dry except for a few small pools.

'Maybe there will be more water at the falls,' he said. We kept on, side by side.

'Vasur, Andal's song?'

'I was waiting for a butterfly to appear before telling you.'

I followed his gaze into the air above us.

'A butterfly?'

'We can imagine what Andal might have felt caught in a cloud of them. Look for a butterfly with a bright red body and matching spots across black wings. I have only seen one and it was years ago—maybe the same kind Andal saw—but then a thousand years is a long time for a creature so fragile to exist.'

'Well *we* have … I mean us, the human race,' I said, tugging his arm. He pulled away just as playfully.

'Amazing, isn't it? A thousand years of human invention, from stone axes to a man on the moon, and yet the verses of a girl fixed on a god still resonate.'

As we walked on, I wondered if there was a part of Vasur still attached to the life he had led before his wife died. I had so many questions, but sensed asking about the past would only result in a shrug of shoulders. I had weathered too many shrug-offs from Marcus in our years together. I tried to remember the man I had fallen in love with, but felt nothing in my body. Marcus was mysterious too, until more and more that mystery detached his life from mine. With Vasur it was different—his mystery somehow held the whole world, and I was included.

'Andal's butterfly, Vasur? Tell me.'

'You are knowing her *Tiruppavai*. Then there is her *Nacciyar Tirumoli*. Andal is no longer an innocent girl in love with Krishna. She takes us deeper in a kind of twilight language. After her wedding dream, there is the seventh Song of the Conch.'

O right whorling Valampuri you need not search for sacred rivers—you dwell in the hand of red lotus-eyed Krishna, you bathe in the nectar of god's own mouth.

Vasur paused and took a long leaf from a tree, rolling it into a tight cylinder. He whistled through one end, making a sound not dissimilar to the calling of a bird we could hear from the undergrowth. The bird stopped, then started again.

'Try,' Vasur said, handing me the leaf, but the sound I made was all breath and no song. He continued their duet until a tiny black-winged creature with a golden breast flitted across our path and out of sight again.

'And the eighth song?'

'Then Andal goes to the Hills of Venkata where dark rain clouds roll in, *like raging elephants*, she says. In the ninth song, she visions the forests of Tirumaliruncolai where the entire grove, every flower, wild fruit, cuckoo, and peacock mocks her search for him. He is everywhere, tormenting her, but still he eludes her. Tirumaliruncolai is where the Kallalagar temple is, the one I would go to as a boy, so I thought one of those verses was appropriate for today because we are climbing a mountain to the same Beautiful Lord, the one, she says, who stands facing east. There are people who think she came here too, as well as there, but who knows? Nobody. No need anyhow. A goddess can be everywhere just as Andal describes her Tirumal, her Krishna.'

Crimson butterflies fill the air of Tirumaliruncolai, a glow vermilion as his forehead. How can I escape this net the lord with beautiful shoulders spreads?

I let the words sink in, more as colour, as crimson and amber, the black cross-hatch of a net, the honey-brown of a lover's skin. As we continued to climb, Vasur's words, 'a goddess can be everywhere,' somehow eddied my past into the present and I was twenty-six again on a ferryboat with my mother headed for an island resort.

'Prise yourself from that man of yours,' she had said. 'Come for a holiday with your mama.' I was still fragile, but the waves of sadness were growing less and less—the one child I had already lost and now the chances of another taken from me too. I had fallen in love with Marcus again—love! How is it possible you can fall in and out of love multiple times with the same person? He had wooed me with his body and those intense eyes of his. Our coupling in streams and under the stars had carried us

across every lifetime we had spent together. And now that there
was no threat of conceiving a child, we could be careless, whatever the time of month. He had flushed me with his Tantric skil-
fulness, head to toe.

'You are moving too quickly,' my mother said—she had
never warmed to him. 'Take some time to think about your life.'
It's not too late, was on the tip of her tongue, I could tell, but
she restrained. Some lives are not that simple, I would have
replied.

The resort was a paradise, but there were warnings of tiger
snakes on the inland tracks and few guests ventured far from its
white beach. I can only explain my impulse to walk to the other
side of the island wearing nothing but a sarong as yearning. My
whole body had caved into a pain that was welling just below
the surface. Mama was right, I needed time alone. Simple tactile
encounters—a smooth shining leaf, sand flowing through my
fingers, paperbark against my cheek. I took my carapace of
misplaced desires and padded barefoot into the forested valley at
the island's centre. Thousands of blue wings fluttered through
the filtered light and shadow of trees. The path curled down and
the light became less. Clouds of Ulysses butterflies undulated
above me like one cognisant breath. I untied my sarong and
walked naked further and further in, to the forest and the clouds
of blue subtly shifting as if allowing for the presence of another.

Oh, my body and mind then, sweet and dramatic.

I had swum without clothes on empty beaches but never
walked naked through a forest. The blue-winged air on my skin
felt sensuous as the sea. Without thinking I lay down in a
tremble of sunlight pooled beside the path. The earth was damp
and smooth against my back and I spreadeagled my limbs. Is it
you doing this? I had asked of myself, momentarily. But it was
not. It was desire without object, and I had fallen into its arms.
One butterfly caught my attention, its wings lit by the shifting
light. I followed its flight, my heart beating a kind of rapture,
until the sun blinded me and I was haunted again. In the air

where the butterfly had darted there was now a child holding fast to a balloon, her legs kicking. Up and up they floated until they disappeared, as did the sun behind a cloud, and I was myself again, plunged into the dark of the forest. Empty. Not knowing what to do, as if a lover had entered me but just as suddenly withdrawn.

✥

Vasur was waiting by the waterfall's one small trickle, the prasadam orange peeled in his hand. He placed segments into mine one by one, their juice the kind of sweet concentrated from sitting days in a summer's heat. Sweet with a hint of decay but I didn't care, I was distracted, my body unsettled by those waves of blue wings and the disappeared child.

We watched clouds tumbling down a ravine in the mountains ahead of us, gathering speed but not yet loosed toward the arid plains we had left behind.

'Shall I give you another of Andal's verses? *The word of the serpent-bedded lord means nothing. I take refuge in him, but he forgets me. He tortures me.* She is pleading this, Saisha, to those dark clouds you are seeing. No matter how strong Andal's longing she speaks it.'

Vasur reached over to fill his palm from the trickling of water. He sprinkled some into my hands, just enough to wash the stickiness of the orange away.

'However deep your despair, you must look it in the eye— then leave it at the feet of the one you've accused. Only then can it metamorphose into love,' he said. 'Like one of those crimson butterflies.'

I swallowed hard. Why that verse? I had taken refuge in the quiet calm knowing of Marcus, but every time he closed his eyes, I felt forgotten. It was self-inflicted torture and a flawed comparison, but torture nevertheless. Vasur saw the abyss in me, and there was nothing godly about it—my nothingness rimmed with catastrophes I pretended to forget. I looked across at the clouds. Small tufts were breaking away and riding the wind toward the plains, toward the sea. For all the time I had spent in Andal's temple, my mind was still a pendulum. All my years with Marcus suddenly felt like a rudderless boat. But I had been reasonably content, hadn't I? We'd had more of the calm after a storm than the storms, hadn't we? He was a good man, a steady man. Faithful. But what had happened to me? I wanted to explain to Vasur who I was, really. Unable to bear a child, then the key to my body thrown away. What kind of fate is that for a woman? But his seeing needed no details. I know that now.

He stood and held out his hand to pull me up. His grip was electric but his smile betrayed nothing.

He turned for a last look over the scant patches of green and miles of rocky earth stretched below us. 'You have to leave everything behind,' he said to the horizon. 'All you think you are.'

We walked, and I settled down into the rhythm of our climb. The forest thickened and the path grew steeper. One foot, then the other. Looking out for tree roots snaked across our path, skirting fallen branches and looping vines.

'Maybe we'll see a giant grizzled squirrel,' Vasur said when we stopped for breath. 'Some barking deer, wild boar, even elephants.'

'Should I be scared?' I jested.

Who was this puckish man clad in a lunghi, making me laugh when half an hour ago I had just about cried? One minute enchanting me with the songs of a goddess in his impeccable English, then tying me in a knot the next. Besides having a wife and a mother, a father who was a teacher, he had revealed nothing about his past, nothing of his life before leaving the world. He walked as if born of the forest.

A tribe of langur monkeys ogled us from a tangle of vines, then screeched warnings through the canopy as they glided away. The temple's concrete steps began, two hundred and forty-seven of them, a sign warned, stretching ahead like a red and white striped serpent separating the banks of green wilderness either side all the way to Kattalagar. Like fuel the taste of a prasadam orange lingered on my tongue. I wondered if Andal really did come here. It would have been a day's trek from Srivilliputtur by bullock cart, then by foot as we had done. Her path from here on was probably more a steep clamber over rocks through a world of ancient trees. Her mind oblivious—the flash of leopard eyes or the crash of a wild elephant somewhere deep in the forest reverberating beneath her feet—her heart fixed on the Beautiful Lord waiting.

I matched my footsteps with Vasur's and the slight sway of his body. My breathing deepened. We climbed silently until almost to the top. Vasur paused for me to catch up.

'Look,' he said, pointing to two mountain peaks in the distance. 'Can you see? One is the face of Tirumal and the other a frog.'

If I squinted and used all of my imagination, there definitely was a crouching frog on top of one mountain and the profile of a regal face on another.

'But no need for frog stories,' Vasur said, 'we are here.'

The temple sat white and imposing on a huge rock plateau. When the sun came out from the clouds, its walls glistened.

'One more Andal song I am telling you before we go inside. Come,' he said, turning to the left. We circumambulated the temple three times, taking in the breadth of its craggy land and vast cloud-heavy sky.

'Lord Kattalagar wanted to marry Sri Andal. He came to Srivilliputtur to ask for her hand, but was too late. So, he stayed here in the forests of Shenbagathoppu, no doubt still dreaming of what she had once offered him, *a hundred vessels of churned butter and another hundred of sweet rice pudding*. And, if he accepted these, she promised one hundred thousand more for every vessel already offered. *Choose my heart for your abode*, she said, *and I will be your slave*.'

I trailed my fingers along the warmed stones of the wall

enclosing the one she would be slave to. Stooping low, we entered the temple's inner shrine, the air of its womb space concentrated, thick with incense, camphor, and ghee. Lord Kattalagar stood tall looking to the east, his all-seeing eyes skimming the tops of our heads. I had only ever seen Tirumal reclining on his serpent bed. Somehow a vertical god commanded a different kind of attention. Was it a risk, standing there before him? He might step down from his pedestal and consume me. But he did not move. Perhaps because of his two consorts, Bhooma Devi and Sri Laksmi, standing like heavenly gatekeepers either side of him. I imagined a third consort, earthborn and beautiful, falling at his feet, her entreating cries, her perfumed garland.

The priest circled Kattalagar's eyes with a camphor flame, then plucked two fragrant buds from the flowers circling his wide shoulders. I fumbled at the bottom of my bag for some coins. We waved our hands across the flame, then bathed our faces with its heat. The priest drew a line of turmeric paste up the centre of our foreheads, then dropped a bud each into our palms.

I turned to go.

'Wait one minute,' Vasur said.

The priest returned with a pot and into our right hands he ladled a warm mound of sweet rice pudding.

Chapter Twenty-Two

Devoted one, detached from the world,
Lady Nappinnai, coral lipped, slender waisted,
give us the fan, free us from our selves
give us the mirror, so we can see

Tiruppavai 20

Our bus from Kattalagar rumbled into town just before dark. I got off with Vasur but said goodbye at his gate before walking the rest of the way home.

'Look, all the cows are lying down,' I said. 'Where I come from it's a sure sign of rain.'

He took my face in his hands, looked into my eyes, and swam his head. 'A good omen, then.'

Light rain did begin to fall as I reached the stairs to my room—a mango shower, Tamilians say, for its teases of coolness and orchards of green fruit growing tantalisingly heavy. Any day there'd be blushes of gold and the hint of perfume that at night intensifies. I stood under the palm leaf shelter of my rooftop, breathing in the rain-sweetened air, listening to the sounds of life: bicycle bells from the dark streets below, the chides of a mother and the wail of her little one from a house across the road, and from inside lit-up windows the clangs of cooking pots and animated conversation. Does India ever sleep? Husbands and wives, children, grandmothers and grandfathers. I was an outsider, perhaps I always would be, but I was comforted.

I thought of Vasur in his tree house on the edge of town, the only sounds for him raindrops on leaf and tarpaulin, the occasional low of a cow, the crackle of flames. A lone man and the constancy of his fire.

'And what do *you* see?' Vasur's words played again inside my head as I turned the key to my room. It seemed like forever, but was barely two weeks ago, the night he was suddenly standing beside me as I looked down into Andal's well. The back of my neck tingled just as it did then. I unhooked the padlock and pushed open my door, shook the rain from my hair before stepping inside.

All I needed was there—my clothes folded on a shelf and doubled up on three coat hangers, one thin mattress on the floor, a pillow and a mosquito net, a candle, and Andal's songs. I looked at the picture of her Bhavati had taped to my wall, white cows at her feet, the tree behind her alive with birds and squirrels, Krishna standing underneath. I imagined her again, a garland of flowers draping her shoulders, making her secret way to the well. Looking into its dark water. Are you there, Beautiful Lord? Can you see me?

I took the room's small mirror from its nail and held it to my face, inquisitive as much as anything, wanting to know who it was Vasur saw. Mostly I gave mirrors just a brief glance, neither liking or disliking, and the older I became the less I was inclined to check, the less the temptation to glance at myself passing a shop front or my refection backlit in a train window as it hurtled through a tunnel. Was it a lack of ego or denial of age? Or was I simply confounded by this changing body I continued to inhabit?

Mirror, mirror on the wall, who is the most beautiful— words etched into the psyche of every Western girl. The lure of being beautiful, for whom? When I first read of Andal's visits to the well, it struck me as more fairytale than myth. But then I saw a popular print at one of the temple arcade shops. Her hair gathered into a beehive knot circled with jasmine, the spangled skirt pleated at her hips, a red bodice barely covering her voluptuousness. All the ornaments befitting a bride were there, and a garland, *the* garland, meant only for a god. She was posing in front of a mirror, admiring her reflection. All of this I saw until one day, passing time, skimming the bangles and baubles of a goddess's marketplace, I stopped and looked again. In the mirror's reflection stood Krishna, wearing the same garland, a peacock feather in his crown and an adoring turn to his lips. Why hadn't I noticed this before? It was just as Vasur had said— a twilight language. Krishna in place of Andal's reflection. She was absorbed into him, into the mystery of the divine, her deepest desire realised. A kind of death by love if you think about it.

Melt my heart. Pour him into me, she says.

In Andal's temple, if you turn right before passing through the last gateway, Kamadeva with his Cupid bow and his consort Rati riding her peacock will usher you to the Ekadasi Mandapam, a hall of mirrors. My first visit was to a room empty of anyone but me and my thousand other selves. I laughed like a child stepping into the mysteries of a circus sideshow, but as I walked the perimeters of countless gold framed mirrors, it was more a case of what it might be like trapped inside a kaleidoscope, a target for one of Kamadeva's flower-tipped arrows. Who would I be matched with? How long would the perfection last before I realised there is no such thing? Lovers, they burn, they fuse, they fall, sometimes right back into the arms of the one who pushed them, they make babies, wander rooms of desire, they leave, return, they try again. Perhaps Kamadeva still draws his sugar cane bow, this god out of time, plunging us into the illogic of another's face that, in the beginning, can seem more worthy of breath than our own. It's true, perception can turn on its head: you want to see yourself through their eyes, not yours. As alluring as the beginning of love is, compared to Andal's willingness to give up absolutely everything—to dive into the abyss forever—we humans tend to deliberate. The many tales of that bridge to the other. Is it safe to cross?

It was full moon on my second visit to Ekadasi. This time my face was lost in a sea of pilgrims because Andal was there with her lover. All the raucousness typical of an Indian crowd hushed to devout murmurings. Priests stood either side, gently pushing their flower-decked swing so every mirrored reflection moved too, backward and forward, and we were there as well, one fused body, one held breath, moving clockwise through the infinity of their love.

'*Vange, vange*,' a priest shouted over us if we stopped a minute too long to bathe in their glow. Maybe the world we inhabit is nothing more than a playground for the gods, I thought as I left for town through the temple tower into what was, perhaps, just a one-dimensional realm compared to theirs, as insubstantial as breath on a mirror.

❧

I shed my clothes and girded myself for a cold bucket bath. What a day we had had journeying to Kattalagar. I had forgotten the exhilaration of wilderness, of trekking into mountains then looking back in awe of the distance travelled. My thonged feet had been pummelled from the hours of a rough stone track, my calf muscles ached, my hip joints felt stiff. I collapsed onto my mattress, damp-skinned and satiated. The last image to float past my eyes was of Vasur's lean body disappearing round a bend of the path we had walked.

I slept long and deep, then fell into a dream. An old man with bowed legs was striding purposefully into a forest and I followed him. The trees closed around us until it was impossible to go further. His calloused hands lifted me onto the back of an elephant.

'Hold tight,' he said, before disappearing.

I gripped a fold of its tough hide. There was a sudden quivering of leaves close to us and I felt the elephant's body constrict underneath me. Two emerald eyes appeared through the tangle of undergrowth. I had seen panther scat, but never a panther. Like a bellow, the elephant's whole being expanded then he blew one warlike rumble of breath before bolting, the drumming of his feet shaking the forest floor, crushing everything in the way, higher and higher into the mountains, until we reached an open plateau of feathery grasses where a stream had unwound itself into a wide pool. I slid down his heaving body and waded in. Cupped my hands and he drank from them.

When I woke, sunlight was already streaming through my one small window. I leaned across and kicked open the door for more air. My room had steamed itself into a sauna. The power must have been cut hours ago. I stretched and sweated, twisted and back-bended, remembering yoga poses from long ago, until my body felt supple as a length of heated wire.

We had made no plans to meet but I was unperturbed. An ease had settled in. A day on my own would be good—just knowing Vasur was near was enough. I would take breakfast at Kathiravams, spend some time in Andal's garden, perhaps shop for some pretty fabric, then take it to the tailor on Nethaji Road. I would visit the dancing girl I had discovered in a hidden alcove of Andal's temple.

She, like the quiet presence of the pregnant woman near Andal's shrine, drew me more than any of the larger-than-life consorts adorning the temple's main columns, seductively ushering us inside. I had found references to nityasumangalis on the shelves of Pennington's library, their origins stretching back to Sangam times. *Nitya*, forever, *sumangali*, auspicious for as long as she is married. They were much more than temple courtesans, they were consorts to god, evergreen brides, free from the shackles of marriage and the exile of widowhood, celebrated in poetry.

Her breasts so high the rib of a coconut leaf could not slide between them, I read, *her lower legs covered with hair as they ought, her small feet like the tongue of a tired dog.*

I flexed and circled my feet under the desk, pointed my toes. These women used muskpods from an antelope's naval to perfume their bodies and sandalwood smoke for their hair. A nityasumangali was learned in music and dance, language and poetry, and the sixty-four arts of love. She lived within the temple walls, serving god and priest, king and patron. It was beholden to men to support these favoured women, their shelter, food, clothing and, of course, their strivings for perfection in all their accomplishments. She was therefore often the cause of grief for a wife whose husband's duties called him hither and thither. She would sulk and accuse him when he returned with the scent of musk on his skin. How to temper the wrath of a wife betrayed? He made love to her, of course, intensely, till she melted in his arms. For this pleasure—the sheer industriousness of her husband—a wife could only utter secret thanks to the wiles of a nityasumangali.

The lone dancing girl I had discovered was, I suspected, of another world and no threat to any wife. I had found an unobtrusive place to sit inside the temple, away from curious eyes. Resting my back against a column, I let the sounds of life fade into a hum—the cock crowing over the temple walls, a priest berating an out-of-line pilgrim, and a woman murmuring prayers.

'Madam, this is not a place for the sitting.'

I pretended not to hear.

'Madam. Madam!' It was the voice of the woman praying. I opened my eyes. She pointed me to another column. I couldn't tell the difference but got up anyway—you never know what the next moment might present—and she left, continuing her song, plastic prayer beads slipping between her fingers.

One terracotta lamp burned at the foot of the column opposite me. There was no god or villain sculpted into its length, but when a small flame leapt up, I saw the flickering of a dancer carved at its base. She was naked, one hand coyly covering her genitals, her hair falling in a long, thick wad reminiscent of a peacock's fanned tail. Kumkuman smudged her forehead scarlet. Her black body glistened from offerings of oil.

Who was her sculptor thinking of? And why here, out of sight? Daily, temple courtesans would have passed him, anklet bells signalling their passage. Their lovely breasts tangled in coin necklaces and strings of pearls, hips tightly swathed in pleats of muslin, their dark-lined eyes playing hide-and-seek with whomever they chose. These he took as models for Saraswati, Rati, and Mohini. But this girl devoid of jewels? Did she even enter the temple? Or did he see her outside its gates, wandering with a begging bowl, singing the praises of some pagan goddess? Or had he only heard of these women living in the mountains alongside siddhars and sorcerers? I sat there opposite her, seeking a clue but she gave nothing. Her eyes were open, but the sculptor had cleverly crafted them so they appeared to turn inward as if to say, why be bothered with the appearances of this world? It is all a dream.

She felt wild, like the forest track to Kattalagar. All I needed to do was to stop and let her wilderness in. I had never spotted the zipping lights of siddhars over the ghats, nor heard the voice of one from his, or her, grave. I didn't disbelieve these stories, but I didn't need them either. Did I?

I left my room and walked to Kathiravan's for breakfast, every muscle in my body shouted *alive!* Vasur's presence whirled inside me. I felt exhilarated, and terrified.

I skipped shopping for fabrics and walked past the entrance to Andal's garden in favour of the dancing woman. I needed her nakedness, her uncompromising inward-turning eyes. I took off my sandals and slid them behind the puja-wallah's door opposite the temple entrance, then peered inside his cupboard-spaced shop, past hands of bananas and sachets of sesame oil. Day in, day out, he sat cross-legged watching the constant ebbs and flows of the temple. He never really smiled, but the subtle swim of his head I always took as a welcome. There was order in the disarray of his wares, small pyramids of powdered turmeric and kumkuman, cubes of camphor, sugar crystals, and jars of cough lozenges. Everything within arms' reach. A lamp, I wanted, to offer at the dancer's feet. I pointed to the piles of terracotta bowls. His response was to break off a banana.

'*Illai.*' I shook my head.

He pointed to the kumkuman.

'*Illai*, no. Just one lamp.'

As I watched him cut a wick to loop inside the tiny clay bowl, I felt the prickle of a blanket. A bangled arm reached across me to the kumkuman and I smelled an earthy mull of wood ash, patchouli, and damp wool. She pierced me with her cataract-glazed eyes before raising henna-stained fingers to her forehead. It was the same woman I had encountered on my very first night in Srivilliputtur, just before entering Andal's garden. Since then I had sometimes glimpsed her, like a shadow, a phantom, but always at a distance except for that first fleeting time and now, as I stood waiting for a lamp. I felt heat emanating from her, then quick sparks, flaring at the base of my spine. The hair on my arms rose as if the air was chilled, not the thirty-five degrees of a Panguni morning. I looked to the puja-wallah, but he was intent on the parcelling of my lamp, acting as if she wasn't there. With a volley of Tamil directed at no one, she drew a line of bright red through her matted, dust-caked hair to the crown of her head, then walked away, blanket thrown over her shoulder, faded red sari hitched to her knees. Swaying her hips, scuffing the dirt with her feet, paying no attention to the stares or wide berths of some in the crowd, she took her time and yet, as suddenly as she had appeared, she disappeared as if into the edge of the shadows hugging the temple walls.

The puja-wallah handed me the lamp, holding up three fingers for the rupees I owed. Who is she? I wanted to ask, but it was impossible with my smattering of Tamil and he with even less of English.

I walked around the metal detector and past the policeman, his baton amiably swinging. I was too unnerved to give him my usual smile. The sparks at the base of my spine had fanned to small flames and were looking for somewhere to go. I took a deep calming breath of cow and hay from the temple's stable, filled my lamp with ghee, and lit its wick from one of the hundreds burning beneath the flag pole. Holding it steady, I carried it to the black stone girl. Watching her flicker to life, I dabbed my finger into some of the kumkuman fallen at her feet and did with it what the milky-eyed woman had done. As I pressed what was left in a dot between my eyes, I felt the sear of her again, her brash voice, neither a man's or a woman's, and I remembered the spear-like scar on her top lip. What was she saying? I uncrossed my legs, then crossed them the other way.

Chapter Twenty-Three

Little kuyil pecking young red buds
warble sweetly in his ear
if you make him come quickly
you will see what I can do

Nacciyar Tirumoli 5:8

It was almost dawn by the time Andal and her father had
finished talking. In slow surreal motions she unrolled a mat
beneath her bedroom window and lay down. Her body needed
the rest even if her mind and heart did not. She closed her eyes
and exchanged them for two of the stars not yet faded, her
mouth for the new moon. She let her face vanish into a sky of
neither night nor day, the soothing imperceptibility of its light
washing the world into pureness and newness; more like heaven,
she thought, than earth. This was how she imagined Vaikuntha,
there where her love reclined on his serpent bed. From gem-
studded palaces and oceans of milk, from the peaks of snow-
capped mountains, the gods played their war games and love

games with mortal men and women who knew no better than to be born again and again into the folly of thinking they lived independent lives. And no matter how convinced Andal was of her destiny, still that one insisted entangling her with his game of hide-and-seek.

Alone in her room, she did what she always did and set herself adrift into the dawn. This day was different. How her fingers and toes tingled. The bright blaze of a fever flushed her cheeks. How strange the sensation rushing like a waterfall up and down her spine, the whoosh of it roaring in her ears. Was it only three days ago she had traced the lines of a new song into the sands of Villiputtur's riverbank? *Why not show yourself? Instead my soul is burgled. The life you breathe into me, this torturous dance of yours.* Her despair spiralled down to the water's edge.

An ocean lay between that day and this. The breeze blowing through her window was his breath, she was certain. Neem leaf shadows shimmied across her wall. It was her dark-skinned lord rising from his bed. She let him have his way with her until morning's light banished their play, leaving her no choice but to get up and begin the charade of life bound to the streets of Villiputtur. Soon she would be free and they would be together for good.

Andal heard the latch of their front gate open and close, the cadence of her father's wooden sandals setting off for the temple. Scents of roasting coconut and steaming idlis wafted through the house. She braced herself for the call of her mother from the bottom of the stairs.

'Andal,' Varaji said as her daughter entered the courtyard, 'do you think the world doesn't sleep? You have rings under your eyes dark as a blackened pot.'

Varaji pulled a pitcher of water from their well and poured it into Andal's cupped hands, once, twice, three times. Mouth rinsed and face washed, Varaji sat Andal at her feet and began oiling her hair.

She kept on as she pulled and tugged its knots. 'Man or god, I don't know, and frankly at this stage I've given up caring which, but no one wants a sallow bride.'

What chance did Andal have to tell her mother the news? Better to wait until she calmed down. They sat at the edge of the well after their bath, loosely wrapped in their muslin shawls. Andal was shivering and Varaji wrapped her tighter.

'Amma, I'm not cold,' Andal said, when what she really wanted to say was, 'Amma, I am to be ...'

'Look how loose the bracelets at your wrists. Who wants a bag of skin and bones in their bed?' Varaji pinched Andal's cheeks before mixing a paste of white clay and water. Her fingers trembled as she painted the mark of a sweet gourd seed on her daughter's forehead.

It was useless trying to talk to her mother when she was in such a state. Andal let her body go limp as a korai grass doll, turning this way and that as her mother wrapped a length of vermilion cloth round her hips three times for an illusion of plumpness.

'Breathe in,' Varaji said as she laced her bodice tight to accentuate the swell of her small breasts. Mother and daughter, each in their own separate worlds. Varaji forgetting her worries fell on deaf ears; Andal closing her eyes and rolling them back, letting her tongue curl up till it touched the roof of her mouth.

Aum Namah Tirumal, she sang under her breath until her body disappeared and the only sounds left on this bright, bright morning were the milky waves of her lord's ocean lapping their world.

'Open your eyes!' She felt the distant pressure of her mother's hands trying to still her. 'Eat, my daughter. Eat!' Her banana leaf of breakfast had turned cold.

'*Aum Namah Tirumal,*' Andal kept singing as the waves swayed the little boat in which she sat. Closer and closer she floated toward Vaikuntha's shores.

Seven nights past, Visnucitta had helped Andal perfect her fourth hymn, Song of the Circle Divination. He strummed his tamboura as she sang its eleven verses, each one ending, *kudidu kudale*—let the circle join. It was a game Andal used to play with her friends Sarvani and Marali, closing their eyes and drawing circles in the river sand as they made a wish. If the circle joined, their wish would come true.

The image of Skandha, the fortune teller, flitted through Andal's mind as she paused to find her rhythm between the notes of Visnucitta's tamboura.

Old Skandha had warned her, 'Be careful what you ask for. The circle is divine. Once joined it cannot be undone.'

O Kutal, may this circle join, Andal intoned loudly as if in defiance of Skandha's warning.

Visnucitta kept playing, his stomach uneasy. He no longer knew what was best for his daughter, and when she slipped out of reach, he felt helpless and afraid. She was deaf to him and blind to the pleading in his eyes. Varaji's frustration was no help either.

Andal cared not one neem leaf about the admonishments of her parents or the recriminations of small minded Villiputerians, but Skandha she could not shake off. He had managed to plunge her hopes into despair. Skandha might have stinky garlic breath but he was wise, everyone in Villiputtur consulted him. She had played the circle game her whole life, wishing for the red-lotus-eyed one, and every time she traced a circle it joined. So why didn't he come? It made no sense.

She had stopped going to the river with Marali and Sarvani. She'd had enough of their prattling on about wedding saris and toe rings. Were it not for Varaji's insistence, Andal saw little reason to ever bathe again. At least she could pour her heart into her songs. Just as she had watched her father turn grown men to tears with his, she felt the same sweetness flood her body, and whoever else happened to be present, whenever she sang hers—even though they were only meant for the ears of Tirumal. The day after her fourth hymn was completed, Andal tucked her feet up on the porch swing. The chores Varaji had set were done. She had already worn Tirumal's garland to the well and back and now it was in safekeeping until its offering at the temple. For the rest of the day, there was nothing to do but breathe in the luscious traces on her skin of his garland's flowers, and when evening came, she imagined these same perfumes circling his wide chest. As for Skandha, he didn't know everything. He didn't know that Tirumal had called her Choodi K Kodutta.

Who should walk past their porch but Sirimai. Andal knew her by name now. It was she who had led the procession for her first blood ceremony. Ever since then, whenever their paths crossed, Sirimai winked at Andal or put a hand on her hip and swivelled so the bells on her girdle jingled. Andal caught glimpses of her at the temple, flashes of silk and silver weaving through the colonnades—she was the dancer who fanned Tirumal and sang him to sleep. Even when Sirimai walked she danced. Andal wondered: if I could inhabit my body like that, maybe Tirumal would notice me.

'Say *venakam* to Andal.' Sirimai reached up to the parrot perched on her shoulder, ruffling its neck feathers. She beckoned to Andal with her other hand. Andal stepped shyly across the porch. The parrot hopped from foot to foot, dipping its head as if to say hello. How pretty and plump she was, her bright green feathers and the long turquoise one underneath her tail.

Sirimai coaxed the parrot onto her hand, then drew her close to whisper something before settling her back on her shoulder. 'You know, don't you, parrots are the ones who carry messages between lovers?' Her eyes twinkled, mischievous and familiar. It was as if she knew how desperate Andal was. 'They can fly to the gods too.'

It was worth a try, Andal thought, watching Sirimai continue down the street, turning every head she passed. All week, Andal worked on her fifth hymn, calling it Sing to Him Cuckoo. In it she tried persuading her imagined bird to take love messages to Vaikuntha. If Sirimai was right, all she need do was offer a bowl of sweet rice to convince the little bird to fly from its secret grove, and if this did not work to tell him how lovesick she was, and if that doesn't work— *you little kuyil dallying amongst flowers, if you do not call Tirumal today I will chase you from here.*

The words came effortlessly. In six days, she had finished. Visnucitta unwrapped his tamboura, adjusted the strings, then started strumming. Andal waited for his nod to begin. Three times she sang its eleven verses for her father and he fell into the spell of them.

'Perfect,' was all Visnucitta could say. Andal beamed from ear to ear and sent secret thanks to Sirimai.

She skipped down the stairs to boil water for their tea, leaving Varaji to her nightly prayers. They drank in silence until Visnucitta looked at Andal in a way that made it impossible for her to look anywhere but his eyes.

'If, as you say, Andal, no mortal man will be your husband, I cannot keep on forcing you. You are telling me I should pray to the Dark Lord about your marriage, the god called Beautiful One, in the mountain temple of Kallalagar in the groves of Tiru-maliruncolai. He is, however, just one of Lord Tirumal's one thousand and eight forms and his temple is five days' journey. You do not make an easy task for your father.'

Andal put down her tea, unsure of his words—husband, marriage, Dark Lord. If this was another dream, she vowed to never wake up.

'Andal! Are you listening? When you close your eyes like this it's as if you are a hundred miles away.'

'Sorry, Appa, I am listening.'

'Each of Lord Tirumal's names expresses an aspect of his divinity. It is up to you to choose which god is best suited for you.'

She swallowed the saliva pooling on her tongue, felt her heart trying to beat its way out of her chest. It was as if all at once one thousand and eight gods filled her body. How could she possibly choose one?

'Let us narrow this down to one hundred and eight of his most sacred temples,' Visnucitta said, 'and each lord inside, his unique disposition, his skills and boons.'

Visnucitta had travelled to all four directions of Tamil country. When he returned from a pilgrimage, Varaji and Andal would sit with him, listening to his tales of the temples he had visited. Varaji massaged his legs. If it was hot, Andal took a yak tail whisk, sprinkled it with water, and fanned him. When it was cold, she kept the fire bright. Andal's stomach churned. If he had asked her this night to pick up a fan, she would have found it impossible.

'Vatapatra sayee is the lord you know best, isn't it? Let us start with him, here in Villiputtur.'

Visnucitta described Lord Tirumal as a baby floating on his banyan leaf, how he took pleasure sucking the toe of his right foot. Andal closed her eyes, imagining his newborn skin, the tickle of his eyelashes, the milky ocean that would surround them. She blushed; as much as she loved him, he was, after all, the god whose garland she wore every day, but no, Vatapatra sayee was not the one. She desired the Lord Tirumal with four arms stretching to his knees, a right-whorling conch at his lips.

'Go on, Appa,' Andal said, and as the moon rode the sky, he described each of Tirumal's abodes, moving in a clockwise direction from Pandya country west over the mountains to the sea; to Venkata in the north where he stands facing east, then across Tondai land to the Chola realms. One by one, Visnucitta described each god until they had come almost full circle. They arrived at the great temple town of Srirangam on the Kavery River.

'Sri Ranganatha is the lord facing south, his body indigo as a monsoon cloud, lotus eyes sharp as spears, lips coral-red. He reclines on the serpent bed of Ananta Sesha and fills Srirangam's garbarigha as if it were the sky.'

The trembling through Andal's body, since the beginning of her father's one hundred and eight descriptions, stopped. She saw him, smelled the sandal paste on his chest, the jasmine flowers circling his jet-black hair. The air in the garbarigha where he lay thrummed slow like the deep notes of a rudra veena.

Chapter Twenty-Four

My honeyed one that Lord of Srirangam—
his beautiful dark curls, his lips, his beautiful eyes
the lotus flower unfolding from his lovely navel

Nacciyar Tirumoli 11:2

Varaji smoothed out three banana leaves and placed half a coconut shell scoop of tamarind rice onto each. The rasaam she ladled smelled light and piquant—black pepper, ginger and jeera —but did nothing for Visnucitta's appetite. The wheel he had set to turning churned his stomach. Last night, Andal had chosen the darkest, grandest lord, the only one in all of Tamil's Divya Dassams facing south. Had his daughter bewitched him with her songs? Of course, temple courtesans married gods, but it did not make them immune to the beds of kings and priests. Andal's idea of wedding Sri Ranganatha transcended the greatest boon of all for a woman, becoming nityasumangali, free forever from the bondage of widowhood. He had fallen into Andal's audacious dream to be seated in the lap of Lord Tirumal, not as a symbolic wife, but *the* wife, alongside and equal to Sri Laksmi and Bhooma devi.

Varaji lifted the kadhai from the fire. 'Poriyal with beans from today's market.'

He could not meet her eyes. She knew, she always did, that something was on his mind. But before he had gathered the strength to speak, Andal blurted it out.

'Amma, we have decided Sri Ranga is the one I am to wed!'

Varaji put the kadhai down and looked one to the other. So, this was why two lamps had burned to the black last night. As a mother and a wife, Varaji felt betrayed.

'It just happened, Varaji.' Visnucitta entreated her with his eyes. 'It had to.' They looked across at Andal, playing with her food, putting one grain of rice at a time to her lips, humming an alap under her breath. 'She will be fifteen in a matter of days. What else can we do?'

'What else?' Varaji pushed her leaf away. 'Andal, if you are not going to eat then at least have curd. There is a fresh pot ready in the kitchen. Take a bowl, then go to your room.'

'What else?' She pinned Visnucitta with her eyes. 'I don't expect you are intending to betroth her to the temple in some ritual of a wedding. You know as well as I do that she is too old for that. No priest or king would have her anyway. She'd end up wasting away in some dark corner, nothing more than a servant.'

'Of course not, Varaji.'

'Sri Ranga? In Srirangam? And how do you propose we arrange such a wedding?'

'This I cannot say.'

'You cannot or you will not? I am your wife, Visnucitta. She is our daughter. Indulging Andal in her dreams might bring colour back to her cheeks, but for how long? It will certainly set the town's tongues wagging again. None of this serves Andal. Marrying Sri Ranganatha? It is a preposterous idea and will only add to her stubbornness. Do not play with her so.'

'Trust me, Varaji. Give me time. The lord has spoken to me

before. He will again, I am sure of it. Have some faith. Was it not you who first coaxed me into believing our daughter was worthy of the gods?'

Varaji looked at him and shook her head. Planning their daughter's wedding should bring happiness, but all she felt was estranged. The barrenness Varaji had suffered in the years of their marriage before Andal suddenly welled up. What use had any of her prayers been? She watched Visnucitta rise and leave their courtyard. Ghee congealed on their rice as it cooled. Tears streamed down her face.

'Sri Sri Laksmi, when was the last time I offered you flowers?'

Visnucitta paced the rows of his garden, his mind a jungle of thoughts. The temple was closed, the gods had lunched and were napping, as was the town. Villiputtur's streets were deserted. Instead of turning right for home, he walked straight across North Street and into the lane of shingle roofs. He looked up to the only two-storey house and saw the shutters were open. He walked purposefully, as if on an errand, in case a pair of veiled eyes lurked. But every other window was draped, every door latched. His pulse quickened and he did what he had vowed he would never do in the light of day.

The perfumed air of her corridor could not mask the treacle pungency of fenugreek in his sweat; blood coursed through his body like a reckless river, and for a moment he forgot the real reason for his visit. He parted the curtains to her room and their eyes met.

Every time he wrote a song in a woman's voice, something happened. It was as if a fifth sense, female, inhabited him. Like the high-altitude air of a mountain coppice, sweet and wild, a way of being that circumvented thought. Sirimai sat up, letting the silk bedsheet fall into a pool between her crossed legs.

Visnucitta started to speak, but she put a finger to her lips. She would not let him embrace her, but instead lay his head in her lap, stilling his hands, slowing his breath.

How much time passed? The call of a water bearer in the street below, the distant sound of a broom sweeping fallen leaves from a threshold. Sirimai stirred. She had her servant leave a pail of water by the door and brought it to the bed. First she sponged his body, and then hers. They drank tamarind juice sweetened with jaggery. Not a word broke their spell.

Visnucitta reached around Sirimai to the curve below her waist. He untied her braid, letting it fall like a mane across her shoulders. He brushed her nipples as if by mistake and felt the dark down of hair on her arms rise. Slow and meandering as a river, they played their love games. They took turns until, it was always Sirimai, with a press of her breasts into Visnucitta's chest or a slowing of his hands with hers, they flowed deep and timeless into each other. No need to rush, nothing to complete. They heard the cart wheels of the milk seller, the *clink-clank* of steel against steel as he beat his cans. It was if they listened to the sounds of earth from far away.

'You are my heaven,' Sirimai said as she left their bed and started to dance, veiling her hips then unveiling them as she circled, measuring her steps to the milk seller's percussion, moving her body in and out of its rhythm, 'my Vaikuntha,' her eyes never leaving his. Visnucitta sat up and called to her.

She wrapped her legs round him, let herself be lifted then eased down. 'When saffron milk is placed on a fire,' she whispered, 'and warmed to the temperature of blood, you dip your finger into it and can no longer tell what is the milk and what is the body.' She closed her eyes and pummelled her soles into him as she arched her back. He knew better than to hold his breath. He let himself be danced by her. She let the dance dance her.

'Now tell me,' she said, shifting from his arms. Leaf shadows inched their way across the floor from the old tamarind tree outside her window. The sun was low, and a breeze blew in from the ghats, cool with evening and fragrant with jasmine.

'Andal has chosen a husband but, Sirimai, I am afraid. What she has asked for is impossible.'

He took a breath. 'Sri Ranganatha.'

'Sri Ranga? In Srirangam?' Sirimai's eyes opened wide with delight.

She sat up, the jingling of her bangles like laughter. It unnerved him. 'Ma, bring chai,' she called down the corridor, 'and sweets! Rain and drought, both can plague the world, but today, my love, you bring news of most-timely rain. This is something to celebrate, isn't it?' Sirimai clapped her hands.

'And all these hours,' she feigned a pout, 'you have been keeping this from me! Why look so worried? Who else but the darkest, most beautiful lord of all for Andal? I am not surprised. Do you remember the year we travelled there together? Half of Villiputtur camped on the banks of the Kavery River. No temple in Tamil country can match Srirangam's. Poets, musicians, dancers flock to its festivals, not to speak of the lakhs of devotees.'

'Yes but …'

'Shhh, don't worry. I have friends there. If it were not for you, I would be dancing in Srirangam for a thousand pairs of eyes, not the handful here in Villiputtur. But how would I survive without the taste of you, Visnucitta? Even if it is only once in a blue moon, *nila nilavu*, no matter, you bring yourself to me when you can. It is the lot of a lover to wait, isn't it?' She ran her fingers through the dark whorls of hair on his chest. 'We ride our way to the gods like two serpents, you and I. I am content enough with that. But for Andal, nothing less than Lord Ranganatha will do.'

The chai was hot and peppery. They took turns feeding each other little pieces of the laddoo balls, letting them melt, sweet and nutmegged, on their tongues. They heard the conch sounding twilight, waking the gods from their nap, calling devotees to the temple. Visnucitta had planned to come for an hour.

'We must keep this secret,' he said, 'at least for now. Send word to Srirangam, but make sure, Sirimai, that it is with a messenger who can be trusted. Whoever it is you know within the temple walls, tell them how gifted Andal is. Her songs are worthy of a king, of god himself. I will not send her there unless she is treated well. Whatever the consequence.'

He looked across at her, those amber eyes in the lantern light lustrous as a tigress'.

Chapter Twenty-Five

Crying she-buffaloes with heavy udders,
hungry calves bound by rope.
The earth is soaked with milk and we
stand ankle-deep in the mire

Tiruppavai 12

Vasur would always have fresh milk in a small copper vessel covered with cloth. I learned to like the taste of it. He taught me to drink without touching my mouth to the vessel's rim. After Kattalagar, he refused to eat anything except *prasadam*. He said those first meals we had in the marketplace were an exception. Our meeting was a kind of destiny, he added.

Rarely did he come to the temple and it was only my impatience—all right, desperation—three days after our forest trek, and no sign of him, that I walked like a woman possessed to Thirumukkulam, past its teerthum and blue pavilion, and through the gate to his banyan tree home.

'Saisha,' he said, looking up from the wooden staff he was chiselling. 'Sit.'

I sat and the world slowed to normal speed. I felt the smoothness of swept earth beneath me, the play of light through the leaves, then silence in place of my crashing heart. Vasur continued working, holding the staff steady with his foot. He didn't look up until he had finished, but I felt his eyes roaming, all the same, every fibre of my being.

He gathered dry leaves and kindling, then made a pyramid. 'I was wondering when you would come.'

'I was wondering too,' I said.

'Better you come here.'

I knew he was right.

'Any time you can be coming. Always welcome.'

And so, most days I did. Sometimes hardly a word passed between us, there was just the pared simplicity of a tree for a roof, a fire, the hustle of traffic left behind. It was a relief. But these things were extraneous to the mystery I felt, my life inter-twining with Vasur's, as enigmatic as those three rivers purport-edly flowing underground for thousands of miles before bubbling up in the ancient teerthum of Thirumukkulam. It was so close that on a clear still day, sitting with Vasur, I breathed in the muddy scent of its pooled water, was lulled by the *slap slap* of women washing clothes at the stone steps where it was deepest, and was soothed, for some reason, by the victory cries of boys and the thuds of their balls and bats on a cricket pitch set up on the caked earth of the teerthum's floor where the water had long ago dried up. There were moments I thought I could stay forever.

Vasur picked up the staff he had been chiselling and began sanding its length with a stone. I told him about my elephant dream the night of our return from Kattalagar.

'The whole world is a jungle, Saisha. Only an elephant is capable of breaking through.'

As I let his words sink in, the relief of the elephant sculpted on the column outside Andal's sanctum flashed through my mind. I described it to Vasur—how Tirumal was standing beside him, two of his four hands gently resting on the elephant's back. I couldn't remember his name.

'Gajendra,' Vasur said. He put down his staff and stone. 'But even the strength of an elephant is not enough to conquer the jungle of desires. In the end, you must surrender,' was all he said, lifting his eyes for one long second to stare into mine.

❧

Each visit, I would buy food for Vasur from the market, oranges and cashews, raisins and puffed rice. I took them to one of the small temples near Andal's and placed them on the priest's tray. He offered it to the deity, the deity blessed it, and the priest gave it back. It was now prasadam and Vasur could eat it. He shared it with the birds and squirrels who shared their home with him. He put cashews and raisins in my hand if he saw I was hungry. I didn't say anything, he just did it. I began to understand the cyclic nature of this kind of giving and receiving. As long as it continued, the world would keep turning. My place in the mystery of what was happening began to shift.

'Yes?' Vasur sometimes asked, after a length of silence. He saw, I supposed, my mind lapsing into its *this* and *that* way of thinking and I attempted an explanation.

'You know how Andal talks to the flowers and clouds. Is she saying they are taunting her because they *remind* her of Tirumal, or are they actually god and *he* is the one taunting her?'

'Both are right.'

'So, there is no difference?' I chirped too quickly.

'There is a big difference.'

Vasur's answers were like a rabbit hole.

'It is depending on you. Do you remember the Chathuragiri siddhar's teaching about devotion and wisdom? When you see everything is god, this is wisdom. When you serve god, this is devotion. When these two meet—!'

Vasur clapped his hands. Once, fiercely and loudly. I practically levitated.

He laughed. 'Better even than—what is it you say in the West—rocket science.'

'Maybe you meant to say, it's *not* rocket science?'

'Yes, you are right. It's simple; this highest of all sciences changes everything!'

I would return to town light as a body with not one question remaining, and some days more perplexed than when I had arrived. Either way there was spring in my step, a sense of purpose, a reason for being.

On that day of rocket science, as I was getting ready to leave —it was milking time and the cows were congregating at the stable door—Vasur looked over at them.

Crying she-buffalos with heavy udders, he said, *hungry calves tied with rope.* He spoke not to me or to the cows but as if thinking aloud. I followed his gaze. *The earth is soaked with milk, and we stand ankle-deep in the mire.*

I recognised the words—they were from Andal's *Tiruppavai*, but for some reason I had only ever skimmed them. The moos of those cows stayed with me as I made my way to Bhavati's house. I idled through the market place. Flower sellers and fruit merchants were closing and two of the street cows had moved in for a feast. The ground was soft under my feet; the air ripe with scents of bruised tomatoes, discarded marigolds, pineapple skins, wilted cabbage leaves. *Ankle-deep in the mire* ... The sounds, the smells, the changing light, the patterns of Srivilliputtur life in and outside the temple, they felt part of me now. Had *I* changed though? Had I taken even one step out from the mire?

Fragments of Andal's songs tumbled in as I played with the bangles at my wrists, slipping them one by one up my forearms, then letting them all fall back together. *In every jasmine blossom I see his smile.* The taunting I had asked Vasur about: was it the flowers or was it the gods? Perhaps, if I am to see the face of god in a flower or a cloud, I first need to transcend the stories in my own head.

I turned into Bhavati's street, stopping to buy guavas from the fruit-wallah's cart. It was mid-afternoon, time for a rest before joining her for the twilight chanting of Tirumal's names. Since Vasur's appearance, we had been spending less time together. Bhavati didn't seem to mind, but it was hard to tell, really. I was conscious of the change, because there was Marcus to consider too. In Bhavati's eyes, I was married to him. She sometimes asked after Marcus in an attempt, it seemed to me, at understanding how it was possible for a husband and wife to spend so much time apart. She had seen me with Vasur, the whole town probably had, despite our attempts at being discreet, and I hated the thought of what she might think. I did not want to jeopardise our friendship. We were at opposite ends of the world in many ways—there was I, questioning my celibacy while she confided her dislike of sex. It was a Tamil wife's duty, she knew, but it was Andal who called to her. How much of our difference was cultural? How much of the ache we both felt came from the same yearning?

Bhavati's English was much better than my attempts at Tamil and we managed to talk late into a night, stumbling sometimes into places where words were inadequate; but then in that lovely silence two people can have, a different kind of understanding happens. When Bhavati asked me the most unavoidable of questions, I told her the truth. I could not have children. There was that look of incomprehension, then the awkward sadness, and I feigned a small smile, shrugged my shoulders in an attempt to put her at ease.

I could have explained that without the responsibility for a child I had more freedom. That it wasn't a big deal for Western women, we were an emancipated generation. After all, these were some of the arguments I had used on myself, never mind being given baby dolls as a child. One of my dolls had even died. I had buried her in a shoebox.

Bhavati fell silent. In the space between us, I felt the twinge of a muscle where I had shrugged and the smart of my smile, then the returning of my own incomprehension.

It was this remembered exchange with Bhavati, and Vasur's recalling of those *crying she-buffaloes* and *calves bound by rope*, that broke through the levee of a story in me, one mire kept stagnant for too long. I put the parcel of guavas down and turned the key in my padlock, trying to dismiss the image of Bhavati's saddened eyes. Sliding back the door bolt to my room I heard something else—the collapsing of an old-fashioned elevator's grille. The hallway smelled of musty carpet. The air of the room I entered was antiseptic.

The cold metallic thrust of the speculum, his clinical fingers gently depressing my stomach, the glare of the spot lamp burning between my legs. When it was finished, I dressed, forgetting, in my stupor, to wipe dry the gel he had used for lubrication. I took a chair in the consulting room, felt the clinging damp in the crotch of my knickers. The room was plush in an olde worlde kind of way, the upholstered furniture and floral carpet, the family photos and a glass paperweight on the gynecologist's desk, the polished carving on his mantelpiece—an Asian girl with a bamboo pole balanced across her shoulders, two pails swinging either end. I turned to look at the man sitting beside me for a hint behind his eyes, for a message in the turn of his mouth, but Marcus was featureless and pale like a ghost.

I had waited patiently, then impatiently, for Marcus to say 'yes' to a child. For twenty-two months I had been taking the pill. I started to nag and then to cry, so desperately did I want to conceive, until, finally, he relented. I washed the last of my prescription down the sink and celebrated. But nothing happened.

The secretary, tweed skirt, white blouse buttoned to the top, comfortable court shoes, brought in a folder, placed it on the doctor's desk, then left as discreetly as she had entered. We waited as he studied the ultrasounds. Three months of tests—my cycle and Marcus's sperm count, the graphs of daily temperatures I had kept on our fridge door so we could have sex to the exact hour of every ovulation.

The gynecologist put the file down and leaned toward us, looking first at Marcus, then to me. I shifted to the edge of my chair. 'We will need to book you in for surgery. Last week's test shows a blockage in both fallopian tubes and my examination today confirms you have a cyst. It's quite large—the size of a grapefruit—growing on your left ovary.'

He held up one of the ultrasounds and I saw them, my tubes, two skeletal wings reaching out from a halved pear and the damming of dark dye on both sides.

I felt the same nausea as the day he had injected more and more dye, because the flow of it into my tubes was not registering on the screen. I remembered the unbearable pressure of it, the stirrups keeping my feet in place and the nurse holding my legs open. The moment before I fainted, I saw the face of a child losing grip of a balloon; it floated up and up, then burst.

'A grapefruit,' was all I said.

'It has been there a long time. My guess is it began as an infection three years ago when you had the Copper 7 removed.'

He paused. Those words hanging in the air like the fetid scent of the wound inside me.

Was he giving me time for this information to sink in?

I looked at Marcus.

'Beginner's luck,' was what he had said, soon after we met, about our first blissful months of reckless-no-precautions love-making. 'But better to be safe,' he continued. He wasn't ready for a family.

Not yet, was what I thought then. I could wait.

He showed me an advertisement in a local paper: *Breakthrough in Contraception*. There was a Family Planning clinic on the Gold Coast. So, I spread my legs for them. And then every night we made our carefree love until the intrauterine device dislodged. 'Get it out,' I had screamed, doubled over in pain, as we waited the hours past midnight on plastic chairs in the emergency wing of a public hospital.

They took it out and sent us home. I started taking the pill.

I turned back to the doctor. He had closed my file and placed the glass paperweight on top. I was too shocked to lay any blame. What would be the point? It was done and there was no running away from it. What were the words my grandmother wrote? *Running away is never …*

'I won't know the extent of the damage until I operate, but the ultrasounds show significant scarring on both tubes. It may be necessary to remove the left one where the cyst is growing.'

I heard sympathy in the doctor's voice. But I could not look at him. I shifted my gaze to the framed print hanging behind his desk. It was a Hans Heysen watercolour, the Flinders Ranges, red and arid.

'Saisha.' I heard the doctor calling me back into the room, but my eyes did not move from the painting.

'I will remove as much scarring as possible, but you need to know now the chances of conception are slim.'

'Slim?' Marcus said, speaking for the first time. 'Can you be more specific?'

I wondered about the gum tree Heysen had painted, how he made it so real. The brittle grey of its leaves, their falling like long tears hanging in the sun. But look how the tree's bark has peeled back and the shine he has given the newly exposed wood.

'Five percent at most,' the doctor said. 'It's hard to say. But miracles can happen.'

A miracle? Red silt stretched to the painting's unforgiving horizon. The sky above it was bleached.

'Thank you,' I said. *Thank you!* We walked into the waiting room, past the smile of the secretary and out to the hall. We stood at the elevator watching the numbers of each floor light up as it ascended to us.

All the tears in the world would not be enough to make things grow again. A taste of brine flooded my mouth and I swallowed as we entered the lift, felt the crumpling of everything inside me. Marcus stood there, just stood there, watching the numbers descend.

❦

Sitting face to face with that pregnant girl carved into the black stone of Andal's house she sometimes defied me to look again into a past I kept insisting was reconciled, just as the kindness and inquiry in Bhavati's eyes had done the day she asked the most natural of all questions. 'How many children?'

If Marcus had wanted a child, I would have moved heaven and earth. I would have opened my legs for another gynaecologist, and another for a second opinion. I would have happily made love any time day or night for a miracle. Surrogacy, a test tube baby, even adoption; she would have dark ringlets of hair and laughing eyes. But Marcus had made it clear: he did not want a child.

If I am honest, he did not from the very beginning. It was my desire, not his.

What was I to do? Leave him? Search for another mate? I had seen other women subjecting themselves to test after test on top of an automated sex life in their quest for one random meeting of sperm and egg. With a clever blink of an eye, I turned what I had been willing to do into an argument against it, if it had to be with another man. I made my choice.

Running away from difficulties is never a way of overcoming them.

We were still making love then, and it was good, and on a

positive note we needn't worry about any contraception. I called it karma, mine and Marcus's, in an attempt to explain away my desire for a child. I razed myself with a word. One neat decision, one strike.

And my body forgets?

❧

Twenty-one years and still the red silt of a painting hanging in a Wickham Terrace consulting room filled me with its arid heat. What had been more primal for me, as a woman: the desire for sex or the desire to have a baby, or was one embroidered into the other?

I shook off my thongs and felt the burn of the roof's cement. It would be hours yet before the day's heat dispelled. I shut the door to my room and pulled the window curtain closed. I didn't care how stifling it was. I wanted heat and darkness like a glove over my body, like a womb. I curled into a foetal position and rocked and rocked. A thousand years ago I might have cried myself into an oblivion of sleep. Tears—what use were they now? But the cramps gripping my stomach and every wave of bile, I welcomed. They felt familiar. I kept on rocking, eyes clenched shut. No desire so no regrets, no need for anyone and no ties to anyone. Just leave me be. Let me go. I reached out and felt my hand trailing through water, my ribs pressed hard against the hull of a boat. Faces, one after the other, began surfacing, staring into me and through me, calling me in. My mother, my father, Vasur, Marcus, a lover from a long time ago, the moon-faced priest from Srirangam, the face of a child I did not know, Bhavati ... tighter and tighter I gripped the boat until everything disappeared.

'Saisha!' I heard knocking from far away. 'Saisha!'

I untangled myself from wet bedsheets, pushed strings of damp hair from my face, and struggled to my feet. The dark was absolute. Where was I?

'Saisha!' I opened the door and squinted into the lantern Bhavati held. She clicked her tongue at the sight of me. 'I was worried, you are staying here when usually we are at temple or …' she paused, 'somewhere else going.' Her hand on my forehead felt cold. 'Some fever you are having.'

Bhavati took me down the stairs and into her bathroom, undressing me as if I were a child, squatting me onto a low stool and ladling water over my body. She wrapped me in a towel and combed medicated oil through my hair. I dressed in one of her cotton shifts and she sat me down on the cool tiles of her living room, then disappeared into the kitchen.

'Curd rice,' she peeped out from its curtained door, 'soothing for stomach.' I inhaled the scents of ginger and turmeric as Bhavati crushed them in her mortar and pestle. The fragrance of the cooling basmati she had pressure-cooked was light and tempting. Food was Bhavati's currency. It was her way of making the world right again.

We rolled the silky white rice into balls with our fingers and popped them into our mouths. The ceiling fan whirred, the pages of a paper calendar flicked back and forth, and a family portrait—Bhavati, her husband, their daughter and son-in-law with a new baby boy—replete with an edging of roses and backdrop of ocean, surveyed us from pride of place on top of the television.

'Come,' Bhavati said after our meal. She pulled the drape back from her small shrine room and we stepped inside.

'Since I was a small girl, only *Andal* I am thinking.' In the half-dark, she took down a jar of ghee from a top shelf and warmed it between her hands.

'Then I am married. But still, Andal is there before anything else. She is there when I wake up and before I go to sleep. When I see our friend Rani, the widow, walking to my house, I see it is Andal coming. When Kartika, the priest's wife, cooks, it is Andal making the fire, tasting the food for salt. When I saw *you*, Saisha, coming to the garden, I am thinking, Andal, Andal.'

Bhavati poured the ghee into a small brass bowl.

Cutting a length of loose woven cord, she said, 'The ragged lady you sometimes see outside the temple gates. She is also Andal.'

Bhavati drew the wick in a circle over the ghee until it was saturated, then struck a match. The lamp spluttered, then a flame shot up tall and steady. Above us the framed print of an Andal smiled. It was a Mona Lisa smile: no matter where we stood, there she was looking into our eyes. The hour must have been late, its stillness amplifying Bhavati's chants of Andal's names. And in the distance an owl would take three minutes to fly, other flames were rising and another voice chanting into the dark of trees. His face, like Bhavati's, like Marcus, and every other I have loved, no matter how imperfect my attempts, they were there—in her eyes.

Chapter Twenty-Six

Cool clouds of Venkata where the lotus-eyed lord lives,
at his feet I am falling, the one who churned the conch-filled sea
if he enters me for just one day—then I can live

Nacciyar Tirumoli 8:7

'Tomorrow, I am going to meet Krishnaveni—a siddhar,' Vasur said. 'There is not much time left.'

I looked across at Vasur, wondering what he meant and who Krishnaveni was.

'One day, maybe two, we will be gone. We will take the train.'

Apparently, it was decided and that was all I needed to know. Vasur walked off toward the stables and I played with the fire in his pit, feeding it, turning the coals.

I felt ready for another journey with Vasur, but was curious all the way home to Bhavati's house. Perhaps she knew something.

'Krishnaveni Amma.' Bhavati swam her head, pressing her

hand to her heart. 'She is south from here, living sixty years in a cave.'

She? A lady siddhar? The thought entered me like a quick shock.

'Will he be taking you?' Bhavati asked.

'Do you think it's a good idea?' It was the first time either of us had acknowledged to the other Vasur's existence.

'Of course, otherwise how will you find her?'

All this time since meeting with Vasur, I had wondered if my cautions were excessive, about what was acceptable and what was not for a Western woman in a traditional Tamil town. Bhavati seemed neither drawn into or hindered by a town's gossip and temple protocol—what mattered was Andal. And anyhow, siddhars were above the law of small-town thinking. That was part of the point.

Bhavati rolled out two mats on the tiles of her living room for us to sleep away the midday heat, and as we lay down the image of the ragged woman flashed before me. There was something siddhar-like about her, the way she swaggered through Srivilliputtur's streets, oblivious to its age-old traditions. Just two days before, she had come up to me as I was walking through the temple arcade. Swaying slightly, bare feet planted apart, she looked through me and I felt that familiar flick of heat again at the base of my spine.

'She is wanting coffee,' the man in the shop opposite said. So I bought her a cup. She took it with one glance of her bottomless eyes, the twist of her upper lip worn like the scar of an old warrioress, then wandered off, red blanket trailing in the dirt. Left in her damp wool-scented wake, I watched her linger in the shadows of the small pavilion, putting the coffee to her lips, aloof to the beggars sitting there day in and out. 'Ma Ma,' they call with hands held up to every passer-by. I had never seen her beg from anyone.

Bhavati and I lay on our backs, letting the fan cool us. 'The lady who stays outside the temple,' I asked, 'the one with matted hair, who is she?'

'Her name is Lalitha. Fifteen years ago, she came to Srivilliputtur.' Bhavati turned on her side, propping her head to face me. 'I am watching her mind wavering and changing. Sometimes I worry. I think to take her to a barber to shave off her hair. I try to buy her a new sari. But she scolds me and walks off. She has no care for the body. Only Andal, Andal.' Bhavati paused. 'This is meaning she is like a master soul.'

There was tenderness in Bhavati's face. 'Once or twice a week, ever since she is here, she does *pradakshina* around the temple. There are people who get afraid when they see her. Some think she has evil. Me? I don't. It is like a mother's feeling, like Andal. A mother can be fierce also.'

'How did she come to arrive here?' I wanted to know everything about her.

Bhavati reached over and touched my hand. 'How did *you* come to be here, Saisha?'

Her question separated my body into two: my head adrift, with the sound of my heart still beating inside it; my bones all of a sudden heavy, fused to the floor on which we lay.

Vasur also knew Lalitha. 'She chose to step out from the world just as I did. We find our way. Hers was to Sri Andal from the beginning. Sometimes a path is as simple as that,' he said, casting his eyes over me as our train *click-clacked* south through groves of coconut trees and ploughed paddy fields. The first proper rains were late, the earth still waiting.

I crossed my legs on the slatted wood seat, disconcerted by the intensity of his eyes. 'What are you saying, Vasur? My path is not?'

He gave me one of his smiles and gestured through the grilles of our window to the ghats in the distance where heavy clouds filled every ravine, where there was every chance solitary hermits sheltered. I imagined entering the mind of a siddhar or holy man—or woman. A mind not tugged this way and that by thoughts, those clouds moving through her, the seasons in her body, each birth and death.

I was not convinced about Lalitha and her path. Part of me thought she might just be plain crazy. I had seen so-called outcasts sifting through dirt and refuse, mumbling to themselves, squatting for hours unaware of the flies feeding from the corners of their mouth, oblivious to the stares of passers-by or the believers, who stopped to press their foreheads to the ground, leaving offerings of cigarettes or a coconut or milk. Where was the line between crazy and enlightened?

'What about Krishnaveni?' I asked.

'She is … how do you say it? The real deal.' He swam his head.

I was eager to meet her. Across the aisle, a small girl tumbled over the laps of a bevy of women. Her kohl-lined eyes were laughing. She was safe and happy, the dark spot painted on her cheek ensured no child kidnapper was tempted by a less than perfect face.

At Virudhunagar Junction, we struggled through the crowd rushing to board the emptying carriages of our train.

'No hurry,' Vasur said, leading the way up the stairs, across two sets of tracks, and down again to platform number five. 'We wait for the Tirunelveli express.'

We walked toward the end of the platform, away from the frenzied buffeting of passengers every time a train pulled in. Vasur squatted, his body agile as a child's, his eyes focused on the ground in front of him. I stretched my legs, revelling in the colours and chaos of an entire continent on the move.

When our train eventually arrived, we joined the fracas, found two seats, and settled in again, the mountains to our right and on either side of the train tracks tall wind generators like white ghosts dotting the plains, *whoosh whooshing* India into the twenty-first century. Scents of spiced chickpeas filled the air as a tiffin-wallah entered our carriage with a tin bowl balanced on his head. Five rupees for a newspaper cone filled to the brim. Then the cry of a chai-wallah, for three rupees the pleasure of milky sugared water poured over a tea bag in a tiny plastic cup, the epitome of modernity. I drew out the pleasure of it with small sips, all the while aware of the family opposite us staring at me as if I had just beamed down from outer space. A smile was all it took to let them know I was as human as them. We fell into the rhythm of the train and the hypnotic passing of time. We sat six to a bench built for four, our bodies rocking against each other as the train propelled us south. Vasur's arms and legs pressed against mine. I felt an aliveness pulse between us and swear he knew this as wholly as I did.

From Tirunelveli station, we took a bus with a rusty floor and ancient suspension headed for Papanasam at the foothills of the ghats. We wound south, then west through paddy fields and villages. Then we walked on a track following the meandering of a river until the valley narrowed and water tumbled and pooled in a landscape of stone. Giant boulders lay strewn like marbles left mid-play by the gods. We climbed steps stained with lichen and splashes of whitewash to a small temple freshly painted in bright yellow and green teetering against a cliff. Its doors were locked. A black statue of Nandi the bull sat on a plinth in front, ever ready to chariot his god, ever devoted to his ascetic Lord Shiva, draped in tiger skin and holding a trident. Shiva, who does not distinguish poison from nectar, whose neck turned iridescent blue because he drank a serpent's poison to save the world. Shiva, the river Ganga flowing from his top knot. Shiva, self-contained, eyes closed to the desire-wracked bodies of men and women, saying foolishness, do not be caught by transient pleasures. Shiva, the god of destruction, whose symbol is a lingam, black and steadfast, rising from the earth.

Here I was, faced with him again. Here I was, falling for another man and this is where he brings me. Vasur touched his forehead to the plinth where Nandi sat then whispered into his ear. I watched the ripple of Vasur's dark skin tightening over his ribs as he leant forward in a bow, the leathered soles of his bare feet, the splayed grip of his toes. He stood back and gestured me forward. What was I going to ask of Nandi?

'Truth,' I silently mouthed, 'the truth,' feeling the breath of it rush off the tip of my tongue like the sound of a tiny chick's wings airborne for the first time. This quickening inside me growing stronger for every day spent with Vasur, threatening the boundaries of a self I had so skilfully patched up.

We hugged the path and turned a corner. We were high now. The air was cooler and clean, spritzed with water, rock, and forest. I stopped to fill my lungs and looked up to a set of steps and a door built into the side of the cliff towering above us.

The door was opened by a young Brahmin priest. He ushered us in to the cave's patchouli-soaked air, the smell of kerosene and candle wax. Before my eyes had accustomed to the shadowy light, I heard her voice from a far corner of the cave, '*Aum Shakti Aum, Aum Shakti Aum,*' like the rhythmic clack of a heddle, weaving the mantra's syllables into every atom vibrating the womb space we had entered.

Her attendant stood to the side of her plastic chair. Still chanting, she peered toward us with milky eyes, the rudraksha seeds of her mala slipping one by one through gnarled fingers. Krishnaveni's thick matted hair framed her, like a halo in the muted light, white as clouds, falling in ropes past her knees. She was dressed in a voile sari the same green colour I remembered Mootai Swami wearing. Her body, soft and round like a mother's, filled the confines of her chair.

'Sri Sri Amma.' Vasur touched his forehead to her feet. He called her name again and she was silent for a moment, as if searching through veils of time, with her eyes, ears, and whole body, for the man who knelt in front of her, then she laughed and patted him on the head. Vasur sat at her feet and they talked and talked like old friends till I heard my name mentioned and she peered again through those veils. Vasur gestured me closer.

Her feet felt cool and wrinkled against my brow. Something compelled me to stay there. Forever, if need be. Vasur took my elbow and sat me up. Back and forth Krishnaveni and Vasur spoke. Her eyes were glazed with thick cataracts but they shone. Her entire forehead was smeared white with ash.

'Amma wants to know if you have children.'

'No,' I said, feeling a twinge of shyness at Vasur learning this second-hand. It felt like a confession. *The truth, the truth*, echoed its way into my head. Vasur translated my 'no'. She took a large pinch of ash from a bowl and asked for my hand. I looked across at Vasur. What should I do, make a tilak between my eyes or draw the three horizontal lines of a Saivite? I fumbled through my bag for a scrap of paper to wrap any left-over ash, to put it on the small shrine I had made for Andal in my room.

Krishnaveni interrupted with more instructions.

'She says you must take it, and not to worry. You will have children. This is medicine for you.'

'You mean swallow it?'

'All of it,' he said. Krishnaveni looked through me with her all-seeing eyes. Thoughts from sceptical to hopeful to ridiculous rushed through my mind—bearing a child at my age was as farfetched as an immaculate conception. But, hey, this was India and anything was possible. But what if it actually happened? Did I really want a child?

Vasur and Krishnaveni apparently expected me to do the deed then and there, so I placed the ash on my tongue and swallowed its silkiness down.

Evening was falling by the time we left. The priest parcelled some prasadam rice for us before ushering us to the cave's door, and there to its right, taped to the stone, was a calendar picture of Andal, a herd of white cows at her feet, the hint of a smile on her lips.

Chapter Twenty-Seven

Nacciyar Tirumoli 6:5

'Take me to Thirumukkulam, Amma. Let's bathe together, just you and me.'

Varaji looked at her daughter quizzically, stopping the words at the tip of her tongue, the tiresome scolds: not sleeping, not touching her breakfast, wandering about the house like a lost soul. Something had changed in the night. A cloud had lifted. Even in the light and shadows dappling the walls of their courtyard there was playfulness, as if Laksmi had sprinkled gold dust.

'*Aum Srim Hrim Maha Lakshmayai Namaha.*' The mantra still hummed inside Varaji bright as the flame she had offered last night. 'I bow to you, great goddess.' She had poured in enough ghee so the lamp burned until morning, and all night Laksmi shimmied through Varaji's sleep.

'Amma!' Andal took a corner of her shawl and wiped the kohl smudging her mother's eyes. 'Did you hear what I said? The cock has not crowed, it is not too late.'

Another Margazhi month had gone. Both of them missed their early morning bath on the edge of town, the way the mountains reflected in the temple teerthum, the ripples their bodies made as they entered its chilly water. Those shy little forest birds venturing close to drink, the sway of coconut palms, the special quiet of the dark just before dawn.

'Why not? Yes, what a good idea. Bring the pot of turmeric, Andal, and pour a small pitcher of sesame oil. Make sure you stop it well.' It was a perfect idea. Flowers, I must bring flowers.

Varaji took Andal's hand and gave it a squeeze. For too long I have felt in the midst of a battle, she thought, keeping house, keeping my husband and caring for our daughter, but where did my heart go? Where did *I* go? Pouring balms of herbs and prayers into my womb, but all I really did was seal the grief away. Varaji pressed her other hand on her belly, felt its roundness, its forgotteness. She kept chanting as they threaded their way through town, their earth edging toward the sun. She took in a deep breath of the sky's changing colours and felt the soft prickling of a lotus stem curling inward from her navel, as if seeking the centre of her being. As she watched the quickening of dawn, she felt the bud of a lotus, crimson as the sky, slowly opening inside her, petal by petal.

'*Aum Srim Hrim …*' Far below, Varaji felt her feet touching the ground, the distant sensation of sand between her toes. There were other footsteps too, gentle and rhythmic, at the centre of the lotus unfolding in her belly, for it was there the goddess had placed *her* feet. With every step Laksmi took, Varaji felt blood swirling, warm and rich, swelling the walls of her womb, and with every breath out, every Aum she uttered, it was as if the goddess was the one breathing through her.

'Amma, we are here.' Varaji felt Andal's hand pressing and releasing hers as Laksmi's feet continued their dance—the pulse inside her and the hand of her daughter, both the exact same rhythm. They took off their veils, unwrapped the muslin from their hips, and dipped their toes gingerly into the water. Two months had passed since the chill of Margazhi's dawns and now the water lapped at their feet like velvet. Varaji gathered a handful of marigolds and held them high as she stepped down. Andal followed and together they waded in.

'Aum Srim Hrim Maha Lakshmayai Namaha,' Varaji chanted.

'Aum Namah Tirumal,' Andal sang, her face bright as a bride's. One by one they placed each flower into the ripples circling them.

❧

Visnucitta's fingers were stained from lamp black. Sheets of palm leaf scrawled with verse covered the floor of his study. He heard the anklet bells of his wife back and forth across their courtyard and the high trilled voice of his daughter playing words into the notes of a new song.

All the celestials arrived, chanting sacred verses, blessing me as bride.

He put his stylus down and closed his eyes.

I mistook your innocence from that very first day, he thought, remembering Andal's delight as she looked up to him through a showering of tulasi seeds, her body dusted from the earth of his garden, her newborn skin glowing red as gurivinda seeds.

Andal's voice lilted up from their courtyard—*draped in wedding silk and flowers, this vision I dreamed, my friend.* He nodded at the *tālam* Andal was improvising and tapped his fingers to its rhythm. She was god's from the very beginning. And now how empyreal her strides toward their wedding.

Last night's vision flooded Visnucitta again. Tirumal had raised the discus in his left hand and let it spin until it formed a circle of blinding light. 'Bring your daughter to the dark-bodied one. Make ready for her journey to me on the banks of the sacred Kavery.' He had entered Visnucitta's dreams before, but this time Tirumal's words were like a sky of free-falling stars. 'I, Tirumal, in the body of the one called Ranga, will take her as my bride.'

The bell on their front gate rang, the metal latch thudded onto wood as it dropped. Visnucitta heard Andal's sing-song voice muffling into the leafy shade of the street. He opened his eyes. Every time she left the house, disappearing into her world of make-believe, turning Villiputtur into the cowherders' village of Vrindavan, he let go of her a little more. He opened the shutters to catch a glimpse of his daughter, straining to hear the next verse of her new song.

Sri Ranga himself had requested Andal's hand! He must tell Varaji the news, ask her to prepare an offering of sweet rice. Tonight, they would take Andal to the temple and seek Lord Vatapatra sayee's blessings.

Cooking smoke curled its way up the stairs, kalonji and coriander seeds tempering in coconut oil. Visnucitta was hungry. He stood at the courtyard entrance, watching her as she rolled a pestle over dried chillies, adding a handful of roasted sesame and a pinch of salt. Her hair, glossy with oil and loosely twisted into a braid, fell between her breasts. She put down the pestle and stretched, coiled her hair on top of her head. How flawless the day, and how sweet the air with ripening mangos. It was almost Panguni.

Varaji felt the heat of her husband's eyes. She took the spices from the fire and poured them into the sambar. Instead of stirring them in, she covered the kadhai and let them infuse. Their meal could wait. She stood up and walked to him. Beneath the scent of jasmine in Varaji's hair, Visnucitta smelled the earthiness of Thirumukkulam's water on her skin. How different to the perfume he had so carefully washed from his body last night.

'We bathed there this morning,' she said, lifting her hand to stroke his cheek. She traced the conch-like curves of his ears, whispering Laksmi's name, stepping closer. She pressed her middle fingers into the orifice of each, the cave of man where all sound enters, music, prayer, the crackle of fire. Her touch was light, but the roar of an ocean filled him. Varaji's body, so familiar after so many years, pulled him close like the mystery of a full moon. He ran his hands down to her hips, then unlaced her bodice as they moved into the sunlight. Careless of food, of sound, of duty, they let their clothes drop onto the courtyard stones. Varaji yielded to each of her husband's wishes, then played with them until Visnucitta yielded to her. She shifted her weight over him, her skin soft like moss and beaded with perspiration. An image of Varaha flashed before Visnucitta's eyes, Tirumal's avatar in the body of a boar, saviour of Mother Earth, Bhooma devi. He had rescued her from the depths of an ocean that covered the world, laying her across his tusks to carry her to the surface. Visnucitta had seen the sea at Thiruvananthapuram once, in the hours before a monsoon storm, wave upon powerful wave tumbling to the shore. Like this Varaji took him—his wife, his mother, the earth herself—until he felt as insubstantial as the froth of that remembered sea.

Chapter Twenty-Eight

Lord with the banner of Garuda, exalted and obeyed,
useless sorrow—these innocent breasts meaningless to him,
bind them tight to his broad shoulders, end my separation

Nacciyar Tirumoli 13:7

'Mother Uluka!' Andal held her lamp high and called to the old owl perched outside her window. She could barely keep the light still as evening darkened around them.

'Tonight, Amma, Appa, and I are going to the temple to ask for Vatapatra sayee's blessings.'

The owl fluffed her feathers and blinked her glassy green eyes, then shifted closer as if to say she was also coming. Andal reached out to stroke her tawny wings, but the owl hopped to a higher branch. She did swivel her neck though, so their eyes met for one long unblinking moment.

'Why don't you call Sri Laksmi and she can come too?'

'*Povaa-aa, pova-aa,*' the owl replied as she de-huddled her head and flapped her wings.

'She says "Yes!"'

Andal clapped her hands, convinced this was the very Uluka Laksmi called upon for her chariot. Most evenings she took up residence outside Andal's window, every now and then swooping down to the street for a morsel of scampering mouse. They had been friends from the beginning.

It was on the morning of this evening that Visnucitta had called Andal to their courtyard. Uluka had been there too, preening her feathers after swallowing a small lizard. '*Povaa-aa, pova-aa.*' She had looked at Andal and nodded her down the stairs.

ʂ●

'Today, you will make your own garland as an offering for Lord Vatapatra sayee. I will bring home flowers. You just tell me what you would like.'

Instantly, Andal smelled the dark green leaves of tulasi, as if she was lying in a bed of them, each aromatic leaf crisp and clean. Lord Vatapatra sayee's favourite. She visualised twining tulasi twice the length of her body, then tying white lotus buds into it like the stars of a Vaikunthan sky.

'Andal, are you listening?' Visnucitta touched her arm, kindness in his eyes. She had fallen into her dreaming again.

'Sit down,' he said. Something in him had relinquished; it was as if, strand by strand, the net entangling both of them was at last beginning its unravelling.

'Tonight, we will go to the temple after evening puja. It is best that you, your mother, and I be alone with Villiputtur's lord. We must ask for his blessing, now the god you desire has accepted your vow.'

ʂ●

'Look, mother owl, at the new clothes Amma has set out for me, how pretty the cloth is.'

Uluka tipped her head to the side and blinked as Andal wrapped three sunflower yellow yards of sheer muslin around her body.

'Listen to the bells of my anklets,' she said, stamping her feet. 'Look how the skirt clings to my hips and hugs my thighs. Amma says I am skin and bones but, old wise owl, if I were to climb on your back and ask you to take me to Vrindavan, in no time at all I will be plump again, drinking the creamiest milk from the fattest cows in the whole wide world, the prettiest of all milkmaids.'

'Are you dreaming or are you getting dressed, Andal?' Varaji's voice carried up the stairs.

'Getting dressed, Amma.'

Old owl shifted one foot to the other. Not a breath of breeze cooled the night. Andal wiped her forehead dry with a corner of her muslin shawl. Steady as her hands allowed, she held the mirror to paint a line of kumkuman straight as an arrow from between her eyes to the part in her hair. Then she saw in the mirror's reflection a swishing and rustling of the leaves behind her, outside where old owl was perched. Andal watched as Uluka spread her wings, then bent low to let a tiny figure, small as a sparrow, climb onto her back. It was Sri Laksmi herself, swathed in pink silk, skin golden as the mirror's polished brass.

Andal turned around just in time to hear her say, 'Take me to Lord Vatapatra sayee,' before the two of them flew toward the temple, leaving the tree shivering and the moonlight tangled in its branches. Andal leaned out the window, but they had disappeared. She squeezed her eyes shut, feeling the air against her skin, warm and lotus-sweet. The moon had soaked into everything until it wasn't night anymore, but neither was it day.

Andal heard the drums over the temple walls and the nasally notes of a flute. It was as if she were a bird too, looking down at the golden dome of the shrine where Lord Vatapatra sayee waited. She imagined drops of nectar dribbling from his rosy lips as he watched the priests prepare a copper bowl of fresh milk, sweet with jaggery and fragrant with saffron.

'Do you remember, little baby on a banyan leaf,' Andal called down to him, 'when you were Krishna and I was your lover? All the milkmaids wanted you but it was me who loved you most. Remember one midnight when we came to you in the forest, shy as a herd of deer? You chose the most brazen of us, the one whose lobes shook with bright earrings, and you carried her on your shoulders to a grove on the banks of the Yamuna. With little ghee lamps, we followed your footprints and spied through the bushes. What I saw there, I should never have seen. Where was her self-respect? You offered her a flower from a tree in heaven and she took it with a face bloated as the moon. How jealous I was. When later you walked up to me with a flower for my hair, I tossed my braid back in disdain.'

'"Only one flower from heaven?" I said. "Is that all I am worth? Bring me the entire tree."'

'And you did! Flashing your lotus eyes down the length of me so my whole body quivered. Like this, you and I, we played our games.'

'Andal!' Varaji's voice was loud with impatience.

'Coming, Amma.'

Andal twisted her hair, then knotted it on top of her head. Sri Ranga's name began vibrating on her tongue as she took the stairs two by two. She stood at the bottom, her arms on fire. *Ranga, Ranga*, his name burned to her fingers, whirlpooled in her belly and down to her toes.

Yes, he had said *yes* to her father.

'I will marry Andal. Bring her to Srirangam.'

Visnucitta caught his daughter, holding her until she stood steady on her feet.

'All you need remember is to lower your eyes like a bride-to-be, and while I pray to Lord Vatapatra sayee you bow at his feet. I have composed a song in the voice of your mother telling how deep your devotion is, and that now the greatest of all Lord Tirumal's incarnations is calling for you.'

Sri Ranga! Andal imagined his sapphire skin against hers. She let Varaji adjust the veil over her head and step by step, with her parents either side, she concentrated on him all the way to the temple.

A priest led them into the low pillared foyer of the sanctum —Varaji carrying a platter of sweet rice, Visnucitta with a hand of yelakki bananas, and their daughter, Choodi K Kodutta, the lady who offers the lord garlands first worn by herself. Andal was draped in the garland she had woven, as artfully as any by Visnucitta, each twine knot invisible, every flower and tulasi sprig perfectly placed.

'We will be safe from prying eyes,' Varaji whispered to Andal as devotees filed past them, their hands filled with sugar crystals. She *cluck-clucked* as she straightened Andal's veil and pinched her cheeks. 'Look at you, wearing his flowers, blushing like a bride.' Tears welled in Varaji's eyes and she quickly brushed them away.

'Bride-to-be, Amma,' Andal said, pretending not to see. For a brief moment, she was the one in control. 'First we have to ask for Vatapatra sayee's blessing.' Her heart thudded hard, as if trying to break free from its cage. Of course, he will give it, she thought, and then my father will meet with the astrologer to settle on a date. The minutes dragged like days. If her heart continued like this there would be no body left for it to beat against.

Andal read the silent incantation on Varaji's lips, *Laksmi, Bhooma Devi, Namaha,* and saw herself standing beside them— the lord's consorts—Sri Laksmi, goddess of abundance, and Bhooma Devi, goddess of earth. But I am going to be his wife.

Visnucitta waited at the sanctum door as preparations were made for their aarti, the *pulup-pulup* of ghee pouring into brass lamps, the priest's whispered prayers. All the devotees gone, Varaji and Andal moved to his side. Tiny black bats darted through the corridors, the stones echoing every wing beat. Each soft fluttering tickled the insides of Andal's ears. She felt something else and turned to see the eagle eyes of Garuda, Lord Tirumal's chariot statue, shifting in the shadows and she swore the stones sang back to her the ruffling of his feathers at the sound of Vatapatra sayee's chortling inside. Garuda: always ready to carry him. Soon she would be riding on his back too.

The priest pushed open the temple doors and their hundred studded bells rang loud as the anklets on a royal procession of elephants. He blew one long note from the temple's conch. Andal's mind emptied of everything except the one waiting for her, his indigo body illuminating the darkness. They bowed at the foot of Lord Vatapatra sayee's dais. Visnucitta then sat to the side, took up his tamboura and began to play, the sound of its five strings strumming over and over like a drone of bees sipping from the dark centre of a flower.

Andal felt the press of Varaji's hand at the small of her back. She stepped forward and dropped to her knees. Carefully, she took the garland from her body and raised it high. *Aum Namah Tirumal. Om Namah Vatapatra sayee.*

'O conch shell, Panchanjaya,' she heard her father's voice, as if from a great distance. 'You are nourished by nectar from the lips of the one who measured the worlds. Your bed is the hand of the lord.'

She risked a glance toward the priest, saw him hesitating at the crib. Never, to his knowledge, had this been done in their temple, offering a garland defiled by human touch. And what to say of the shameful stories about this girl whispered in every corner of Villiputtur—but Visnucitta's dreams, his wisdom and songs, had brought unimagined riches to their temple. He should not be doubted. Nevertheless, just to be safe, the priest muttered a quick prayer of penance before circling the exalted one—ever playful, big toe in his mouth, his imperial smile—with the garland the girl had worn. Andal watched him lay it over Lord Vatapatra sayee's chest, one of its lotus buds brushing the divine one's rosy cheek. She felt it too, as if it were her cheek, and shuddered with the velvet pleasure of it before lowering her gaze.

Three times Andal prostrated, then three times twice again. Would he grant her wish? Would he let her marry an avatar other than himself?

She stood up, her legs like blades of grass in the wind, her mind like a panicked bird. A hand took her elbow, an arm circled her waist, guiding her to the centre of the garbarigha and to the end of his bed. Her body trembled and she did not know what to do with it. The weight of an arm gently lowered her down. She dropped her forehead to the stones.

The sharp scent of camphor, the biting sweet of ripening bananas, the smoke, the thick heat—Andal's head began to spin, her skin tingled all over as if a swarm of black bees had come to sup the pollen dust left from his garland. She had not an ounce of strength to shake them off. Lord Vatapatra sayee's lotus eyes were the only light now in the shrine's darkness. Words, where were the words she had practised? Everything swirled, her body was sinking, heavy and heavier into the stones. Her teeth were clenched for fear of what she needed to ask. She forced her mouth open and the wall of air pressing down on her rushed in, causing a gasp so loud it set off a screeching and careering of the tiny black bats clinging to the niches above.

'Lord Vatapatra sayee,' her words tumbled out, 'by my bare feet half a moon's cycle away on the banks of the Kavery River, you lie on your serpent bed as Lord Tirumal's avatar, the great Ranga. It is him, more than any other incarnation, I wish to wed. This is my vow, but it can only be so by your grace.'

It was as if all the garbarigha's air was absorbed into him and not a breath of it left for her. If he did not answer, what was she to do?

She turned to her father, but his eyes were closed, his fingers strumming the tamboura over and over.

My daughter, like a ladle slipped from its handle, like a kuyil bird she repeats the lord's name. Sri Ranga. O Vatapatra sayee, tran-scendent on your banyan leaf bed, the whole world secure in your belly. Look how she falls into trance. Please listen to her.

Andal crawled to Varaji and clutched the hem of her skirt. 'Amma, take me home.'

'My child,' she said, from a thousand miles away, as Andal began beating her head against the stones as if she could beat an answer out of them. Varaji took her daughter's head and rested it in her lap, rocking her, letting her weep.

'Sri Ranga is the only god who faces south and I am here, Amma, here in the south, waiting for him. Why doesn't Vatap-atra sayee hear me?'

She kept rocking Andal, wiping her daughter's tears, tears enough to fill the Kavery River itself.

Chapter Twenty-Nine

You alone I desire O lord
my breasts rise and fall for you
—I am caught between despair and joy

Nacciyar Tirumoli 5:7

At the bottom of the stairs to Krishnaveni's cave, we took a narrow track forking off the path, leading further into the gorge. We had been travelling since early morning; I was dusty and sweaty, in need of a bath and a soft place to rest—unlikely, given Vasur's quickening steps. Further and further we walked, away from the tiffin houses of Papanasam, probably stoking their cooking fires for a night's trading of dosas and sambars.

My legs dragged. Vasur had probably read my mind but remained his usual unfazed self. He did slow down a little though, throwing me one of his smiles.

'It is not far. I am taking you to another cave and nearby there is a pool for bathing.'

Down a set of ancient steps chiselled into a bank was an

expanse of iridescent water dappled with twilight, deep and beckoning.

'Kalyanyi Theertham,' he said, untying the cloth bag from his shoulder.

'But first we visit the home of siddhar Agasthya. We leave our things here.'

You are nimble as a mountain goat, I thought, clambering behind Vasur over more rocks and around the pool, buoyed at the thought of diving into it, my weariness gone.

'Watch your head,' Vasur said, his voice muffled by a small waterfall. I followed him behind its cascades to a low ledge and on the other side was a small dry square of earth. The sun had disappeared and what light was left fell in shadowy ripples down the rock face in front of us. Vasur knelt at a low entrance into the rock and took a terracotta lamp for each of us from a neatly stacked pile. He curled in two wicks and filled them from the bottle of oil left there for pilgrims. I watched, lost for one safe minute, thinking of the thousands of shrines and temples all over India, each of them tended, incense, fire, and water.

Vasur held out one of the lamps and I paused, unsure about taking it—unsure about saying yes. I would gladly have abseiled a cliff face with nothing but one rope, but a cave with an entrance as dark and small and primitive as this? I was claustrophobic; I knew the symptoms: cramps in my stomach, palms turning clammy. Vasur prised my fingers open and put the lamp in my hand. Stay close, his eyes said as he struck a match and the wicks hissed into flame. My heart thumped double time, but it was not from fear, it felt more like fearlessness. Something whirred inside my chest, like the tremor of a compass needle.

I had watched Vasur, had felt him with a kind of hunger, the whole day since leaving Srivilliputtur. He was, I realised in that moment, more than one finite man. He was more than just a sum of parts crouching in front of me. He was the tree under which he slept, the path we were walking, he was the blind beggar singing for alms, he was Krishnaveni, he was the cave we were about to enter. And me—he was me too.

I followed Vasur in. The rock above us glistened as we tunnelled six, seven, then eight body lengths. The cave elongated out into a womb-like space soft-lit by the steady flame of a solitary lamp burning on a small hewn shelf, and behind it the black silhouette of a lone lingam. We sat, and as my eyes accustomed to the light I noticed a row of snakes carved into the wall opposite, their black hooded heads smeared red with kumkuman. *Nagas*—nature spirits, guardians of wells and springs, of shrines and underground rivers, bestowers of fertility. We were clay bodies in the belly of earth. Eyes open or closed, it didn't matter. Time did not, could not, exist in such penetrating silence and stillness. The air we exchanged from inside out and outside in filtered through rock and water, the pores of our skin; it was air hummed through the bodies of siddhars, their centuries of incantations, their bones buried in dust.

Vasur melded Krishnaveni's mantra into the dark, *Aum Shakti Aum, Aum Shakti Aum,* his voice entering me like a slow flowing river, more vibration than word, until I could not distinguish between the sound and the periphery of my body, the earth and these legs beneath me, numb as if crossed a long time ago. His chants faded into before time and I disappeared. Forever, it felt like, until the bright turquoise body of a parrot darted behind my closed eyelids, its head and breast golden, its beak scarlet.

'*I am caught between despair and joy,*' a girl's voice sang. '*Oh beautiful kuyil, what do you gain by hiding?*'

I opened my eyes, as if there really was a parrot to see. The lamp on the shelf was dry but the flames of ours still burned. I felt the weight of a hand on my leg, the gentle pressure of five fingers calling me back. Slowly, I returned into the familiar of me, moving my fingers and toes until they tingled. Despair and joy, my gatekeepers—I had carried them like some kind of authenticated gemstone—joy and despair. They were stilled. All that remained was a small whirlpooling in my stomach.

'Come.' Vasur's hand moved to my back, then lifted me to my knees. 'Put your forehead here,' he said, guiding me to the lingam. I rested my arms around the circular channels of the *yoni* on which the lingam sat. It was soft, from countless offerings of sesame oil and ghee and pillowings of melted candle wax. The lingam smooth, from layerings of unguents massaged over it, of turmeric paste and sandalwood. As I pressed against the lingam stone, a kind of shining penetrated my forehead, pulsing like the throb of an ancient instrument. I heard the rattling of a drum but could not tell if it was real, if it came from the lingam or from the flick of the nagas' tongues. I could not tell, at first, if the sensations flooding my body were of heat or the burn of ice. If it was the lingam trembling, or me. I could not tell. I felt Vasur's hand at the base of my spine, steadying me, and the heat, yes it was heat, intensifying there. I had no strength left to call upon, to escape or to stay. I rocked back and forth. I pressed my head harder against the curve of the lingam until a low groan gathered like a storm cell, as if torn from the insides of my belly. If I opened my mouth, all of me would pour out. I did not want this, and yet I dared myself. Take it, a voice said, the entire universe is here in the coupling you are holding, Shiva and Shakti, creating and sustaining. Let them roar through you. Let them cut you free.

❧

Sounds of water flowed toward me. I was on my hands and knees again, crawling in pitch dark. Drop by drop, water on rock, closer and closer. There was the scent of animal on my skin, and from the rocks above my head another smell, familiar, from the temple in Srirangam. Above its giant winged Garuda, guarding the entrance to the inner shrine of Lord Ranganatha, lived a colony of bats, their droppings smearing the columns and flagstones, pungent like fungi and the damp rotting of fallen trees. I recoiled from this smell, as I did from my own body's fermenting if I ever went too long without a bath. But feeling my way out from the cave's dark, these scents felt elemental. I wanted to be wrapped in them, cocooned and succoured. I wanted to be born from them.

'Slowly,' a voice said as I slipped out into the air. I gripped Vasur's hand and stood up tentatively, blinking through the veil of water falling between us. Step by step, we retraced our way to Kalyanyi Theertham, its deep waters rippling like hammered silver and a trillion stars above.

Slowly, the only word uttered since leaving the cave. And before that? All I knew was the raw sensation in my throat and how thirsty I was, and hungry, but it didn't matter. *Slowly.* Vasur was already at the water's edge stepping out from the folds of his lunghi. *This*, I whispered into the night. I undressed and waded in, the ripples of my body marrying the circles of his. I threw my head back to the sky and laughed at all those stars, then dived into their reflection, my hair unravelling like waves of sea kelp.

Like two night creatures, we played, Vasur and I, letting the water do with us what it willed, our skin sometimes lightly brushing, our bodies diving back into the infinity of the mirror holding us. All those stars, and no moonlight. I felt for a rock flat enough to sit. How good to be alive to the elements of air and water, the call of a night koel from deep in the forest, the sight of Vasur taking one last dive then springing over the teerthum's rocks toward me. Should I cover myself? The thought hovered, only briefly.

Vasur placed the leaf parcels of prasadam from Krishnaveni between us and rolled the first bite-sized ball. He held it to my mouth and popped it in without touching my lips, rice studded with peppercorns and slivers of ginger, each grain tasting like some kind of miracle. We took turns feeding each other, a small ceremony of gestures, of gratitude for our time together, and, strangely, I felt, for whatever was to become of us. Then we drank from the pool, although I hesitated, to Vasur's amusement, until he assured me it was pure enough. 'Even for foreigners,' he said, 'even though once you were not.'

I looked at him for an explanation, but he gave none and I felt suddenly vulnerable. There I was, bent over the water, my ungainly breasts trailing its edge, my face a dark Delphic reflection, the glint of the crystal beads round my neck like a mockery of the stars above. I drew my cupped hands out, splashing the mirror into pieces, this body of mine turning to wrinkles and folds of flesh. All the magic snatched in an instant. How foolish was I? What was I thinking, careering into unknown forests and caves, believing I was somehow invincible, that sensuality was mine again, that it was my birthright as a woman? I panicked, looking for where I had left my clothes, and in my panic, brushing my wet hair out of the way, I caught my hand in the twists of the necklace's copper wire.

As I watched its beads scatter like falling stars down the rocks and into the water, her voice surfaced in me again, *despair and joy*, insistent, unrelenting, uncompromising, holding me between them like the taut string of a bow.

'Saisha!' Vasur pulled me to him, taking my hair, my silvering, tangled hair, twirling its wet strands then coiling them on top of my head. His hands drifted to the nape of my neck where the beads had been clasped. He held me close, staying there until my weight surrendered into his.

'Don't play with me, Vasur.'

'I am not playing.'

He kept holding me.

'*Pálálilaiyil tuyil konda paraman valaip pattirundénai,*' Vasur's hushed Tamil entered me fine as breath—*He sleeps on a banyan leaf and I am tangled in his net. He dances with a water pot balanced on his head. His mindless teases spearing me. Bring me the cool blue basil garland he wears; place it soft around my hair.*

A faint scent of woodsmoke rode the night. Wisps of mist rose from the pool at our feet. A quiver of wind like a rush of arrows swept through me, and fleetingly I wondered how alone we were, if there were siddhars in the cliffs above us, or a goddess in the guise of Kama Deva stepping across the water. But the warmth of the stone beneath us was real, my breath rising and falling, the sighs escaping me, the sky of stars whirling behind my eyelids, the hands tracing my body as if it were a landscape.

Despair and joy stood either side, old friends, they said, you can trust us—their siren cries.

'Stay with me,' Vasur said, his lips at my ear as he pulled me away from them and into his lap, crossing my legs round his back. Every wound I had held like a torch for my existence he peeled back and kissed, then said go. How exquisite to know his body with mine and that there was no difference in the end, one from the other. We were five senses joined in a kind of bliss that knew nothing of doing. Only life awakening then falling away, then another breath. In each moment an eternity. In each, a death.

We slipped back into the water, both of us gasping at its dawn chill. 'This is a pool of solar fire and a well of lunar nectar,' Vasur said. 'It was here the siddhar Agasthya had his vision of Shiva and Shakti's wedding.'

We submerged ourselves three times in a final prayer to them. On the third time, I opened my eyes and caught a glimmer below of two drops of light, two crystal beads disappearing into the silt of the teerthum's floor.

I remembered my visit to Srirangam, aimlessly wandering its streets, and my encounter with the umbrella man—his prophecy of a disappearing necklace had come true. And how my entry into the inner sanctum of a lotus-eyed god was refused—Non-Hindus-Not-Allowed, the sign mocked—the thick scent of those bats in the air. But there Garuda knelt, never wavering, ever ready to chariot his lord to wherever he was needed. Maybe there was no need to return to Srirangam. Wherever you are, there is god.

I climbed from the pool and sat cross-legged in the first rays of the sun, basking in a trident of water, rock, and Vasur redolent on my skin. A play of morning light stippled my closed eyelids. And what of Andal, I wondered as the day brightened, of her vow to wed Ranganatha?

I lifted my face toward the sun, bathing in its warmth, aware of the tiny spangles of water clinging to my eyelashes. The transparency of light washing through my eyelids deepened into a shimmer of gold and from this shimmering she appeared. Not as girl or poetess or goddess, but a fountain of water flowing up from the core of earth.

'You stepped into me last night,' she said.

The sun moved an infinitesimal inch, and she was gone.

Chapter Thirty

The sweetness springing from his mouth—only this nectar
can dispel my pain—bring it to me—let me drink the divine

Nacciyar Tirumoli 13:4

All of Villiputtur was awake. Women had been up before dawn, sweeping the street between Andal's house and the temple, sprinkling it with water then fine white sand. Flower wreaths lined the way, and outside Andal's house townsmen had built a tall canopy with banana trees at each of the four directions, its roof thatched with white palm fronds and trumpet flower vines.

Varaji flitted from kitchen to courtyard and up and down the stairs. So much to do and already the sky was flushed pink. Wives from neighbouring houses had come to help with the final preparations. They wrapped sambar spices in banana leaf packages, measured husked and rinsed rice enough for two weeks, and stacked lentil cakes and sweet millet cakes then tied them with string. Fresh ghee was ladled into small kettles to hang from the yokes of the bullock cart. Lentil chips made with yoghurt, dried vegetables, and pulses. Tins of cumin-spiced jaggery mixed with tamarind.

Varaji appraised the neat piles of provisions for the hundredth time. 'How many kadhais are there?

'Tanti-ji,' a voice came from the steps of their well. It was Sarvani. She and Marali had been Andal's inseparable friends forever, playing their imaginary cowherd girl games on Villiput-tur's riverbanks—at least they thought they were games—until their friend began falling for longer and longer into her make-believe world. How many times had they waited for her to come back? Gossip in the town grew. She was mad, some said, possessed by evil asparas. Varaji had no choice but to summon the *velan* to spirit these demons away. And when, after the velan's visit, Andal's behaviour continued just as before, Marali and Sarvani's parents had no choice but to forbid them from seeing her. But they were returned to the fold now in their grown-up anklets and pretty clothes, thrilled to be helping Varaji with her preparations. And even more thrilled that Andal, bride-to-be, had asked them to accompany her to Srirangam.

Varaji hurried across the courtyard as she called a reminder back to the women: 'Double-check we have enough cow dung cakes for the cooking fires.'

Visnucitta crossed her path, his arms laden with sandalwood sticks and stalks of cardamom. Two servants followed him, one carrying pots of honey and the other balancing a cage on his head. A black-striped civet paced inside. Whenever he hissed, with a show of his sharp teeth, sprays of musk punctuated the air. There were piles of offerings and wedding gifts waiting to be packed, cones of cinnabar and blocks of kohl, fans made from deer hair, and the long white tusks of a mountain elephant. Varaji caught her husband's eyes and for a moment everything else disappeared. This was their daughter's day and her love had rekindled theirs.

'Almost ready now,' he said, holding her with his eyes.

'And the puja supplies? Have they been packed safely?'

Visnucitta nodded.

'Tanti-ji.' It was Sarvani again, this time insistent. Varaji hurried on, her body flooded with warmth. So many details, but I can hold them all, she thought. A vision of a boat anchored at the shoreline of a vast sea flashed inside her. The boat was filled to the brim with pots and sacks of provisions. She saw herself climbing in, motioning to a fisherman to untie the rope. No matter how burdened she felt, there was always this milk-white ocean waiting for her. She trailed her fingers through its waves.

'Like this, Tanti-ji?' Sarvani asked as she twisted Andal's braid into an elaborate knot. Varaji nodded. A ray of sunlight played at the edges of her daughter's feet. How empty their home would soon be without Andal's songs, her pleas and antics.

Sarvani joined Marali squatting on the steps of the court-yard's well, waiting for Varaji's next instruction. Andal stood bare-breasted, a thin petticoat tied at her waist, oblivious to the fussing around her. How a tide can change, Varaji thought, and how loyal are Andal's friends. They never stopped loving her and now see their reward. What an honour to help in her bathing rite.

Marali was given the task of collecting Andal's gift from the shrine room, a sari from the king of Madurai himself. How word had travelled, from Pandya to Cola country. It was unprece-dented, the marriage of a girl from Villiputtur to the lord of Srirangam. It was Sirimai, Villiputtur's chief temple dancer, who brought the gift to their house. She knew the king well and was often summoned to his palace to dance.

Varaji had felt slightly flustered by Sirimai's unannounced visit. They sat together in the front room in awkward silence. Sirimai took out the package and gave it to Varaji with a conspiratorial wink, just enough to break the ice.

'Open it,' she said.

The anticipation was delicious as Varaji loosened the ribbon. She drew a sharp breath in; it was luminous and the perfect colour for her soon-to-be-wed daughter.

'A gift from King Vallabhadeva,' Sirimai announced with more than a little fanfare.

Varaji was speechless. The king?

Sirimai took a sip of tea and helped herself to a ladoo.

'This morning, a palace courier delivered it to my house. Of course, you know it is no longer a secret. The whole town is atwitter about Visnucitta's dream—Lord Ranga accepting Andal as his bride. Well, in the king's note he said he also dreamt. Lord Ranga came to him, the very same night!' She paused for drama and another sip of tea.

'This sari. I have never felt such fine thread.'

'Indeed. The gifting of Andal to Sri Ranga is a fortuitous alliance for King Vallabhadeva. He is an astute king. Trust me, Varaji-ji, the sari is a small gift only. As we speak, he is having a pearl palanquin built to carry Andal to Srirangam.' Sirimai swam her head from side to side as only a dancer could. 'Such generosity, Akka.'

Varaji filled Sirimai's cup, blushing at the nityasumangali's affectionate address.

'And, Akka, one more thing. The king will be accompanying us to Srirangam.'

Us? So Sirimai means to say she is coming too? Calculations of food, pots, pans, and servants reeled through Varaji's head. And now the king? O Mukunda! Laksmi! Vatapatra sayee!

'Don't worry, Akka, all will be provided,' Sirimai said, as if reading her thoughts. 'The king will have his own retinue.' She licked the tip of her fingers. 'Such fragrant ladoos. Am I tasting rosewater?'

'Please, Sirimai-ji, let me wrap the rest in a parcel for you.'

'Thank you, Akka. You are kind. You have been a good and gracious mother for Andal too.'

Marali unfolded the sari and it fell through her hands like water. Varaji watched the girls as they draped Andal, pleating the silk, then draping her again until she was enveloped in a sea of emerald green. Varaji took the small bangles she had tucked into her bodice, specially made for her daughter's delicate wrists, and threaded them over each of Andal's hands, three coral, two jade, three coral—how prettily they jingled. Andal's eyes opened wide at the sound. All at once they laughed, the four of them together. What a day this was. They laughed until they began to cry. Until a conch bell sounded over the gate.

Varaji lifted the last yard of silk circling Andal's shoulders and veiled her head. 'No one must see your face until the day of the wedding. Only your father and I, and the women.'

Andal knelt to touch her father's feet at their front door. 'Bless you, my daughter,' he said, garlanding her with red water lilies. Priests from the temple lining the path to their front gate blessed her too, first with drops of sacred water, then the pure-white flames of camphor. The conch sounded again as they entered the street and the townspeople crowding both sides surged forward for one last look at Choodi K Kodutta, the lady who offers the lord garlands first worn by herself.

Andal glanced up into the branches of the tree outside her bedroom. Uluka sat motionless, head half-tucked into her tawny body, just one eye open and directed at her. As the first clouds in months blew east over the mountains and the sun began brightening their world, she felt the shadow of another bird's wings. It was Garuda, churning the sky from pinks to indigos, soaring higher and higher. She knew, as sure as the sand beneath her feet, that he was carrying news to Sri Ranga in Srirangam that the girl who loved him was leaving Villiputtur. Soon she would be there.

Unaware of the crowds pressing around her and the shouts of the priests berating them to stand back, Andal sang to her vision as Garuda dissolved into the sky. *Bring me close to the glow of his fiery discus but do not scorch me. Let me be cooled in the gathering of his Vedic light.*

Varaji was quick to take hold of Andal before she fell.

'Marali, bring water. Hurry!'

She looked across at Visnucitta, her eyes full of fright, and together they guided their daughter toward the palanquin. Andal turned a final time to the house she had grown up in and the streets she had played in. All the hours spent with her lover, all the songs sung through her. And no matter how abandoned and desperate she had felt, she knew this day would come. How verdant the world looked through her silken veil, yet how illusory.

Chapter Thirty-One

For goddess earth draped in moss, deep in the ocean,
with no shame he took the body of a filthy boar.
Oh bright lord of Srirangam—the words you spoke then
—can never be wrenched from my heart

Nacciyar Tirumoli 11:8

'Appa?'

Virudhunagar Junction seethed with passengers.

'Appa—' The voice was insistent and close. I turned to see a woman catch up to Vasur. She was a head taller than the panic of bodies around us manoeuvring copious pieces of luggage from a train to the platform against the wall of impatient passengers pushing to get on. She was handsome, the bone structure of her face like his.

'It's me, Roshina.' She attempted to bend down before him, but he took her hands and they stood face to face, all the desperation around them disappeared, the moment cutting into me like a knife.

'Appa,' she said over and over. Was it disquiet I saw across Vasur's face or the looming of a memory, like ink-stained fabric long ago ripped into two, the sound of its tearing still visceral? There were tears in the woman's eyes. A small girl clung to the end of her sari, thumb in her mouth.

Appa. The word crashed its way through my head.

'It really is you,' she said.

I didn't know where to look. For the first time, Vasur seemed unsure of himself—a father. It threw me. The little girl looked across at me, her eyes a deep hazel, while the woman, determined, had managed to drop to the ground, the crowd miraculously parting around them, to touch her forehead to Vasur's feet. The girl buried her face in the drapes of the woman's sari.

'This is Kodai. My daughter—your granddaughter, Appa. Kodai, say hello to Thaatha.' She peeked out from her hiding place.

I had not thought of a family beyond the wife Vasur had so fleetingly mentioned. Vasur was tied to nobody—except me. Now here I was at a train junction, a crossroad for everywhere else, standing at the periphery of a circle, of three lives suspended, all the years gone missing spiralling to life again.

The little girl put her hand into the one held out for her. The train they had got down from rumbled forward like some giant beast. The crowd around us started to thin.

Roshina—what a beautiful name. A glance passed between us as she dried her eyes with a corner of her sari and I took the edge of my dupatta to wipe mine. She smiled a timid smile, then returned to her father and her daughter, their reunion like a kind of gravity, pulling them into a vortex that would not, could never, be broken, and I did not know what to do with my hands.

Our train to Srivilliputtur was not due for another two hours and Roshina's, to Trivandrum, for three. We walked to a lone tree at the end of the platform. Roshina took my hands, listening to the sound of my name on Vasur's lips, and repeating it. She was young enough to be my daughter, Kodai, my grand-daughter. And who was I, this foreign woman travelling with her father? Curiosity palpated the space between us. Vasur spread his blanket for us to sit. I watched Kodai mesmerised by the bare-chested, barefoot man sitting across from her until the screeches of slick muddied hogs scavenging near the tracks distracted her gaze. Two white butterflies fluttered above the mud and I followed them, their persistent search for a place to settle erratic in the air. A fattening sun pixelated into shards of gold as it moved toward the rim of our world.

'I am married now, Appa, with one daughter only. We live with my husband's mother in Pondicherry. She is a widow. Little Kodai, so many times was asking after you and Amma. But what was I to tell her?'

Pondicherry. The name unrolled itself like a bolt of cloth from Roshina's lips to my grandmother's album. Of course, I had looked for it on a map, a town once occupied by France, less than two hours south of Chennai, but I was only slightly inquis-itive and had had no inclination to visit despite my grandmoth-er's time there. I had found my own path, just as she had.

'Truth is best,' I heard Vasur say as he leaned across to tousle Kodai's hair. 'Let her grow used to it. She will because you love her. You are a good mother, I can see that,' he said. 'Was it wrong of me to leave after your mother died? I am sorry if you think so.'

There were more tears in Roshina's eyes. She kept shaking her head, and I couldn't tell if it was in a yes or a no.

'You had grown up. You had started college.'

Roshina dried her eyes and smiled an embarrassed smile to me. She glanced at her watch—two hours were going to pass in an instant. Back and forth they talked, some of the time lapsing into Tamil, their tongues loosening as they mended time with small stitches of events and places and names—Roshina prof-fering the most, pausing every now and then to encourage Kodai to tell about starting school, animals, favourite games. Vasur listening, responding more with liquid gestures and connection of eye than words. And me, interpreting from their expressions, from the tone of their voices and the rush of rolling syllables like music from ancestral lips, a falling into fragile ease, possible happiness.

When it came time to board our train, I sensed panic in Roshina's eyes. She pressed a piece of paper into Vasur's hands, closing his fingers over it with a beseeching look. Vasur then bent down to Kodai for a final goodbye.

I wanted to say, let's all of us stay here for a night, there'll be other trains. But it felt presumptuous.

'Do you have email?' I asked Roshina as we were pushed and pummelled toward the train. Email, of all things; it felt as insubstantial as a thin thread stretched between Srivilliputtur and Pondicherry.

'Of course,' she said, scrambling through her handbag for pen and more paper. 'We must keep in touch. My father …' she paused, looking down at Kodai, intent on each of her grandfather's words, 'he is doing what he has always wanted to do. It is not uncommon, you know, in India, when a husband or wife dies, their other half leaves too. But it is hard, I am telling you. Knowing he is alive, yet no longer part of us. I was surprised he even acknowledged us.' She took the loose end of her sari and veiled her head.

'Maybe this is because of you,' she said. I shook my head in one of those yes or no responses. The train lurched an inch and the crowd surged forward in false alarm.

'May I have your attention please,' the loudspeakers crackled. 'One-six-one-two-seven Guruvayur Express now ready for departure.' The words scratched the air. 'Wishing all passengers a very happy and comfortable journey.'

Vasur had already disappeared into the carriage.

'You please send mail to me,' Roshina said, scribbling her address. I held her hands in mine, wishing for all the world our time did not have to be so short, and as the train pulled away, I attempted a reassuring smile as if it might stem the distance of those turning wheels.

&

'It is nothing new, this separation from loved ones,' Vasur eventually said as we snaked through a landscape of thorn trees and the occasional tilled field baked hard under Panguni's sun.

'Yes, but …' There was no point in arguing. I didn't have the energy, and of all times Marcus had to chime in, his monotone voice inside my head. 'You want everything, you make excuses, but it's not up to you.' All it did was make me defiant. I shifted my gaze higher through the grilles of the train window to the peaks of the ghats backlit by a disappeared sun, their outline razor sharp. A world free from diesel fumes and noise, canopies of ylang ylang and springs of pure water … With a rush of metallic air, our carriage entered a tunnel, then was out again. I squinted into the light and there I was, my face transposed over the world whizzing by in a dirt-smudged window. But whose eyes were they, and whose lips? The matted hair at my shoulders. She smiled at me, opened her mouth, waggled her tongue.

The train suddenly pitched to the left, propelling Vasur's body against mine, pinning me to the window. I felt him like a shock. Less than a day had passed since Kalyani teerthum. Immersed in its water, he had wrapped all of me in his arms and held me present, telling me stories of the earth goddess, Bhooma Devi. How she reclined in the pleasures of heaven and yet wanted to know what it felt like to have a fallible heart. How to love. Standing at the edge of Vaikuntha, she had heard the crying of men and women from the violet-blue orb of earth spinning below her. God could not console her. In his munificence, he granted Bhooma Devi one birth in that mortal world, from the soil of a temple garden.

'Stay with me,' Vasur's eyes had said as a universe flowered in my belly, spread tendrils through my veins, grew roots down my limbs. The memory seared into me as the train carried us closer and closer, home to Srivilliputtur, our compartment filled with the thick scents of hessian and sweat, masala and wilted jasmine, and the sharp reek of ammonia every time someone unlatched the urinal door.

'Stay with me.' His voice vibrated through me like strikes of a bell. I listened to his telling of how, long before the earth had even been born, Varaha the boar, an avatar of Tirumal, had rescued Bhooma Devi from the bottom of the ocean, carrying her safely into the light on his tusks. And when Varaha opened his mouth, Bhooma Devi looked inside and saw the creation of the world.

Images of that world played across the tissues of my eyes— mountains of molten lava emerging from the sea, green valleys and silt-rich rivers, drought and flood, chaos masquerading as destiny, layer upon layer of existence spinning from formlessness into form into formlessness—as the train rocked us closer and closer and those storm clouds over the ghats darkened. I saw these things and, instantaneously, their wavering—even Vasur. He was there, of course, but I put my hand on his arm, to feel his warmth, just to make sure.

Chapter Thirty-Two

Andal's wedding party stretched the length of Villiputtur. People flocked to the streets, scattering marigolds in front of the procession so when the petals were trampled the way turned into a mosaic of bright golds and yellows. As Villiputtur's temple tower grew smaller and the tumult of percussion and hundreds of voices faded, Andal fell into the rhythmic sounds around her palanquin, the footsteps of the four men carrying her, the occasional whinny of a horse, the wheels of chariots and bullock carts, and the *thump-thump* of Madurai's royal elephant at the front. King Vallabhadeva, shaded by the brocade of a tasselled umbrella, surveyed the entire procession from his regal throne.

Keeping the Malalaya mountains to their left, they travelled through forests of banyan, ivory wood, and champak. Silk-cotton tree fruits burst open in the midday heat, and Andal drew her curtain an inch to watch them floating like little white clouds. Fields of millet and mustard surrounded every village. They forded streams and followed the willowy course of deeper rivers until they found a safe crossing.

Word preceded them and they were always welcomed. Women squatted in thatched shelters by the side of the road, waiting. 'Cool water,' they called, balancing clay pots on their heads, 'perfumed with blue iris.' They filled the cupped hands of the thirsty party and teased the young servant men, bending a little lower so their round breasts almost spilled from their bodices. For this they received extra betel leaves in payment.

When approaching villages at nightfall, they were given a temple's keys. 'Honoured guests.' The village elders bowed. 'Please shelter here and when you leave, carry our prayers to Srirangam.'

King Vallabhadeva's men pitched a canopy, lining it with carpets and cushions. Visnucitta joined the king for meals. 'Bring your tamboura and sing for us!'

Sirimai was there too, sitting to the side, her head demurely covered, giving the king ample time to coax and flatter her before getting up to dance. Andal stayed in seclusion with her mother, Marali, and Sarvani.

Sometimes the wedding party camped by a river. On the night before Madurai, a troupe of women from a nearby village mimicked bird calls through the banyan forest to announce their presence. They took baskets from their heads and unpacked white-skinned purple-fleshed yams, fresh-speared fish sprinkled with pepper and ginger ready for frying, thorny cucumbers full of juice, and thick yoghurt made from buffalo milk.

'And toddy, fermented from our coconuts.' They winked. 'After feasting, we will dance.'

Varaji swept the ground for them to sit.

'Sarvani, tell Marali better she keep Andal company. Take her these,' she said, plucking a sprig of grapes. 'Make her eat.'

The men sat separately and were served first, dish after dish, until they were satiated. The food was spicy and charcoal sweet. Lit by the flicker of cooking fires, scavenging animal eyes dotted the surrounding forest, their tongues lolling with saliva for fish bones and the blackened skins of yam thrown to the dark. The women cleared the men's leaf plates and plumped their cushions.

'Recline,' they said. 'Digest, smoke your hookahs, talk philosophy, politics, markets.' They left them to it and ate what remained.

The village women took jasmine strings from their baskets and threaded them into every woman's hair. They formed a circle and counted clockwise, each woman given a note. Sa, ri, ga, ma, pa, dha, ni. Sa, ri, ga, ma … Three more were needed to complete three circles. Varaji hesitated, should she call Andal and Marali? It had been too long since she had seen her daughter dance. She looked across at the men engrossed in their talk and too far from their circle to distinguish one woman from another. A hand brushed hers, and she turned to find Sirimai stepping into the circle.

'Akka, I will be the note pa.' She squeezed Varaji's hand. 'Did you think I would miss this?'

Varaji felt herself blushing and thanked the shadows Sirimai did not notice. 'Quickly,' she said to Sarvani, 'bring Andal and Marali.'

Holding their arms in a crab's grip, they circled the fire, leaning in, leaning out, perfuming the air with jasmine as they swung back and forth. Each woman sang her note in turn, taking the octave higher, bringing it to the earth and singing low from their bellies, then starting over.

Breathless and laughing, they moved from the fire. 'Let's dance the Kolattam!' one of the women cried. Pairs of wooden clap sticks were handed out.

'Krishna!' Two perfect syllables called into the night. Varaji glanced across to her daughter. Each time the blue-skinned god's name was sung, she shone like the moon, the women's delight adding to hers. Finally, she was understood and here, on the way to her wedding with Ranganatha, all the verses of her *Tiruppavai* were coming true. Andal crossed her arms side to side, striking the sticks of the women beside her. Sirimai shimmied into the middle, stepping out a circle for Andal, sixteen and at last betrothed. The faster they moved, the more still Andal became, the more joyous her face in the centre of their dance.

&

Talking drums drowned the call of birds, the ripple of streams, the chants of trees, as they neared Madurai, city of pavilions and lotus streets. The king is coming! The king is coming! Women put down their cooking pots, men left buffaloes yoked to their ploughs. But who was the girl? they asked. Is it true what they say? An incarnation of Bhooma Devi? Betrothed to Lord Ranga?

All the clamouring was nothing but a faraway hum to Andal's ears. Even the pleasures of King Vallabhadeva's palace when they arrived—a marble bath of milk, delicacies served on silver platters, her bed of swan down. It was the scent of earth she wanted, its moist furrows sweetened with rain, not the cloy of sandalwood smoke or the precious oils anointing her. How could musk taken from an antelope's navel compare to the pungent green of tulasi?

The next day, a fleet of boats ferried them across Madurai's wide Vaigai River. The procession's horses, bullocks, and even the elephant were tethered to the boats and made to swim. Visnucitta looked back to Madurai's four temple towers, brighter than a monsoon rainbow. They were one third of the way to Srirangam. He was suddenly filled with unease and felt loathe to address it. He caught Sirimai's eye, two chariots ahead, behind the king's elephant. He wanted to believe her assurances. What would happen to his daughter when he gave her away to the greatest god of all? Girls disappeared all the time into the bowels of a temple. She would not survive it. The whole story had grown out of proportion, had taken on a life of its own, and he was more to blame than anyone. His dreams—were they real? Did Lord Ranga really speak to him? The king, however—what did it matter if a king's dream was a little manufactured? His gift of a pearl palanquin was a small price to pay for the stability of a kingdom. Without him heading their procession, it might have been possible to turn back. Even if it meant paddling a boat upstream for the rest of his life. Dreams and myths, the search for love, and the body's desire for it: they were traps and he had walked into every one of them. He watched a servant tug at the nose ring of the last bullock, its black back glistening as it clambered from the river.

Ancient cork trees surrounded Kallalagar's temple. The men were eager to set camp, then bathe in the spring at the foot of the mountain.

'Goddess Rakia is there. Ask anything, she will give it,' one of the servants said as he tensioned a canopy rope. Visnucitta turned to face the temple. If only, if only …

The moon was neither full nor dark and not a pilgrim was in sight. At Visnucitta's request, Kallalagar's priest agreed to open the temple's garbarigha. Andal had only dreamed of seeing the god they called Beautiful One, but as she entered all the excitement was winded from her and she fell to the ground like a bird plummeted to earth. So dark he was, and tall. She felt him above her like a heavy cloud.

'You,' he said, 'crumpled there on the stones, are you ready for Sri Ranga?'

The Beautiful One demanded and questioned, shredding her foolish expectations as if she were nothing but a rag.

'Have I not suffered enough by your hands?' Andal lifted her head and cried a cry that brought tears to her father's eyes, and there was nothing, *nothing*, he could do.

'My hands?' the Beautiful One scoffed. 'It is in your hands!' Andal felt his voice pound inside her head. A fierce gust of wind tunnelled into the garbarigha, extinguishing its one camphor flame. The priest gasped and scrambled in the pitch black for a light.

'When you are absorbed into me, nothing is left. If you fear the darkness you find yourself in now, then better return to your world of fancy.'

Andal felt his blackness and sobbed as the shroud of it swallowed her, but then she felt it swallow her fear too. She was worthy. She knew this as surely as she knew the place where her father had found her, a girl-child born out of the earth.

With all her strength she sat up. 'If your words are true, then my birth is false!'

The priest fumbled and struck again, the camphor hissed into flame and a rat scuttled from the light.

'Appa.' Andal turned to her father. 'Tomorrow, we leave at dawn.'

Their way was lined with tiny lamps. Villagers clamoured for a view of their king, resplendent on his elephant. They sang *bhajans* and pressed melons and bananas into the hands of the accompanying priests. But the girl, where was the girl? they asked, peering into every chariot. When Andal's palanquin appeared, they fell silent. They glimpsed a shadow of her behind pearl embroidered curtains, sitting still and erect, the profile of her face looking straight ahead, her hair piled into a regal knot magnificent as the hump on the back of Shiva's bull.

Chapter Thirty-Three

All my desire burning for a bandit's love—
if I see him I will wrench from their roots these useless breasts
fling them at Govardhana's chest, put an end to this raging fire

Nacciyar Tirumoli 13:8

We walked from the railway station to town, Vasur's bare feet silent on the bitumen, the flip-flopping of my thongs. My thoughts wound like weft round a shuttle, looking for a way in. But what was there to say? A peacock's insistent calling cut through the night. The temple's floodlit gopuram beamed bright as a lighthouse above the dark shadows of mango trees. Scents of hay and cow and fermenting fruit layered the air.

'It is all a divine play,' Vasur had said, somewhere between Rajapalayam and Srivilliputtur, 'between the three qualities binding spirit to each human body.'

He had looked past me into the dark stubble of cotton fields outside our train window, pausing, making sure the words found me.

'Three natures we are having—*sattva*, *raajasa*, and *taamasa*—goodness, passion, and destruction. All are from god, but god himself is not in them and they are not part of him. Always changing, and always god only. So, you please live accordingly, Saisha. Desire nothing but god. Anything else and you will be chained to endless births and deaths.'

Vasur's words made no sense, they bounced here then there, looking for a home. And truthfully, I did not want them, lulled as I was, my desire appeased—temporarily, I knew, but still. What was Vasur trying to do with his words of wisdom? Land me in a place where I had no need of him? I wanted to shake him. He would take my arms and pin them across the dark whorls of hair on his chest. I would melt into him and there would be no passengers, in this carriage of my desires, to witness how he lay me down the length of our green seat ...

I looked up with a start to the woman opposite, oblivious of me or my musings, a silent mantra on her weathered lips, the little boy beside her picking his nose. Oh! I wanted to taunt the god Vasur spoke of, to heckle him, to call his bluff—go on then, have your divine play, take your fill. I looked out the window, calming down into the *clickety-clack* of the train, letting the constancy of the wind rushing through our window play with me instead, cooling my dusty skin, ruffling my tangled hair, until: *all my desire burning for a bandit's love* wove into the rhythm of the train like some capricious homecoming song. Now who is taunting whom? Andal's words teased themselves into the wind, her desire and despairing for a god, and mine for a man, until one last winding of track before the lights of Srivilliputtur came into view.

Vasur stopped at the entrance to town and took a tiny envelope folded from newspaper out of his bag. 'Vibhuti, from Krishnaveni Amma,' he said, 'sacred ash, the one you have already tasted. You keep it for later.' He put it into my hand before slowly tracing three lines across my forehead, his touch filled with heat, a slight trembling in his fingers.

'I am invisibly inking you,' he said, 'your desire for life, fear of death, and whatever ties you to the world. All three Shiva will destroy.' Piercing me with his eyes, Vasur took a step back into the cloud of humming insects caught under Srivilliputtur's first streetlight. There were drops of sweat beading his forehead. I wanted to reach out and wipe them away, but he took another step, the distance between us faltering for the fleetest of moments.

Then, without a word, he took off down a narrow track, disappearing into the darkness and I stood there, the moist residue of his fingers turning cold. How I wanted to follow him, but he had made it clear I should not.

Buses careered down Thirumangalam Road and across South Car Street. Butterfly wings beat fast in my stomach. Andal's temple garden was still open and her silver-rimmed eyes too, her image as primeval as earth, solid as stone.

My mind is lost but he utters nothing, not even, 'Have no fear'.

Bhavati would be home, her chanting of Tirumal's thousand names finished. I stood stymied at the crossroads. Temple garden or my rooftop refuge in Bhavati's house? I turned right then left, then left again, reached up and took the key from its hiding place, and unlocked the gate.

'Saisha, you are home. Come! Are you hungry?

Sit!' she said, turning on the fan.

I looked across the room to the curtains draping the entrance of Bhavati's shrine room. 'May I go in?'

Bhavati swam her head, turned the gas down under a kettle of rice, and joined me.

A faint remnant of perfume pervaded the air—Andal's garland, its dried flowers, the tulasi leaves crinkled. *Do just this,* Andal sang, *place his sacred garland cool on my body.* It had been given to me on one of those days when you expect nothing, then the whole world falls into your lap. The priests were on their way from shrine to shrine, the morning's rituals almost finished, and there I was contentedly cross-legged in her garden.

Every morning, the same cycle of offering begins again. After the door to Andal's shrine is first opened, the temple's cow milked, and Jaya Malika has raised her trunk then bowed at her feet, a fresh woven garland is given to their goddess. The flowers she had worn the day before and through the night are then wrapped in a damp cloth and carried on the head of a priest to the inner shrine of Tirumal and offered to him, just as he had asked of her—Choodi K Kodutta—a thousand years ago. And now the priests were returning with the garland that Tirumal, all of him—Vatapatra sayee, Lord Ranga, Krishna—had enjoyed wearing, its scent infused with the perfume of their queen. With a smile and small flourish, the priest placed Andal's worn garland into my arms: dense woven tulasi leaves between bands of velvet wine-dark petals and white mullai buds tipped pink. The weight of it was luscious in my lap. Filled with tenderness, I carried it to Bhavati's house and offered it to her.

We lit one lamp together and sat, the scent of Bhavati's steaming rice wafting in, the night's street noise fading to a hum. Bhavati's soft chanting, *Aum Srim Srim Kodaiyai Namaha*, washed through and through me until I felt a pooling of water behind my closed eyelids. I saw Roshina's daughter—Kodai— her wide hazel-flecked eyes full of wonder. I felt the feather touch again of her small hand in mine, curiously familiar. My heart whirred. Then my hand was empty again.

Empty.

Waves of warmth slow-rippled through my body as if lulling the grasping that was rising in me, and in its place I felt an ocean of gathering clouds. Through them surged a four-masted bach, its sails billowing, and at the helm my father, his hair gingered gold. When he was alive, he was more at sea than he was at home. Strange, he should come to me now with that blue eagle tattooed across his chest. How I would run into his arms when he strode through our front door and he'd lift me up into its unfurled wings.

He reached out to me over the milky water and I wanted

more than anything to feel his hand on my cheek. But instead, he bent low, took a thread hanging loose at the hem of my skirt and gently pulled. I turned with it as it unravelled, my feet swivelling, my body balancing on the smooth back of a giant mythic tortoise. Thread by thread I am undone until nothing of me is left. The tortoise dived into the deep and a woman emerged through the ripples left in its wake. She had long curls of raven hair and skin the rich red colour of earth. She dipped her hand into the milky sea and took a sip before calling to the eagle on my father's chest. *'My father, Visnucitta, heard the Lord of Srirangam's promise. "Love me and I will love you in return."'* She moved closer and whispered into the eagle's ear. *'"Nothing else is worthy of belief."'*

I opened my eyes to the leaves and flowers of Andal's garland in front of us, trying to make sense of that flood of images. The woman appearing out of the waves, was she Andal or was she Bhooma Devi, or do they inhabit the same body? And my father? I was seventeen when he took the pipe from his mouth the night before he died. 'Be true to yourself, Saisha,' he had said. I didn't know he wouldn't be there the next day and these words were for that reason. They were the only words of his I remembered, and the eagle on his chest, etched one drunken night at some Mediterranean port before I was born. Those mythic wings spread across his fair skin, a man with sea in his blood, who sailed the world, who could fly from death back to life to protect a daughter.

Two truths—a whispered promise and my father's last words—one from a god and the other from a man. They felt linked, like a circle. I searched the garland draped around the framed print of Andal, as if it held the key to joining them. We pressed our foreheads into its papery petals. The flame of the lamp flickered high then low.

Every morning the same circular path is taken, the garland worn by Andal offered again, and again, her fragrance abiding through myth and time, from celestial realms to a small garden pavilion. Watching the play of lamplight and shadows across the face of a goddess, I brushed my fingers over the faint imprints of her flowers on my forehead. Truth is truth, she said, smiling, and there really is only one. Its source is love. But there is one difference too. The gods need do nothing while earthborn ones have a choice. It is up to you what is made of the life you are given.

❧

I knew, when tomorrow came, that I would go to the banyan tree where Vasur sheltered. I also knew he would not be there. A longing welled inside me, too impossibly deep to be bearable, and yet there I was in a body that kept on breathing, its five senses transmitting my place in the world. Those three lines he had traced across my brow? Maybe they were nothing more than a map to being. 'Anything else and you will be chained to endless births and deaths.'

Bhavati had once told me how she could not bear her husband's advances—her only desire was for Andal—but she did, she said with tears in her eyes, it was a wife's duty. I wanted to be as honest, to say how much I had struggled with celibacy. All the years I yearned for more than Marcus was willing to give, or was capable of giving. I wanted to tell her on this night how profound it had been with Vasur. But it seemed an admission of frailty, of being less than perfect in the eyes of a friend, and of a goddess. Of wanting less than god. Oh! But it was the truth.

'Andal is seeing god in everything,' Bhavati said as she extinguished the lamp's flame with a sweep of her hand, '... in you also.'

As we sat over our leaf plates, I told Bhavati about meeting Vasur's daughter Roshina, and that she had a daughter and her name was Kodai.

Bhavati's eyes lit up at the sound of those two syllables.

'Kodai!' she said. 'It is Andal's birth name and is having many meanings—gift from the earth, the one with beautiful hair, a garland of flowers. Meaning of Andal is one only: she who rules, because the lord refused any flowers without her presence inside them. It is a name for a queen. For a goddess.'

Kodai—she was Andal and she was also Roshina's daughter. Vasur's granddaughter. Bhavati waited, watching me. I let the sound of Kodai's name settle inside me.

'And Vasur, was he happy?'

'Yes, he was, it seemed, but there was distance too.' I paused, prickles of foreboding under my skin, disbelieving for a moment what had happened between us, and then meeting his family, all of this just hours ago.

I told her about Krishnaveni, how I had swallowed the ash she had given me with the assurance soon I will have children. Bhavati raised an eyebrow and we both laughed, for the relief of a few seconds, the fan whirring above us, wicking away Panguni's sticky heat, its festooned streets and fertility rituals, marriages made in astrologers' heavens.

'But something happened, Saisha, between you and Vasur?' Bhavati entwined her fingers and pressed them to her breast. 'I am thinking this tonight as soon as I saw you.'

'Yes,' I said, blushing like a teenage girl, eyes pinned to the remains of the rice on my banana leaf.

'Kamadeva's arrow was finding you. Having love—like medicine, isn't it? Maybe one time is all you are needing, then the key will be fitting. The door opening.'

The curtains to Bhavati's shrine room wavered in the briefest of cool breezes blowing in from the street.

&

I slept through dawn, through Jaya Malika's loping up the stairs to Andal's shrine, the milking of the cow, and the procession of Andal's worn garland carried on a priest's head, down the temple arcade, past her garden to the inner sanctum of the storm cloud-hued one. I slept deep and dreamless till the sun hit the roof of my room and I began to sweat.

There were autos on the street waiting for a fare, but I wanted to walk to Thirumukkulam, to feel those three kilometres solid under my feet, dependable, even if there were eyes of strangers peering at me from their dark corridors and latticed verandahs, generations of lives as usual, a certain certainty wrapped in their laws of karma and the will of their gods. I was just a foreigner to them, a passing cloud, an oddity escaped from her zoo, nothing more really, in their days, than a distraction. I stopped for a coconut water, the *thwack* of the wallah's machete disturbing a cloud of drunken flies from the spiny split skin of a jackfruit on his table. *Thwack!* jolting the *thud thud* of my heart. I shooed a fly from the tip of my plastic straw and drank.

I stopped at Krishna's Internet Cafe and booted up one of the two computers, 'in excellent working order'. It clunked to life like a tired horse. I pressed *receive* on my internet server and a page of closed envelopes filled the flickering screen. I had neither the inclination or fortitude to open any of them, even the two from Marcus sent since I checked three weeks ago.

I should write to him, but not today.

I typed in Roshina's address and sent my greetings. 'I am on my way to see your father,' I said. 'Did he tell you where he was staying in Srivilliputtur—under a huge banyan tree near Thirumukkulam?' I visualised him still sitting there. And wondered about the chances of a reply from Roshina. I was never sure in those days how reliable computers were in these dodgy cafes, especially one called Krishna, the most mischievous god of all. I pressed send before any chance of a power cut or viral invasion.

Tiny birds skittered in the thorn trees on the outskirts of town. Thirumukkulam's teerthum was a glassy blue, the boy's cricket pitch half-submerged. The first proper rain had fallen while I slept. Water now lapped at the base of the small pavilion in the middle. There was the *slap slap* of women washing laundry on its steps, and squatting at the water's edge on the other side I saw a lone woman dressed in red. I kept on, to the rusty gate into the dairy and its grove of trees. There was laziness in the air, cud-chewing cows ambling between patches of shade and three wiry old men sitting on a porch smoking beedis. I waved. One of them got up and came toward me, shaking his hand above his head and toward the gate. I had played the scene out already and knew this was no signal I should go, he was telling me Vasur was the one who had gone. Where? I asked with upturned hands. He swam his head and to make sure I understood led me to the tree and pulled the hessian curtain aside—the dappled light, the makeshift shelf balanced in a tangle of vines, and nothing there of the little Vasur possessed. Inside and outside around the fire pit, not one fallen leaf or print of a bird. Vasur, the old man seemed to be saying, had swept before he left. I looked at the crescent strokes of dirt and imagined his firm grip round the broom's woven handle, his lithe body bending, circling the banyan's roots. I looked up into the spread-eagled branches of heart-shaped leaves, and could have wept, but didn't. The old man wandered off and I took the broom of twigs from where it leaned near the entrance and swept my footprints away. As if it were that easy.

The day was so still, the laughter of the women like some foreign song as they beat their soapy clothes on the stone steps. I did not know which way to go. To keep walking toward the mountains, take the first bus to Kattalagar? I knew the way, but every broken tree would remind me, every waterfall. I turned toward town. There was a small temple on the other side of the teerthum and I remembered one Margazhi morning, squashed in a sea of women, singing Andal's *Tiruppavai*. The priests had given us a prasadam of grapes, apples, bananas, and oranges all mushed together. Bees hovered above our heads as the sweet, sticky juices ran through our fingers and down our arms. How naive my delight and wonder then, the myth of Andal's life and her thirty profound songs—everything was Andal and I had superimposed her seemingly innocent love onto mine.

The teerthum's whitewashed walls shone in the late morning sun. The woman I had seen on my way to the dairy was still squatted at the edge. As I came closer, I recognised the faded red of her clothes and the bangles covering both forearms, her ropes of matted hair dangling in the water. Lalitha. I climbed down the steps and sat a few feet away, her presence, like every other time, triggering a shiver of fear down my back, and intrigue too, strong as the pull of a magnet. I kept quiet as if approaching a wild animal, not wanting her to run but neither to face me with those searing eyes. I needn't have worried; she was mesmerised, gazing into the water at her feet, cupping her hands into it and drawing them up, staring intently into her palms until all of it had drained away. Then she returned her gaze to the water before trailing her fingers across the surface. The ripples she made circled out and eventually lapped at my toes. I looked down at them and there, inches away, was *my* face settling clear as a mirror as the ripples subsided.

Lalitha hummed a kind of laugh, the sound a woman might make when caressed by a lover, and I turned to see her, her eyes closed, chin tilted up, rapture soft on her cheeks and in the turn of her lips. Then I saw what she was feeling. It was the play of light. Shimmering and rippling, reflecting, refracting. Mirrorings of sun and water dancing across her face. A game of hide-and-seek, of a god's wooing, at once tangible, then intangible; never predictable. Lalitha in a prism of sunbeams, her existence as ephemeral as forever is infinite.

'Divine play,' Vasur had said, simple as that. I let the tears come and watched them *plink plink* into Thirumukkulam's water. Tiny whirlpools for a fraction of a second spun with light.

❧

Day two, day three, then the next and the next. The rituals and routines of temple and town slowly lulled my heart back to shape. But still, on my way to the temple from Bhavati's house where the road turned right to Thirumukkulam, my heart missed a beat and my body wanted to go that way, but my mind knew better. Vasur was gone.

Panguni celebrations had notched up now the moon was waxing. I glimpsed chariots queued in the wings, a swan, a prancing horse, an elephant, a mythic mountain, all of them hand-beaten and polished to gold except the wooden skeleton of one. In a few days, there would be men ankle-deep in flowers, weaving garlands over its frame and tying hundreds of strings of jasmine buds into curtains for their queen. A palanquin for Andal's wedding day.

Three months had barely passed since my first time alone in Srivilliputtur. I had fallen into Margazhi's rituals and pageants, its unashamed theatre lush with flowers and jewels and fancy dress. I had almost drowned in them. Perhaps there were moments when I did. I had revelled in my fight for freedom too, but skated on, assured, knowing there was someone across two oceans thinking of me, needing me. I was alone, but at the end of the day I wasn't.

And love? *Caress my body and soul*—weren't these the very first words of Andal's I had read? If she commanded her chariot bearers to stop and through those jasmine curtains asked of me, the foreigner, what about love, what would I say now?

I had seen Lalitha only once since our encounter on Thirumukkulam's steps, ten days later near the temple walls. Her feet scuffing the dirt, the sway of her hips, her whole being intent on a kind of communion with whomever was listening. She stooped to pick up a marigold most likely dropped from a procession and held it above her head, lips moving.

One flower or the *one hundred vessels of fresh churned butter and one hundred vessels of sweet rice pudding* Andal offered. When a heart draws no boundaries over the life it is given, maybe offering one flower, or having one encounter, is enough.

Or perhaps Lalitha, in her prism, felt the gentle rain of a hundred thousand flowers covering the earth. I stood there

watching her, imagining, then walked to the end of the temple
wall and turned left to the dusty screens of Krishna's Internet
Cafe.

Dear Marcus, I was composing in my head as I entered its
doors. It has been an intense few weeks. I'm sorry I haven't
written but you know what it can be like here. Everything going
out the window …

Still considering what I needed to say and how to say it, I
pressed *receive*. Roshina's name bounced onto the screen three
times. Her first email sent the day I had first written to her, the
day Vasur left, ten days ago.

Greetings Saisha Akka,

We usually call elder person as akka, so can I call you
Akka? Thank you for your mail. How are you? Appa told me
Andal is the reason you come to India. I am also first seeing
Goddess Andal every morning. Now I am seeing you too,
Akka, and I am happy Appa knows you. You are welcome to
my home. Please come. Kodai is asking too. I conveyed your
email to my husband and he is giving his welcome. His work
is in the French Institute at Pondicherry. Technical adviser.
Did my father tell you there is a statue of Andal there? She is
ancient and beautiful. We will go together one day. But you
are in Srivilliputtur itself! By Andal's grace only, I am
thinking. My husband is asking why you have a French name
when you come from Australia? I am praying to Goddess
Andal we shall meet again.

With sweet regards, Roshina

I clicked on the second mail, sent a week later.

Dearest Saisha Akka,

Tonight, I am taking a train to Sivakasi. Maybe you have
news already? Appa is in hospital. They called me. He was
found collapsed on the road near Watrap by one kindly

person who took him to Sivakasi public hospital. Luckily, Appa must have kept my home number with his possessions, otherwise ... with no family member a hospital cannot admit the patient. I am really worried, Akka. Please reply.

A pop-up Rambo character took over half the screen, the limp body of a woman over his shoulder, a sword in his hand. I felt sick. I pressed escape, delete, escape, but the screen was jammed.

'Another computer?' I called to the boy at the front, the broken wheels of my chair scraping like chalk on slate. He dragged his eyes away from whatever game he was playing to point to a desk at the back of the room. My hands went clammy as I waited for it to boot up, then waited another eternity for connection. Watrap—Marcus and I had stopped there with the professor on our way to Chathuragiri. That must have been where Vasur was headed. And Sivakasi. I had passed through it many times on a train. It was not far from Srivilliputtur. An hour at the most.

I opened Roshina's third mail, sent the night before.

Dear Saisha Akka,

I am trying one more time. Please if you can come. Appa is very poorly. Some septicaemia, the doctor says. Maybe from kidneys. Yesterday I am arriving. At first, he did not recognise me. He has high fever and just now they are giving him drip. So many patients crowding the room and only one doctor coming. I brought some food parcels but he is refusing. At least I can bath him and bring clean bedsheets. Please come, Akka. Please.

Chapter Thirty-Four

Indra and all the celestials arrived
they chanted sacred verses, blessed me as bride,
Anthari draped me in wedding silk and flowers
this vision I dreamed, my friend

Nacciyar Tirumoli 6:3

A cool breeze rippled the Kavery River. Visnucitta took his shawl and wrapped it around Andal. Tomorrow they would cross to Srirangam.

He pointed upstream to the Sahyas mountains. 'Lord Tirumal stands on the highest peak, a mace in one of his right hands, to protect all the life he is creating and a spinning discus in the other because that is the cyclic nature of existence.'

Visnucitta dipped his fingers into the water, then lightly touched Andal's forehead. 'In his left hands he holds the conch, Panchanjaya. When he puts it to his lips, life is breathed into the world. On the tip of his other index finger sits a lotus, and there at its centre rests the cosmos. Honey streams from the soles of his feet.'

Visnucitta paused, a faint qualm in his throat, wondering if Andal had already escaped his arms, no longer needing his stories, needing him. But she took his hand and held it tight.

'Go on, Appa.'

'This honey is the source of the Kavery River and that is why its water tastes sweet. There are others who say the Kavery is the Viraja River of Vaikuntha. Heaven, Andal, we are about to cross over heaven.'

Srirangam's seven temple towers rose up from the island's orchards and pleasure gardens, hundreds of lamp flames flickering to life inside them. They heard King Vallabhadeva's elephant trumpeting downriver and laughed when they saw him spraying the mahouts. The men lay him down in the mud and he groaned as they massaged him, twirling his trunk in the air, spraying them again if they stopped. The men were soaked and happy. They had journeyed long days to be here and the air was festive.

'Andal, my darling, cover your head.' Varaji joined them on the banks of the river, lifting her daughter's veil over her curls and drawing it down to her chin. The fine muslin covering Andal's eyes turned the river into a mirage and the towers into the wings of swans. 'Oh, but Amma, I want to see.'

'Soon enough,' Varaji said, sadness edging her voice, 'soon enough.'

Letting the river lap their feet, they watched the sky changing, a bank of clouds gathering in the west, saffron, then magenta, then indigo, until night took them into her belly.

Ginger and chilli sizzled the air. Varaji heard her name called to the fire.

'Can we stay a while longer, Appa?'

Visnucitta took her head and rested it on his shoulder, lifting her veil with a cheeky smile. 'What use are stars if they can't be bright? See those twelve stars just above the horizon?'

She followed his eyes, scanning the sky. 'I can see four in a triangle.'

'That's the head, Andal. Now look to the left, see its body flexing like a fish, then the whiplash of its tail.'

'Is it Makara, the crocodile?'

Visnucitta nodded. 'Let me listen to you telling his story.'

So she sang to him, pinching the lobes of her ears to reach the right notes. In less than one turn of earth, she would be lying in the arms of the lord who wears crocodile earrings, Makara's looped tail brushing her cheek.

'For a thousand years, Gajendra the elephant struggled to free himself from Makara's jaws. Both of them, Gajendra and Makara, were once upon a time great kings, but they suffered from ego and enmity and so were born as elephant and crocodile in the muddy waters of samsara where lives are lived over and over. Close to death, Gajendra finally surrendered. He held one lotus flower high with his trunk and cried, "Lord Tirumal, only if it be your will, save me." With one strike of Tirumal's discus, Makara's head was severed. Because of Makara's deed, Gajendra was liberated. And so, Tirumal liberated Makara too! Do you see, Appa? Even cruelty can be cause for liberation.'

'Yes, my daughter, liberation has its price, no matter the time it takes. A thousand years, or just sixteen.' He paused, turning toward her. 'I know it has not been easy for you, Andal, but ...' The words he wanted to say caught in his throat ... that he had watched her unerring devotion grow since the day he had found her. Visnucitta looked away, his eyes following the river, the river flowing to the sea. He brushed the tears from his face and tried to gather himself.

Andal tugged at his arm, finishing the sentence for him. 'But now look where we are, and Lord Ranga, on the other side of the river.'

Andal listened to the cheerful sounds of her wedding party having their sunrise bath. Mud velveted her toes. Sarvani and Marali stood either side, shielding her from wandering eyes. She heard her father's prayers asking for forgiveness and for all three troubles to be removed—difficulties caused by one's own ignorance or the ignorance of others or because it was the will of god. She submerged herself three times before taking a sip from the river. It was true. She tasted honey.

By the time their prayers were finished, the men had loaded the ferry boats, and as the wedding party drew close to Srirangam, Andal saw through her veil an entourage of priests waiting for them. Salutations were made, first to the king, who was then whisked away.

A priest led the wedding party to a pavilion on the banks of a bend in the river. 'Here you wait for the temple astrologer's conch call, tomorrow, when the moon's ripening is imminent.'

'The girl,' Andal overheard him say to her father, 'should remain in seclusion. A room has been prepared for her.'

Even Varaji was not allowed. But she was never far away. If not sitting outside Andal's door, she was in the kitchen warming milk, sweetening it with molasses, or grinding coconut flesh into cream and sliding cups through the grilles of Andal's window. For the sake of her mother, Andal tried to drink whatever she was brought even though it made her stomach churn. One of the servant women brought a jackfruit from the market and started to split it open. A sound of retching came through the grilles of Andal's window and Varaji, beside herself, berated the woman to take it away.

Poor Amma, Andal thought, how she wished Varaji could know what she knew. Soon her mother's body would start to swell. Perhaps all the nausea she was feeling was nothing more than saving her mother from suffering it? Sri Laksmi had promised Andal, the day she and her mother bathed, just the two of them at Thirumukkulam. And if Varaji's wish was not fulfilled, why then, she, Andal, would soon be as an equal, wife and consort to the lord. She would scold Goddess Laksmi for telling tales, then make things right herself.

Alone, Andal sat with her thoughts. The day took forever and night's slow, torturous minutes were not much better. Varaji slid another cup of warm milk through the window. 'Let the sound of the river dividing heaven and earth lull you to sleep.'

But sleep refused Andal. Her legs were restless, her feet, if ever they stilled, soon itched from swarms of invisible insects with tiny feathered legs. She paced the room until the moon crept in, then she sat in its path, letting it move cool and soft through her body. When the moon left, she lay down and listened to the river, her mind emptying into it, and she stayed like this, without thought or form, and flooded with light.

Not a breath of wind disturbed the surface of the river as Varaji and Sirimai led Andal to the steps of the pavilion. Sarvani and Marali followed. Behind them, the wives of Srirangam's five sages carried vessels of herbs and spices, resins, oils and unguents for her bath. Chanting sacred verses, they began preparing Andal for her wedding.

The first of the five wives stepped forward to loosen the muslin wrapped around Andal's body. It was still dark, but Andal felt the whole world bearing witness to her nakedness. She drew her hair across her breasts, but the second wife took her hands away.

'Do nothing,' she said, gently gathering Andal's curls into a knot on top of her head.

Marali poured sesame oil into the first wife's cupped hands. She trickled it over Andal's skin in tiny rivers. The second wife massaged Andal with a paste of turmeric and gooseberries, her face, neck, and shoulders, down to the small of her back, turning her round, circling her navel, massaging her legs. Andal felt the world turning too as the first rays of sun tinged a fleet of clouds gold, and the same light played shadow games with the lapping of the river near Andal's feet. The gooseberries tightened and tingled her skin and the scent of turmeric, like fresh ploughed earth, infused every cell of her body. She felt more alive than ever, as if this last day on earth was her first.

The third of the five wives drew water from the river, adding an equal amount of rosewater for every pitcher. The fourth wife held a wide sieve made of brass high above Andal's head and the third wife slowly poured the river water and rosewater into it. Andal felt every drop on her skin, she heard every tiny splash onto the stones at her feet. The first wife dipped a neem twig into fine white rice powder and carefully polished Andal's teeth. Then she took a pinch of cinnamon and clove powder and brushed her tongue. The second wife warmed musk-scented *punugu* oil between her palms and untangled Andal's hair with her fingers. They led her inside to the coals of a fire where the dark resin of eaglewood was melting and with a fine ivory comb dried Andal's curls over its aromatic smoke.

As the sun rose, the shadows of the pavilion columns grew shorter and the stones warmer. Sarvani and Marali took white whisks made from yak tails to fan Andal as the fifth wife stepped forward to anoint her with sandal paste. It was cool and fragrant as the air of the Malayan forest, and yet, Andal felt her body start to burn, her legs tremble.

'She cannot drink until after the ceremony.' She heard the words as if from miles away.

'Sit her down. Lord knows how she is to survive this.' Was it Amma? She felt the familiar touch of a hand on her forehead.

'Take a breath … now take another.'

'My flower,' said another voice. A paste of saffron was pressed over her breasts.

Andal opened her eyes to the circle of women around her. More had gathered at the pavilion entrance, intonations of Tirumal on their lips, over and over. It was all a dream, Andal thought, looking down at her golden skin, to her little plum breasts, her tiny waist. 'Like a bamboo stalk,' Marali, never afraid of telling the truth, had once joked. Her wrists still slender enough for threading on child-size bangles, her ribs poking out like some ancient fretted instrument. But she was glowing, her skin smooth and creamy as butter, and she was breathing again.

With a shimmy of bells, Sirimai approached. 'There you are, bride-to-be, returned to us.' She gave Andal's cheeks a little pinch. 'Wait till you see what the king has gifted for you to wear.'

Andal returned Sirimai's smile, even though she sensed hesitation in it.

She took the hands of the most beautiful of all temple consorts and lightly squeezed them, reassuring whatever doubt it was flashing across her worldly face.

'I am ready.'

Chapter Thirty-Five

*Have you seen my Dark Lord? I am nothing but a plaything to him
the noose of his cool lotus eyes pulls me hither and thither.
Yes, we did, cavorting in Vrindavan, that mighty elephant calf
beads of sweat covering his body like a coat of pearls*

Nacciyar Tirumoli 14:4

Casuarina trees lined the entrance to Sivakasi's hospital, their
bruised needles carpeting its driveway. In the midday heat, the
scent of its leaves was oddly familiar, of sand dunes and heath,
the salty air of a place I had once called home. In a few hours,
like most other thresholds in India, the leaves would be swept
away. Again. What was the point?

What was the point of holding tight to anything?

The hour the bus took from Srivilliputtur had been an eternity of ear-splitting Bollywood and a rage of lip-chafing, hair-
tangling wind through every window. There was no point
emailing Roshina when buses left every ten minutes, but as I
climbed the hospital steps, I realised I did not know Vasur's last

name. Corridors spilled in every direction from the front counter. There were people on the floor, on crutches, in wheelchairs, and crushed toward the two unperturbed nurses at reception. It was chaotic as a railway station. I pushed and elbowed my way in like everyone else.

'Name please.'

'Vasur. I need to see a man called Vasur.'

'The surname, madam?'

'He is having a fever. Some septicaemia.'

'Last name, please.' She swam her head, all the time in the world, and I had none. Round and round we went. I pressed for the ward where he might be staying. I pleaded. The nurses conferred. 'It is not possible unless registering with patient's last name. Sorry, madam. Hospital policy.'

I dropped my forehead into my hands, felt the welling of tears, sweat trickling down my back. The two women squeezed either side of me seized their chance, and with a deluge of Tamil I was returned to the injured and the resigned. It was nothing personal; I was as much a casualty as anyone else. I slumped down the back wall, curling myself into a ball to wait it out, for some strength to surface, a miracle. Vasur had plainly walked from my life, yet here I was. I buried my pounding head … *the noose of his lotus eyes,* my tangled thoughts, bracing myself against the hospital's bedlam, waves of the afflicted and urgent visitors, their constant coming and going, their clamouring voices.

'Excuse me, madam.' The end of a braid glossy with coconut oil brushed my knee. The second nurse was bending down, her soft voice at my ear. 'You can try Ward 10, to the left side.' She pointed. 'Maybe he is there.'

I straightened myself, my dupatta, my tear-streaked face. The corridor was lined with stretchers, the air bleached. Ward 10. I swung through the doors to a cavernous room with two long rows of iron beds, each one shrouded in mosquito netting. Family members sat cross-legged on the beds and floor with tiffin tins of food set out like picnics, every clang of metal on metal and moan of pain amplified by the concrete floor and walls and tin roof. The reckless spinning of ceiling fans billowed each bed's net like the sail of a boat tossed toward a storm. Vasur, Vasur, I chanted under my breath. Please be here. Eyes followed me as I walked down the row of beds. I felt caught in the vacuum of their stares and started to panic. Caught in a net. One of those butterflies Vasur had described in the forest of Kattalagar, its red body and black wings beating toward light. We never did see one. They are rare now, he had said, possibly extinct.

Vasur, where are you?

Only one bed was empty, stripped of sheets. I sat down on the cracked vinyl of its mattress, knowing with dogged certainty that Vasur had been there. I called his name.

The man on the next bed turned his rheumy eyes in my direction and waved toward the door. 'Night time leaving,' he said. 'Lady with small girl coming after.'

I ran my fingers over the bare pillow, willing him back. How, if Vasur had been found collapsed on a road, would he, so soon, be capable of going anywhere? Where was Roshina and what should I do now? I watched the fan spinning above my head, my limbs heavy as rock, my mind in a fever.

'*Puviyeerppu* is the word for gravity,' Vasur had once explained as we sat under the banyan's leaves. Why now this Tamil word in my ear? '*Puvi,* meaning earth and *eerpu,*' he had said playfully, 'is meaning attraction.' Then he told me how gravity in South India is less than anywhere else on earth. 'You are lighter here,' he said. 'Less *eerpu* to enslave you.'

Get up, I told myself.

Through the louvres of a window, I caught the flash of a white-breasted bird settling on the high branch of a tree in the hospital grounds. I strained to hear its song above the sounds of the ward. It was a bulbul, wearing a crown of jet-black feathers. The professor had pointed one out to me in the lantana of

Chathuragiri's foothills, the splash of deep-red under its eyes and tail. '*Keek keek-pettigruu*,' he mimicked. 'He is saying, "pleased to meet you".'

There was a nest of twigs in a fork below. A child's hand reached up into the periphery of my vision—a girl standing on tiptoes, two ribboned plaits tossed behind her back. She had seen the nest too and was calling to the couple a few steps away, a man I had not seen before, his arms around the woman —Roshina.

Little Kodai tugged at her mother's sari as I ran toward them. 'Amma, look, *Periamma* is here!' She peeped out from behind the man's legs as Roshina and I embraced. In between our tumbling of words, she introduced me to her husband Adithya. His eyes were the same hazel as Kodai's.

'Please don't worry.' He took my hand firmly in his. 'We will find him. I arrived now only and have a car for us.'

'But how, Adithya? Appa left here hours ago. The doctor warned me …' Roshina's voice trailed off. She bit the flesh of her hand. 'Appa took out the drip, and left all his belongings behind. He could be anywhere.'

Anywhere, anywhere. The bulbul above us continued its singing.

I took a risk. 'Do you know Chathuragiri?' I asked Adithya. 'Is it possible we can drive there?'

He looked from me to Roshina and she nodded. My heart raced.

'If Vasur was picked up at Watrap, then Chathuragiri must have been where he was headed. Watrap is the last town before its foothills,' I explained, remembering the clarity in Vasur's eyes when speaking about his months in those forests and the old siddhar who had taken him under his wing.

❧

Kodai nestled between Roshina and me in the back seat. Adithya sat in front with the driver. I recalled as much as possible of my conversations with Vasur: his years with Mootai Swami and the six months at Chathuragiri.

'More than twelve years ago he left,' Roshina's voice trembled. 'It was my first year at college and I was living with an aunty. Appa didn't even say goodbye.'

What I had told her was scant, but it was something at least, to fill the chasm left in the wake of a mother dying and a father disappearing.

'Then we met.' Roshina put her hand on Adithya's shoulder. He lay his palm over her fingers.

'And Kodai came like a gift, didn't she?' he said.

At the sound of her name, Kodai peeled her gaze from the world rushing by, insistence in her voice. 'Periamma is taking us to him, isn't she?'

Roshina's sadness dispelled for a moment. 'She is calling you Periamma—the meaning is aunty.'

Kodai bounded onto my lap and pressed her nose against the half-opened window, her excitement tempering our fears, just a little. 'When are we going to see him, Appa?' Adithya reached across to tuck the loosed strands of his daughter's hair behind her ears.

We lapsed into silence, all of us looking out at the patchwork of muddy fields. At every lone figure we passed on the side of the road, Adithya asked the driver to slow, and each time—no, it was not Vasur—to speed up again.

Adithya's English was different from other Tamils. His vowels were softer and it was not as clipped. I looked at his hand still holding Roshina's. His skin was lighter.

The car swerved around potholes and clunked over corrugations in the bitumen. It was a vintage Ambassador and so were its shock absorbers. It was better to stay loose than seize up and we bounced around the cabin like four rag dolls while the driver kept an iron grip on the wheel.

We stopped for fuel at a village called Mulli. It sounded like Mullai when Adithya pronounced it. 'Mullai,' on the lips of garland sellers at Andal's temple gates, their strings of sweet-scented creamy buds that every woman threads through her hair. I looked for signs of it but all I smelled was petrol and burning rubbish. Adithya and I waited beside the car while Roshina took Kodai to find a toilet.

'Your accent, it's unusual,' I said.

Standing a head taller than most Tamil men, Adithya took the cigarette from his mouth, blowing the smoke away from me into the wind. 'My father was French,' he said, fixing his eyes to the other side of the road where a cow sat in a sliver of shade. 'He met my mother in an ashram in Pondicherry. They lived together but never married. He would come and go from France. He took my mother and me there when I was five, to a small village near Toulouse where his parents lived. You might say they adopted me. My father was an only child, so I was it. Without me, their name dies.' He drew in another breath of smoke and looked up into the hazy blue of a Tamil afternoon. 'Adithya Didier. I used to lie in bed under those different stars in that different world putting those two names together. They made sense from the very beginning. France is my home as much as India.' He tapped the cigarette's ash into the wind. 'We return there most years. Roshina is not sure about it, yet. As for Kodai, six years old and she spans the world as if born to it, switching from Tamil to English to French like a true linguist.' Adithya took one last inhale before stubbing his cigarette with the heel of his leather sandal. 'And what about you, Saisha?'

Perhaps it was the combination of nicotine and diesel. I felt giddy and leaned against the car for balance. In my grandmother's photo album—that hint of laughter on her face all those years ago, and me cocooned in her arms—the mountain behind us was less than an hour's drive from Toulouse. Her sepia eyes steadied into mine. She may as well have been standing there with us, her lace-up boots coated with Mulli's dust. *Saissa de Congost.*

You will be Saisha, my mother wrote in the christening card she had taped onto the opposite page. I give you your grand-mother's name but with one letter of difference. There are those, like your ancestors, who walked through fire for love and others, like your mama, who cross oceans. May you be blessed in choosing what is right for you.

I heard my name called and looked up to see Roshina and Kodai on the other side of the road, Kodai waving a bottle of GoldiSpot and a packet of masala crisps. Intensely present one moment, lost in imagination the next; the lot of a child, bubbling and pooling like a mountain spring, all of life at her fingertips, the winding river ahead inconsequential. Skipping impatiently at the kerb, waiting for the last car to pass, Kodai tugged at her mother's hand. Out of time, my own mother's voice came streaming toward me, the haunting of her lullaby words weaving into the songs of cicadas. *Cara ma filha,* she used to whisper in the old language of Occitan. *Non oblides pas jamai, l'ostal ont son nascuts ta maire, la maire de ta maire e totes los que las an davançadas*—my darling, never forget the house where your mama was born and your grandmama and all your ances-tors before her.

Adithya's hand was on my shoulder. 'Saisha, are you okay?'

I sank into the leather of the back seat, grateful our conver-sation had been cut short. The seeming collision of our pasts was too much coincidence, too much to take in. Yet here I was, speeding toward the jungles of Chathuragiri with Vasur's family. With every kilometre, he felt palpably closer, or was this just hope masquerading? Did he even want to be found? I wound my window down all the way, lay my arm against the cool steel of the Ambassador's body.

'Watrap will take another half-hour, then the foothills of Chathuragiri ten kilometres more,' Adithya translated the driver's estimates.

Time and space reduced to numbers so we can more easily navigate, but what would happen when we arrived? My heart started its racing again. Desire again, like a raining of arrows in the dark. And Roshina? Her blood ran deeper. Her sadness bled into me, but there was nowhere for it take hold. Nothing I could say. The gravity Vasur had explained—how light we can be in one place and how heavy in another—that's only the half of it. *You roll the ball of play in your lotus-red hands.*

I had found verses in the ancient Vedas suggesting the earth was round and there were forces at play keeping the cosmos in harmony. The sun and its planets, heaven and earth. But none of this would have mattered to Bhooma Devi when she asked to be born here. There was more at stake. The fragility of a human heart. And even if Andal had known why an apple falls to the ground, she refused to be bound by the same principle. Her resilience was love. *Lion on the cosmic ocean taking care of all creation. You recline on milk-waves, in bracelets we sift river sand. You rescue Gajendra when he calls, then torture us. Please do not destroy our sandcastles.* All the sandcastles Andal had insisted on making, every handful of sand damped and moulded, then all of its towers fallen down, over and over until carried by a river and merged into the sea.

We turned right at a T-junction. The sign pointing left said: Srivilliputter Ten Kilometres. I looked back through the dust-smeared rear window for a glimpse of Andal's temple and there its shimmering tower was, like a hand raised toward Vaikuntha. Almost eight months ago, on the day we left for Chathuragiri with the professor, I had turned to look back at Srivilliputtur from this same junction—a strange ache in my belly, for a goddess I hardly knew. And here I was again, already dreaming another sandcastle.

Adithya suggested we stop at Watrap's police station. 'You never know, small towns have few secrets.'

The driver double-parked and Adithya and Roshina got out. I leaned through the window, watching their animated discussion through the station's door, Kodai's head heavy in my lap, her cheeks dusted with masala salt, her small hands sticky from the GoldiSpot.

They returned to the car, Adithya's hands thrust deep into the pockets of his jeans, and yes, the police did remember a man matching Vasur's description. He was found half-conscious near the bus station.

'They contacted the Samaritan on call for pick-ups of the destitute and dying,' he said. 'Watrap is on a mission to clean up its streets. They didn't actually see the priest when he came, but they gave me his address. He runs a Jesuit hospice near Dindigul.'

'This is no help for us,' Roshina said, wringing her hands. 'If Christian hospices find out someone has a family member, then they are not seen as real destitutes and are dropped at a public hospital instead.'

'I can't imagine your father would have gone willingly. But we can call them.'

None of this was relevant. If Vasur had escaped from the hospital, it wasn't like he'd be knocking at the gates of a hospice. We were going around in circles, wasting time. Plastic bags snapped in the wind like phantoms, betel juice streaked the walls of shopfronts like splattered blood. There were people everywhere.

'Have the police seen him since then?' I asked. It was a useless question.

Adithya shook his head. 'It's full moon and there are thousands of pilgrims passing through Watrap on their way to Chathuragiri.'

Overnight, its sleepy streets had turned into a circus. Balloon-wallahs, wind-up-toy-wallahs, tiffin-wallahs, palm readers.

'Vasur would have known this,' I said. 'There is no way he would go to Chathuragiri now.'

The three of us squatted on the kerb in front of the station.

Kodai asleep in Adithya's arms, Watrap's pandemonium faded to a blur, each of us in the cave of our own thoughts. Was this it then? Even the wallahs gave up on us. Three chais in clay cups arrived and a Limca for Kodai ordered by a kind policeman. We must have looked a despondent quartet amid all the full moon revelry parading toward their mountain of prayers. The tea was strong and sweet. As I sipped, a sound rippled its way in, falling bell-like through the cacophony. I looked up into the cataract eyes of an old man, his dreadlocked hair piled into a hive on top of his head, his weathered skin hanging dark and loose off his sparrow-frame, and in his hand a copper bowl of coins, Shiva's name stopped at his lips. He planted his trident and eased his back straight. Roshina took some coins from her purse, but he waved her hand away. He stood there looking at us. Considering. He gestured at me, and then turned to Adithya with a question. Back and forth they went in Tamil. I heard Vasur's name. Then I heard mine.

Roshina knelt to touch the ground at the old siddhar's feet and he raised his hand in a blessing. He turned and pointed. There were tears in Roshina's eyes. She held her hand across her mouth, then pressed the other against it. Adithya stood with Kodai still in his arms and gestured toward the car. She woke up, her cheeks flushed, wet locks of hair across her forehead. The siddhar placed one foot against the knee of his other leg and balanced, staring through us. Kodai looked at him, wide-eyed, then noticed the bottle of Limca and wriggled herself free to take a long draught through its straw before seeing Roshina's tears and the expression on her father's face.

'Amma,' she said, tugging at Roshina's arm, her bottom lip trembling.

'What did he say?' I looked from Roshina to Adithya and back again.

'Let's go,' Adithya said, and we followed, ploughing through the crowd to the car.

'But what did he say?' I needed to know.

The driver made a U-turn, his hand never leaving the horn as we drove against the surge of pilgrims. Adithya had squeezed himself next to the driver, and the siddhar propped his elbow at the window, his hive of knotted hair pressed against the upholstered roof, his trident held upright between his and Adithya's legs. The air of our small cabin thickened to pungent and sweet, of wood-smoke and earth and sandalwood. Motes of ash flew from the siddhar's skin as wind rushed through the car. Sandalwood—I breathed it in, remembering Vasur telling me how only when a sandalwood tree is cut does its perfume come. Every bump in the road jangled the bells tied to the prongs of the siddhar's trident.

'All three sufferings, Shiva destroys,' Vasur had said the last time I saw him.

Adithya turned to us. 'We are taking another route into Chathuragiri's forest, through Saptur.' The road stretched ahead, red and dusty, before abruptly disappearing into jungle below a jagged horizon of mountains. 'The siddhar says few people go this way and on full moons it is only a handful who retreat here. Any other time all you will find is the scat of wild dogs and boar, panthers and tigers. Not a safe place, the siddhar says, unless you are old like him and having nothing but a body to lose.'

The siddhar chuckled at this and tamped his trident between them. Clearly, he understood English, but was not about to speak it.

'Villagers only enter to scavenge for firewood,' Adithya added to diminish the siddhar's strange humour.

The driver swam his head, then mumbled to Adithya.

'He is saying we need to listen to what the local people know.'

'But we don't have time to stop,' Roshina said.

Adithya nodded. 'On the few field trips I've taken, I've learned it can be hard separating superstition from fact in the minds of remote villagers.'

'Please, Adithya, what was the siddhar telling you in

Watrap?' I leaned toward the front seat, attempting to keep frustration from my voice. 'I heard him say Vasur's name.'

Either Adithya didn't hear or he didn't want to answer. Kodai was wide awake and huddled up to me, both of us suspended in the tension of the air, of Roshina and Adithya, and the portent held in the body of the stranger sitting in front of us. I was as much a child as her, then, neither of us properly understanding where we were going, Kodai's lips quivering and a feral pawing at my ribs.

The road turned to gravel. The driver changed to low gear as we began to climb, his white Ambassador like some foreign beast as the jungle closed around us, the air a layering of diesel fumes, clean drifts of chlorophyll above, and below the dank sweet of leaf decay.

Adithya turned again and reached for Roshina's hand. He looked at me.

'The siddhar said Vasur was on his way to Saptur when he was found in Watrap. They had met just before the Samaritan arrived and the siddhar said he should come with him to his cave, a good distance from the main pilgrim path, but Vasur refused. He wasted no time disappearing into the crowd when the Samaritan's van appeared. And now even the siddhar has had enough and is escaping too. So many hundreds of thousands coming for Panguni's moon. Some say the crooked lingam will shift on its axis and there are extra auspicious boons to be had.'

The siddhar spoke again and there was more back and forth with Adithya. I strained to hear him above the spluttering of the car. To hear Vasur's name again. As if that was all the assurance needed for us to find him.

'Once the forest track begins, there is a cave near a spring less than two hours' walk,' Adithya translated. 'This is where Vasur wanted to go and where the siddhar is heading.'

'Two hours!' Roshina said. 'How was it possible for Appa to reach Watrap, let alone walk two more hours into the forest?'

The siddhar swam his head and mumbled.

The car crawled up the last ascent of road and stopped at a locked gate. We prised our sweaty bodies from its leather seats.

A uniformed forest ranger sauntered out from the cabin on the other side. He acknowledged the siddhar with a swim of his head, turned the key in the gate's padlock and waved him through, then moved to lock it again without so much as a glance at us.

Adithya stepped forward and was met with an abrupt look from the ranger.

'Are you having a permit?'

The siddhar stood on the other side watching, balancing on one leg again, steadfast as a tree.

'No, but we are looking for someone.' Adithya drew Roshina near him. 'Her father.'

The ranger threw me a cursory glance. 'Foreigners not allowed.'

The siddhar spoke up in Tamil, and then Adithya joined in. I heard Vasur's name on the siddhar's lips. He and the ranger exchanged a look that sent dread through my bones. The ranger paused, then asked Adithya to ask Roshina to take Kodai back to the car, but Roshina refused and Kodai's feet were planted.

I took Kodai by the hand. 'Shall I carry you then?' She reached up, clasping her hands round my neck. I lifted her and she wrapped her legs round my waist. 'Let's go over there and see if we can find another bird's nest.' I pointed to a rough clearing beyond the car, mustering hope into my voice. She held me tight. 'Tighter,' I said, pulling her close, as if her need might assuage mine.

There were birds above us in the few remaining trees, a chorus of them singing away unperturbed by the disturbance below. We stretched our heads back and searched through the filtered light. We watched for wisps of their wings through the bright and the shadows and the slight shuddering of branches.

'Look for forks in the trees,' I said, feeling my longing grow as strong as hers for a nest.

Then one mournful cry rang through all the other forest songs we were hearing, and Kodai—this small alive child in my arms with the name of a mythic girl from a thousand years ago —buried her face near my heart. I walked us further from the car and the gate, and the echoing of that cry, and the steady eyes of the siddhar, till we reached a pool of light where trees had once stood. Lianas lay on the ground like some rough woven vessel of the gods. I stepped us into the middle, felt Kodai's eyelashes like tiny wet wings against my skin. I pressed my lips into the curls of her hair.

Chapter Thirty-Six

Have you seen that confounding one, darkest of clouds
his heart black as his body—we cannot grasp this mystery.
Yes we saw him, encircled by friends in the woods of Vrindavan
a vast midnight sky bright with galaxies of stars

Nacciyar Tirumoli 14:7

Sirimai raised an eyebrow at the commotion billowing outside the pavilion.

'A mix of the pious and curious,' she muttered, thinking nobody was listening, but Andal, so heightened were her senses, heard everything—the mahouts' sticks thudding against the thick hides of their elephants, and as the beasts stamped their feet, a thousand tinkling bells raining into the noise of the crowd shuffling and elbowing for a view. Andal wanted to run. Run through the temple streets and seven towers to the golden dome and dark cave where her bridegroom lay. But the women held her like a captive bird, pounding their insects into cochineal, mixing them with plant resins, and painting her hands and feet.

They swept her hair, heavy and glossy with oils, into a top knot like a crown tilted on her head.

Varaji and Sirimai unfolded the wedding sari, muslin fine enough to thread through an ivory needle's eye. Andal stood as still as was possible while they draped and tucked its nine diaphanous yards. Tears welled in Varaji's eyes when the first sage's wife rubbed turmeric paste on the gold brocade at Andal's feet for an auspicious union. Andal felt her sorrow as if she were the mother and Varaji her daughter. As Varaji smoothed the fall of the wedding sari's pleats, Andal sensed a pausing in her mother's fingers.

In Varaji's basket of keepsakes was Andal's very first dress. It had yellowed over time, but she still remembered how white as milk it looked against her daughter's dark skin the day Visnucitta brought her home. Andal's wedding sari was dyed a deep ruby, but she felt the same fine weave and feather-weight of the dress her baby girl had worn. The brocade of Andal's sari was familiar too. She had marvelled at the same tiny gold stitches as she picked out the sticky seeds fallen from the tulasi in Visnucitta's temple garden, the morning he found her sixteen years ago.

Andal knelt and touched Varaji's feet. 'Amma, the feelings visiting you are the depths of love and sorrow Bhooma Devi wanted to experience. You were the one who told me her story, remember?'

Varaji's tears turned to weeping. Sirimai took the corner of her sari and gently pressed Varaji's cheeks. 'Akka, the priests are waiting. Where are the ornaments for your beautiful daughter?'

Sarvani and Marali brought the camphor chest of coral and pearl necklaces, golden bracelets and girdles, bell-studded anklets, two nose jewels, and rings for ten fingers and toes. The five wives fussed and adjusted until Andal felt the gold's weight heavy as earth bearing down on her.

'Give me your hand,' Sirimai said. She threaded one final bracelet. 'My gift to you.' Andal felt its smooth circle of fine beaten gold shaped in the likeness of a crocodile, with topaz eyes and pearls for the teeth gripping its swirling tail.

'Whenever you wear this, think of me. And think of Makara the crocodile too. In a sense we are one and the same, twisting and turning in this life and, god willing, may it be cause for liberation in the next.'

Sirimai, the dancer, audacious one. For the first time she could not look Andal in the eye, could not joke and scoff as if she were the queen of the world. Instead she sang, each verse echoing through the pavilion and out over the river. One of the women crowding the entrance for a view of this bride, all the way from Villiputtur, took a pair of finger cymbals from her bodice and began to play. Andal recognised the words of her father.

I had one daughter and now all the world praises her. I nurtured her and now the red-lotus eyed One is taking her away. Will noble Yashoda, mother of Krishna, welcome her home?

Marali took out the last ornament. With trembling fingers, Varaji held it high, capturing a shaft of light in its facets before placing the sapphire at the centre of her daughter's forehead. Sarvani circled Andal's hair with a garland of lilies, then the fifth wife offered a tiny pot of deer musk.

'No more—please.' The morning had been layer upon layer of powders, pastes, and potions. The sweetness of the lilies was nauseating, the musk, cloying. 'Dress me in as many ornaments as you like, but at least let me go to Lord Ranganatha wearing the scent he loves.'

The women at the entrance stopped chattering, stirred the air with their silence. Certain traditions a bride must honour. But an old lady with a basket of tulasi sprigs on her lap took no notice, intent on the final knot to the garland she had twined. Andal looked across at her and breathed in its fragrance, earthy and green as life itself.

'Can you not tie a length of tulasi around my top knot instead?'

Varaji looked on helplessly.

Sirimai suppressed a smile. 'Andal has a point,' she said, tender and a little cheeky, then motioned to the woman. 'Aunty, bring me your garland.'

❧

The temple astrologer's conch trumpets. A pair of swans nesting in river reeds near the pavilion lift off at the sound. Andal catches a glimpse of the swans' bright red eyes as she steps out into the sunlight, their white wings beating the sky, their long necks stretched taut as they honk as if in reply. She takes small steps through the purifying water of spilled coconuts. She feels him, his breath, the fire in his lotus eyes. He has left his bed and is pacing the temple, leaving lotus flower footprints in his wake. Ananta Sesha glides beside him, uncoiling his one thousand hoods like a royal umbrella.

'I am coming, lord. I am coming.'

Varaji helps her daughter onto the bridal pillow of salt and mustard seeds, every grain a blessing, each minute seed shifting, conforming to the shape of Andal's earthly body. To the reed notes of a nadaswaram and the clear clay beat of mridangams, eight men lift Andal's wedding palanquin onto their shoulders. *Soon I will stand beside the purest one. Siddhars are bringing water from four sacred rivers to bless us. They will tie our wrists with yellow thread.*

The bearers sway side to side in their *pahandi* gait, rocking her as if she were riding an elephant. Sirimai dances the procession forward. Andal hears her proud voice leading the women in their hula-huling and hymns to Lord Ranganatha. The bells of the courtesans' anklets and chimes of their finger cymbals call householders to the street. Like a dream, Andal watches them through gauze curtains as they clamour for a touch of her palanquin, begging the priests to take with them their offerings of fruit and incense. *I am still only bride-to-be,* she thinks, yet how eager they are to elevate me from earth to heaven.

'*Bhooma Devi Namaha*,' a woman chants and another responds, '*Aum Namah Tirumal*.' As their chants merge one into the other, Andal loses sense of where she begins and where she ends. The soles of her feet, the tips of her fingers—how far they feel from her heart. Her body is tiny as a mustard seed, but when she takes a breath the whole world fills her.

When the palanquin bearers pause, Andal holds her breath. When they step forward, she can breathe again. Closer and closer. As they carry her into the shadow of the first tower, Andal feels every brightly coloured god and goddess on its four sides stop their play, their battles, and their lovemaking. Who is this girl? they ask as the procession passes beneath them. Some of them leer and others look ferocious, but when the bells of the tower begin to chime, a thousand pairs of eyes light up.

'Are you well?' she hears them say.

'Yes, I am fine. Have you seen him?'

'Yes, we have, *trailing his robe of yellow silk, that frisky calf, his fragrant hair brushing those broad shoulders like a swarm of honey-drunk bees*.'

Through the second tower, the third, and then the fourth tower called Renga, the mundane world is at last left behind. Three elephant bulls draped in brocade are waiting, their hides a swirl of coloured chalks. King Vallabhadeva's elephant sways with impatience and a flock of parrots lift from the trees at the clattering of bells chained to his giant feet. Srirangam's head priest, then the king, take lead of the procession, circumambulating the golden roofed garbarigha, moving closer to Lord Ranganatha just like the right whorling conch he brings to his lips.

Andal smells the saltiness of the eight men carrying her penetrating the sweetness of the palanquin's flowers. *The gods do not perspire*, she remembers her father's words, *their eyes never blink*. Involuntarily, her own eyes look back and back, up into the space awaiting her, to the one who is calling her from her burning body. *Their feet never touch the ground.*

Conches, flutes, cymbals, drums. Nearer and nearer they circle. At the hall of a thousand columns, Srirangam's courtesans pause for a dance in honour of a girl, the one whose garlands god desires. With white whisks they wave her procession through the fifth tower, then through the sixth tower—Andal's father Visnucitta, her mother Varaji. Sarvani and Marali, and Sirimai with her retinue of temple dancers, and all those who have aspired to love, no matter their stories, their imperfections.

The bearers lift Andal's palanquin from their shoulders. A braceletted hand parts its gauze curtain, guiding Lord Ranganatha's bride from her pillow.

'Slowly, slowly,' Andal hears a voice slip through the last remnant of time.

Her feet touch the memory of earth.

Epilogue

She followed me from Srivilliputtur to Australia, and waited as I bided time. Ancient Tamils say the smallest denomination of time is a *nimesa*—a blink of the eye. Eighteen blinks, they say, make one *kastha*. The seconds, minutes, and hours it took for three months to pass was how much time it took me—she was there in the kitchen as I tempered spices, whisked curds into milk, brewed tea. She was there when I dived into the ocean, opening my eyes underwater to catch the sunlight marbling the brim of her world.

Andal was there when I said goodbye.

What do you say to the man you fell in love with twenty-six years ago? What do you say to him when the skeins of memories, of your love and despair, have unravelled? We walked to the end of the garden we had built and the stream at the bottom of the valley where we swam. We faced both our kitchen chairs to the window with the view of Wollumbin and marvelled at its peak, free from cloud. There was little to say. Marcus knew, he said, this day was coming, just as I had. He had found an ashram half a day's drive south. They were looking for a carpenter. It suited him, the hours of silence and meditation, separate quarters for unmarried men and women, and the ocean, of course, only five minutes away. He put what he needed in his Kombi and I packed what I needed in an old sea chest of my father's. The rest we gave away.

'I'll ship the chest to France for you,' he said and we held each other, and all our years together, for one last time with a love that felt strange because it really was that simple.

She followed me to Occitania in the south-west of France where snow still lay lacy and luminous on the peaks of the Pyrenees as summer penetrated deep into the thawed gardens of a village called Montségur. Sunshine bounced through the windows of my stone house like a friend. Sometimes, on Montségur's breezes, I even heard the tintinnabulation of anklets beneath the *swish-swish* of saris, back and forth from her temple.

I discovered Andal in unimagined places. In the rose vine, at the bottom of my garden, twining through the branches of a pear tree. She dressed in raiments I thought only possible in India, pinks and magentas swathed over bodices of bright green and sienna, blues and violets hemmed in gold. And she was there in the voice of a small girl playing hide-and-seek among them. Laughter in her hazel eyes.

I climb Montségur's mountain and find inside the ruins of its castle a garden of feathery white yarrow, cucumber-scented borage and clusters of velvety mullein. I follow a mossy trail to a small grassy plateau and sit. The pollen hunters are already humming from bud to blossom and I watch one fat bumblebee disappear into the centre of a crimson orchid, feasting like a drunkard, the day hardly begun.

Beautiful Lord, Andal sings, *black bees, dark as your red-lotus eyes, drink from lotus buds. On high Tirumaliruncolai cool ponds are covered in flowers. I am bewildered. Show me the way to refuge.*

I have no names for many of the bird songs in the thicket of ancient low trees behind me, and in the oaks and birch clinging to the rocks of the gorge below, but if I listen, I can hear the trill of one and the response of another, and a woodpecker's *ta tapa ta*, like the finger taps on a mridangam drum. I let my mind empty into the resonance of his notes, beak upon wood. I close my eyes and am lifted into a spiralling of wings, through cloud drifts and across oceans, lowlands, hills, forests—the moist breath of a once upon a time lover on my skin.

I can see the earth at the edge of the sky, slowly spinning, a violet-blue orb wreathed in white. I test the ground beneath me with one foot; it is not solid. Nothing is. And yet, in the lake before me there are reflections of mountains. I let my dress fall and step away. I loosen my hair, slip the bangles from my wrists, and wade in to my waist, then further until I am floating. *Drift your limbs wide*, she says. The lake ripples around me, and I let go into her. My fingers and toes, arms and legs, my womb and the scars of my womb, my tongue, my eyes, breasts, heart.

The gods, they do not blink.

But my eyes do.

Slowly, I open them to waves of daisies dotting the grass where I sit. A play of warm light, sounds of water drumming on rock far below. Migrations of tiny snails with translucent yellow shells make their silvery path across the earth as Montségur's church bells begin to chime. I count twelve, but they do not stop at twelve. Seasons repeat; wildflowers open, lose their petals, turn to seed. The wind takes them. The bells keep ringing as I step back through the castle to the mountain's cliff face.

Far below is the tiled roof of my grandmother's house, and at the edge of the village, two figures knee-deep in long grasses, waving into the sky, dancing their kites, tiny triangles of colour snip-snapping, their tails of coloured ribbon trailing like rainbows. Roshina with a cardigan buttoned up over her sari, and Kodai, her hair escaped from her woollen beanie, wild in the wind. Adithya will come soon from Pondicherry. He will bring cardamom and coriander, tamarind and tulasi. There is a mortar and pestle in the kitchen.

Glossary

aarti—sacred flame offering

abhishekam—ritual libation for deities

acharaya—teacher, guru

Agasthya—revered as Tamil's first siddhar, author of hymns in many Vedic texts

Akka—term of affection for an older 'sister'

alap—musical opening, often improvised, of a raga

ama—yes

Amma—mother

Anthari—Goddess Durga, Vishnu's sister

Appa—father

Araiyers—lineage of reciters of the Divya Prabandham

aspara—heavenly courtesan

Aum—sacred mantra / sound / symbol of the universe

avatar—an incarnation of a god

Azhwars—twelve poet saints, including Andal, who dived deep into the divine

bhajan—devotional song

bhakti—devotion

Bhooma Devi—earth goddess

Choodi K Kodutta—epithet given to Andal: she who gave that which she had worn

darshan—seeing, blessing; an exchange of vision between god and devotee

dosa —a thin savoury pancake made from fermented rice and dal

dupatta—traditional scarf draped over women's shoulders or as a veil

garbarigha—womb-space, sanctum sanctorum

gopika—cowherd girl

gopuram—pyramid temple tower

Govardhana—Krishna in the form of a sacred mountain

Govinda—another name for Krishna, incarnation of Vishnu

gunas—the three qualities of matter, building blocks of nature

idli—fermented rice steamed into cakes for breakfast

illai—no

jnaana—wisdom

kadhai—cooking pot

kajal—natural based eye-liner made from soot and oils

kastha—eighteen blinks (nimesas) ancient Tamil denomination of time

Kodai—Andal's birth name

kolam—floor mandala painted with rice flour or coloured chalks

korai—nutsedge weed / nut grass

kumkuman—vermillion powder made from turmeric and lime

kundalini—coiled energy / shakti at the base of the spine

kuvalai—blue water lily

lingams—sexual organ, symbol of Siva

mandapam—columned temple hall

molucca—smooth shiny seeds used for games and oracles

mridangam—low toned double-headed drum

mullai—jasmine

Nacciyar Tirumoli—Andal's second composition of fourteen songs, 143 verses

nadaswaram—loud double-reeded wind instrument

naga—mythical semi-divine deity half-man half-serpent

Nalayira Divya Prabandham—anthology of the Azhwars' four thousand poems

nimesa—one blink of eye, an ancient Tamil denomination of time

nityasumangali—girl dedicated to a temple, evergreen bride, consort of the divine

paddy—rice

Panchanjaya—Vishnu's sacred right whorling conch

payasam—sweet rice pudding

Periamma—aunty

pongal—pounded savoury rice for breakfast, or sweet

poriyal—fine-diced, spiced vegetable dish

pradakshina—clockwise circumambulation of a sacred place

prasadam—food blessed by god

puja—daily worship of god

punugu—perfumed oil from the glands of a civet cat

puthu—steamed cylinders of ground rice and coconut, sweet or savoury

raajasa—emotion, passion; one of the three gunas

rasaam—spicy tamarind-sour broth taken toward the end of
a meal

sambar—spiced lentil and vegetable broth

sanandhi thalam—sacred oil used in Andal's abhishekham

Sangam—between 3rd c. BC and 3rd c. AD an age when poetry
flourished

sattva—truth, goodness; one of the three gunas

shakti—divine female energy

siddhar—holy man, ascetic

taamasa—darkness; one of the three gunas

tālam—Carnactic musical term for the rhythm cycle of a song

tamboura—gourd string instrument to keep pitch

teerthum—place of sacred water (also called tank)

Thirumukkulam—temple teerthum (tank) on the edge of Srivilliputtur

tiffin—a snack or light breakfast

tilak—adornment above the centre of a woman's eyes

Tirumal—Tamil god of Sangam Age origin having aspects of
Vishnu and Krishna

Tirumaliruncolai—sacred temple site near Madurai

Tiruppavai—Andal's first composition of thirty verses

tulasi—sacred basil

uthappams—savoury rice and dal pancake

vange—come

Vaikuntha—heavenly abode of the gods

Vaisnavite—follower of Vishnu

Varaha—incarnation of Vishnu as a boar

Vatapatra sayee—incarnation of Vishnu as a baby on a banyan leaf

velan—exorcist, curer of lovesick girls

veena—double gourd string instrument

Veli— temple on the outskirts of a main temple

venakam—greeting, hello

vibhuti—sacred ash

Villiputtur—Andal's birthplace (the *Sri* later added in honour of her as goddess)

Vishnu—universal Hindu name for the god who has a thousand names

wallah—person in business

yali—mythical monster with lion's body and elephant trunk

yoni—womb/vagina, symbolic partner of the lingam

Acknowledgments

As a child Andal played with molucca beans, no doubt divining her future. These smooth shining seeds can travel across oceans. Who knows for how long and how far. Some call them *cœur de la mer*—heart of the sea—and when found on seashores they are treasured as amulets. As I wonder where to begin my thanks for all those who have helped this book find its way into the world, I think of them rolling through Andal's fingers. There is mystery at work in our lives. We carry the dreams of our ancestors. We arrive at crossroads. Andal was waiting at one of mine and I followed her. It was a path I had neither searched for nor anticipated. My heart is filled with gratitude for the songs of this mythic girl and revered goddess.

My affinity with India was kindled long before *Andal's Garland*. I have one cherished photo of my father, born in Simla, having his first bath in Srinagar's Dal Lake. There was peace in Kashmir then. People called it Heaven on Earth. Rabindranath Tagore's poetry and Rudyard Kipling's stories were the loved books of my maternal grandmother, who yearned to visit India. Her unfulfilled desire instilled my curiosity and it was my mother who read her books to me. She understood the potency of storytelling, and of imagination. I offer my parents and grandmother, each, a garland.

It was in the early seventies at the Australian National University that the inimitable Professor Basham introduced me to the Vedic texts of ancient India, while the exuberant Professor V N Shukla opened another world, a different concept of time, through the language of Hindi. Its past, present, and future tenses were the key to begin understanding a culture I had loved since childhood. Their teachings were my foundation.

From the past to the present. Above all I offer my profound affection and gratitude to the people of Srivilliputtur and Srirangam, who welcomed and guided me during my visits in the six years it took to write this book. To Srivilliputtur's temple priests and Araiyers and to the kindnesses and graciousness of the many women who included me in their daily devotions of Andal: without each and every one of you, none of these pages would have been possible.

I am indebted to the translators of Andal's Tiruppavai and Nacciyar Tirumoli and also Periazhwar's Tirumoli—C G Balaji, R Bangaruswami, Vidya Dehejia, D Ramaswamy Iyengar, Vankeepuram Rajagopalan, S L N Simha, C Sitaramamurti, P S Sundaram, and Archana Venkatesan. In the early days of the manuscript, their translations from Tamil into English, many of them with commentaries, were invaluable for my understanding of Andal. Their work enabled me to create interpretive translations of my own for use in this book. And thank you also to Anne Mie Tacq and Richard Pigelet for their assistance in finding Pierre Herisson for his translation of one pivotal sentence into Occitan.

To the dedicated staff at Madurai's theosophical library, Sri Ramana's library in Tiruvanamalai, and Pennington public library in Srivilliputtur: with their help I found translations and commentaries of ancient texts and out-of-print volumes, many of them unavailable through other means. V Perumal's *Glimpses of*

Tamil Culture, is one. A K Ramanujuan's translations of Sangam poetry in *Poems of Love and War* and Saskia C Kersenboom's *Nityasumangali* are another two of the many incredible resources I discovered in my search for the truth about a long ago India. Krishna Deva Raya's *Amuktamalyada* is a text that will forever remain close to my heart. Dr Srinivas Sistla's sublime translation of this sixteenth century work allowed me a window into an age of harmony with nature, of refinement and exquisite beauty. My imagining of Andal would not have been possible without this inspired account of her life. Sri Aurobindo Ashram's *Collected Works of The Mother* should also be mentioned. Thank you all.

Andal's Garland might never have been born were it not for the generosity of five women who offered me a precious 'room of my own' for intensive periods of solitary writing time. In Australia, Libbie Nelson, Christine Olsen, Rachel Stone, and Jessie Cole; and in France, Hanne Rorth. Bouquets to each of you.

To Peter Bishop at Varuna, who understood what I was attempting to do—even when I didn't—that *Andal's Garland* moved more like a poem, not a straight narrative, so 'normal' did not apply. Thank you, Peter, for teaching me trust and for sharing something David Malouf said: 'I have an infallible memory for things that didn't happen.'

To my writers group, past and present members, a circle of loyal women warriors dedicated to their craft: Jessie Cole, Siboney Duff, Michelle Granieri Taylor, Lisa Walker, Jane Camens. Where would I be without you? Our vicissitudes and victories. Our Save the Cat moments. Special mention to Michelle for initiating a brainstorming one bushfire-smoke-filled drive home. By the time we reached Woodburn, we had a name for this story. And special mention to Sib who, on another writing retreat, left her desk to drive me to the nearest country hospital. It was only day two and I took a fall on a forest track. You thought my wrist was broken, and you were right. It was a memorable and dangerous week and we renamed the mountain outside our door: Shiva.

To my first readers: Denise Beckton, Jane Camens, Jessie Cole, Tess Parsons, and Anjali Walsh. Huge appreciation for your astute and sensitive insights, and your encouragement. And to Laurel Cohn for your wise, precise eyes and aerial view. Thank you in spades.

Heartfelt thank you to Dettra Rose, Helena Norberg-Hodge, and Kate Veitch: three special links in another circle of women. Your support through the terrains of this book taught me faith.

To Odyssey Books, and my publisher Michelle Lovi, a huge thank you for believing in my story and bringing it to life.

And so the Molucca beans come full circle into love and gratitude for my extended family. When we all happen to be in the same room at the same time, it's the best catastrophe ever. It is an honour to be part of you all. To my sister Catherine for her understanding of deadlines and milestones and the importance of celebrating, and my brother Jason for being a maverick.

And to Mr Peter, my life partner and champion. My other half. My cup full. For being my constant, most of the time. For understanding my exits into solitude and to India. As I write this, the Brazilian Cherry tree in our garden is flushed with white buds. In less than a month we will feast together again under its branches.

About the Author

Helen Burns' interest in Eastern traditions turned serious in 1975. She devoted three years to Asian Studies with a major in Hindi at the Australian National University, until the call to venture deeper overtook the need for a degree. Since then she has encountered teachings of Indian saints, living and dead, from tombs within temples and mosques, to ashrams where the world flocked. From all-night qawwalis at the feet of Sufi saints in Rajasthan, to lone sadhus in mountain caves. From extended silent meditation retreats in Australia and Myanmar, to the midnight dance-divinations of Araiyers in Srivilliputtur. Helen has practised as a Herbalist and Iridologist and created several businesses catering for what was once known as the New Age. She now divides her time between a tiny house in Byron Bay, a slightly larger abode in Far North Queensland, and India wherever it takes her. *Andal's Garland* is her second book.

www.authorhelenburns.com

 facebook.com/authorhelenburns

 instagram.com/helenburnsauthor

www.ingramcontent.com/pod-product-compliance
Lightning Source LLC
Chambersburg PA
CBHW050802190726
48285CB00005B/1757